Sing!

Michael Curtin is the author of *The Cove Shivering Club*, *The League Against Christmas* and *The Plastic Tomato Cutter*. He lives in Limerick, Ireland.

Sing!

Michael Curtin

FOURTH ESTATE • *London*

This paperback edition first published in 2002
First published in Great Britain in 2001 by
Fourth Estate
A Division of HarperCollins*Publishers*
77–85 Fulham Palace Road,
London W6 8JB
www.4thestate.com

Copyright © Michael Curtin 2001

10 9 8 7 6 5 4 3 2 1

The right of Michael Curtin to be identified as the author of
this work has been asserted by him in accordance with the
Copyright, Designs and Patents Act 1988

A catalogue record for this book is available from the British Library

ISBN 1–84115–605–1

Typeset by Palimpsest Book Production Limited,
Polmont, Stirlingshire
Printed in Great Britain by
Clays Ltd St Ives plc

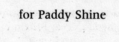

for Paddy Shine

CONTENTS

Part One

Droney	3
Flow Gently	8
Ignatius Valelly	16
Walter Nix	29
Madeleine Brown	40
Nellie	52
The Convent	67
The Whole Coastguard	71

Part Two

The Coffee Table	85
The Letter	88
After Father Cletus	92
London	100
The Drop Out	109
I Spy	114
Madness	120
The Abyss	130
The Coffee Table Players	141

Part Three

And Many, Many More	149
The Concert	166
Full Company Sketch	186
Sing!	201

Part One

DRONEY

Peak cap day was by no means unusual in the life of a Jack Droney.

He woke and read the backs of his hands. BGC. That was a regular. Buy Griddle Cake. SCB. Scout Confession Boxes. He eased his feet out of bed and onto the floor and examined the *aide-mémoire* on his thighs. CB off TB. Chaw the Balls off Toots Books. He opened the wardrobe door and pushed his underpants down to his ankles and bent to look through his legs. The mirror image mnemonics read: SOC. Sing One Cornetto.

Droney straightened slowly. He told me there was no point in waking and rising with calculated moderation if some morning he was to be found with his underpants around his ankles and cause of death due to reading his own arse in the mirror.

On his way up to the Redemptorists a woman gave Droney a look because he grinned and rubbed his hands together and incorporated a little skip into his stride at the thought of my sour puss when he delivered the peak cap. I traded under the name 'Toots Books'. Droney called me the bibliophile, with the messengerboy tongue.

All I'd said to Droney was: 'Jasusbastarinfucking rain, where would I get a peak cap?'

'Go into any church and try the confession boxes.'

'I should have known better than to ask you.'

According to Droney, there wasn't much of a sense of humour around. That woman who gave him the look was probably firing on all pistons herself but you had to keep everything in today. Only last week, the security man with his walkie-talkie, when Droney put his head in the door of the shop, hadn't gone in any further than his foot on the mat that said 'WELCOME' and asked politely: 'Excuse me, young man, is it the policy of this store to prosecute pilferers?'

A frozen 'Yes it is.'

'I'll try someplace else so.'

No response.

Waiting for Mass to end in the Redemptorists, Droney stayed at the back of the church and idled over the literature. 'The Devil at Discos'. When he was a young man it had been 'The Dos and Donts of Company Keeping'. Only last week at our coffee table we had been joined by a transient who conjectured that today they fuck first and maybe a week later, when the girl is walking towards him on the footpath, the fella says to himself, I know that one from someplace.

Why would anyone want to believe in such gloom?

There were only about twenty at Mass and the priest didn't have an altar boy. In a few minutes Droney was alone in the church. He opened the doors of the confession boxes. No luck.

St Joseph's was all locked up after the early Mass and wouldn't open again until evening unless there was a morning funeral. With the shortage of vocations there was no one to mind the ranch. It only made a couple of columns on the inside of the local paper the last time the parish priest left the doors open, when years ago it would have been front-page sacrilege. The priest was encouraged by the crime figures being down (in an election year) and risked it one morning, testing the waters like Noah sending the dove out who came back, and lo, in her mouth a freshly plucked olive leaf. And lo, five poor boxes were plucked plus the antique clock from its eminence thirty feet high up on the wall of the main altar.

Droney slipped on the puke in the porch of the Augustinians. He had to clutch the holy water font to stop himself falling. The

4

prostrate wino wheezed: 'Look where you're going, you graceless, sick-faced churl . . . givusafag . . .'

It was past time for Droney's own first cigarette, time wasted traipsing the town for a peak cap with nothing to show for it but a shoeful of gawk, and now he had to waste more time opening the packet of Gold Flake to tantalise the heap on the ground. Droney had heard the touch of education in the wino's vocabulary, the intellectual-down-on-his-luck for whom Droney was usually a providential sucker.

But 'sick-faced'.

Droney bent down with the cigarette as bait until he was close enough to grab the bottle of cider and pour it over the mottled face. Then he stood up and kicked the wino in the thigh and barked at him over his yelps: 'Who's sick-faced?'

Droney went out to the front steps to have a smoke. He had the shakes of the quiet man having been driven to violence. He wanted to kick himself for having kicked a wino who was only in the church porch because the chamber of commerce had had him fumigated off the streets.

But 'sick-faced'.

Droney masticated on the state of the church while he had his fag. The august was gone from the Augustinians and he wasn't only thinking of winos in the porch. Inside, where he had once hung his surplice, there had been a lockerful of operatic Masses – all now elbowed out to grass by folkshite.

Droney liked to hold forth. The church was on its knees with only the command of a few spinsters and dodderers and priests saying Mass without altar boys. It will all be paid for yet. Just look at the faces of the people passing in the street. Busy with the pain of having got on, not needing guidance now. Post-Catholic pluralists they thought they were, in the way that you couldn't buy a head of cabbage without being called a consumer. Was there ever such bollix? Try to give them a smile and they back off suspicious that anyone not stressed out of his mind must be dealing from the bottom of the deck . . .

Droney stood aside to let a hardy, country-looking man who could have been ninety pass into the church. Droney watched him take off the peak cap and dip his fingers in the holy water as

5

though there were no winos in the porch – a man of resignation by the look of him who had seen more changes for the worse than most. It wasn't a confessional job, just a prayer in passing, kneeling slowly in the third row from the back, cap on the seat beside him. Kneeling himself, Droney used a biro to flick the cap onto the ground and it was all done in less than a minute including a stop to lob a pound and the packet of Gold Flake onto the wino's belly.

Stretching the original terms of reference but I wouldn't know until he'd tell me, maybe in a few months' time. So, peak cap got. Only that nice old gentleman would go home bareheaded and get the Alzheimer's look and there would be talk behind his back of inspecting nursing homes.

I was too busy for Droney to CB off TB for having doubted the provenance of peak caps. Droney sailed the cap over browsers and bookstalls to land on my table. He stood just long enough in the doorway to give me his mad grin before jinking away from my 'Excuse me!'

Droney went to the labour exchange. He counted seventeen people waiting in the enquiry section, holding their numbers so that they would know who was next. He pretended to read a poster on a pillar so that he could watch the crowd size him up. As a child he had learned to see himself as others saw him. Today he was dressed as a bit of a character. Today the crowd could take in the old overcoat with the belt of twine and the jeans and the wellingtons and the cravat flowering through the coat. All he needed was a stick and a herd of cattle to be a drover. He cultivated the incongruously long hair surviving from the seventies style because it covered half the port wine stain on his face. Looking at Droney head on, without the camouflage of the long hair, the deformity blotched almost all the right-hand side of his face, including the ear and a profile of his nose and the complementary portion of his upper lip. It hadn't faded with age. It was ugly.

Armed with the disfigurement Droney sang. He sang with his hand on his heart, standing now facing the people:

Just One Cornetto
Give it to me
Delicious ice-cream
From It – a – lee

A few shook their heads and smiled. Some looked at the floor. But Droney struck gold with one young fella who clapped and stamped his feet. And Droney nursed the glimmer of a people dancing in the streets and shouting out loud when they made love and singing without looking over their shoulders and a tablet mountain in the European Community – with no takers.

When Droney came back to the bookshop the peak cap was already a pet. I was wearing it indoors, sitting at my table over the dusty tome of the racing page.

I said: 'Well, what are you up to besides robbing confession boxes?'

'Toots, you could say thanks. I've been brightening up the lives of the people.'

'Annoying the people. Sticking your head into places saying daft things. You should be locked up. Does it look all right on me?'

'How can people settle for their names being robbed?'

'What does that mean?'

'I was up at the labour exchange. The queue sits down with everyone holding a number and when the number lights up at the hatch they know they're next. Any time I was ever in a waiting room your name would be next. A receptionist or a nice nurse would say, Mr Droney the doctor will see you now.'

'Now is the time the doctor should see you all right. What were you doing in the labour exchange?'

'I went up there to sing "Just One Cornetto".'

'Why did I ask. The saddest thing of all is that I believe you.'

One of my blue rinses came in then. I knew she was good for half an hour pawing the embossed paperbacks. I said, 'I'll see you at coffee.'

FLOW GENTLY

Droney bought the griddle cake in Mother Kelly's Doorstep. He put his hands in his pocket and found no fags. He had to hunt for a corner shop that sold Gold Flake. In answer to the tinkling bell, a skinny, stooped old granny came out of her kitchen and wasn't a bit put off by being out of Gold Flake. 'But I have Afton,' she said, tending the packet in *fait accompli* fashion. Droney went to the pub next door and ordered a glass of water in the exercise of a right handed down in folklore. He sat in the snug and lit a fag and read the packet:

> Flow gently Sweet Afton among thy green braes
> Flow gently I'll sing thee a song in thy praise.

An innocent Afton brought Droney back to his childhood, and there was Mr Hassett standing outside the gate of his coalyard as he watched the children tipping around. I was one of those children. My aunt had a shop in the neighbourhood. The goals were chalked onto a gable-end wall. The footpath stood in for the goal mouth and the pitch was the street. Any uncoordinated archetype – me when I was on a message to my aunt – did for goalkeeper but Jackie Droney had to be knacky enough on the wing to chip a dead ball onto the heads of the master class centre-forwards. The neighbourhood parents were growing out of having children and the motor car was beginning to breed so that we were the last of the street footballers.

In summer Mr Hassett wore a dark serge suit and waistcoat

and a black tie under a starched white collar and black boots and a cloth cap. In winter he added a black old crombie and a sack for his shoulders. In place of a watch a whistle hung from his waistcoat chain. The customers came with handcarts, boxcars and prams. Mr Hassett sold coal by the half-hundredweight. His assets were a scale, two twenty-eight-pound weights, a shovel, a coarse sweeping brush, the yard and the shed, and a hut to accommodate Miss Godfrey, who sat on a bar stool at a tall desk and took the money and wrote the dockets and put the dockets on a spike. When Harry, the bagman, was idle there was room for him to squeeze into the hut out of the rain and take a few pulls of his nobber.

When Jackie played on the wing nearest the coalyard Mr Hassett gave him the wink before he blew the whistle so that Jackie would win the race to be sent across the road to my Aunt Madge's shop for Mr Hassett's twenty Sweet Afton. Where anyone else would get a penny for the job Mr Hassett gave Jackie a threepenny bit. Sometimes Mr Hassett blew the whistle twice. That was the signal for a raffle for a sweet. Jackie always guessed right because Mr Hassett kept the winning number in his head.

Children not from the neighbourhood, passing through on the way home from school, were stopped by Mr Hassett holding out two closed fists. 'Guess which hand,' Mr Hassett would tease a child and the child would go home with a sweet and a pat on the head.

Sometimes when Mr Hassett didn't need to blow his whistle for his Sweet Afton or his raffle he blew the whistle anyway when Jackie was on the near wing.

'Jackie, will we go to Clonmel for a drive and have a swim in the sea?' Jackie believed him. 'But you'll have to run up home first to get permission.'

Jackie ran up home and ran back down: 'My mother says you haven't got a car. She says there isn't enough sand in Clonmel for an egg-timer. She says 'tis landlocked.'

'Aha, that's what your mother thinks. But you see, I know a secret beach. Only I forgot the car is having a puncture mended we'd go now at a hundred miles an hour and bring back a bucket of sand to show her.'

9

Another day: 'My mother says you're only codding. She says Calcutta is in India, half the world away.'

'Aha, I knew she'd think that. But you see, I know a short cut. Only I just discovered the crown wheel and pinion is banjaxed we'd drive there now and bring back a baby elephant and then see what she could say.'

Or: 'Jackie, I have it. Get your togs and we'll drive to Kilkee. Hurry. Run up and ask your mother and bring a light raincoat in case we're caught out.'

Jackie had been to Kilkee on one of the excursions that his father organised from Finucane's pub across the road from the coalyard. Kilkee had sand. Kilkee had sea. You could drive there and back on the same day. Mrs Droney switched to the attack: 'All right. The togs are in your bottom drawer. Take my own towel and your plastic mac. And tell Mr Hassett I said to thank him.'

Mr Hassett looked at Jackie with the togs and towel and plastic mac. 'We're after been hit by a disaster. I went to check the car and the fill and draw sedimentation tank is leaking. But we'll go another day if it stays fine. And will you tell your mother I said she's a card.'

Soon enough Jackie knew where every place in the world was and whether or not you could get there by car if you had a car and could drive. But Mr Hassett played on. 'Jackie, would you like to come to Calais?'

'I'll have to ask my mother first.' Jackie said it to humour Mr Hassett because Mr Hassett missed Jackie's old innocence and still gave Jackie the wink before he blew his whistle for the twenty Sweet Afton.

I was there this day on a message to my aunt. I was two years older than Jackie and, like the rest of the soccer gang, never let Jackie know that Mr Hassett was pulling his leg. I went around the corner with Jackie for a minute and then we went back and Jackie said: 'I can't. My mother said I wouldn't be back in time for tea and that you can't drive to Calais, you'd need a boat and 'twould take days.'

'Aha, that's what your mother thinks, Jackie. You see, what she doesn't know, I have a hovercraft. And I built it myself. Christopher Cockerel sent me the plans.'

'Where is it?'

'Where is it? It's in my own private dry dock.'

'I'll go so.'

'Hah. Jackie, you don't go to Calais just like that, you know. It's not like Kilkee. I didn't mean today. Another day when we're ready. You'll need to get a penknife that has a corkscrew attached and loads of stuff so that we'll be prepared. And we can't go 'til Sir Christopher goes first so that he can have the limelight. I'll make out a list.'

Having emerged from his mother's regency in negotiations with Mr Hassett, Jackie did not expect Mr Hassett to follow through with the provisions necessary for the expedition to Calais. It was more likely that Werner Von Braun would have been in touch, leaking secret lunar transport specifications.

But the whistle blew. And it wasn't Mr Hassett's.

The game was over.

The mirror Jackie looked into most often to see himself was that of his father's eyes.

Timmie Droney drove the Holo Mineral Water truck. The owner of the Holo Mineral Water Company was a Holohan. It was the age of red lemonade. But the bottle of Holo had the colour of brown sugar and cost two pence cheaper. The canard persisted all over the city that Holo was manufactured by farting into a barrel of rainwater. The son of a Holo truck driver should have been in for it. But the nearest bully would have clocked anyone who made a crack when Jackie was around.

Timmie Droney had his own protective coloration. He was spared because he was a thorny wire. His lamb's blood above the door flowed from the caveat that he could not be in the wrong. He was famous for bringing the gavel down in Finucane's pub with the clincher: 'Right. You and me outside the door.'

Timmie Droney was always in action. While he made the deliveries of Holo he whistled. At home after his tea he would jump up and shave out of the basin and put on the Brylcreem and change into his good suit and go to the football pitch to manage Finucane's inter-pub soccer team.

11

At Finucane's Timmie Droney was the spokesman for all the drinkers and at the same time the management representative on behalf of the Finucanes. He took the range out of the kitchen for the Finucanes and put in a fireplace, not noticing or thinking about noticing whether or not the range in his own house was *passé*. He ran the excursion bus to the seaside, deciding what time it would leave and return, where it would stop, who would sing and in what order. He organised the 45 drives and the Christmas draw.

When the government ministers or shadow cabinet came to town to speak from the back of a lorry at the O'Connell Monument Timmie Droney had to leave the house early to get a place in the front row of the mob so that he would know what he was talking about when he went back to Finucane's to start a fight.

He had his own special spot where he liked to stand with his pals to watch the St Patrick's Day parade. He'd say to Mrs Droney, 'Take him up near the Tech where he'll get a good view.' And he would say in Jackie's presence, 'Has he his exercise done?'

The girls around the road used to fight to take Jackie out in his pram.

When Jackie made his first communion, my Aunt Madge called him across the road and gave him half a crown. She'd given me two bob. Otherwise her rate was a blackmailed tanner for a customer's child.

The older Jackie told me that nobody could make scrambled eggs like his mother. Her griddle cakes would have put Mother Kelly's Doorstep out of business. Those Invisible Menders today could not turn a shirt collar like Mrs Droney. Bitten by the teeth, compared to Mrs Droney everything was a fraud. He asked his mother once before she put the light out in the bedroom to kiss the port wine stain and make it better. She kissed it. She said, only God can make it better. But he might want you to be special.

Mrs Droney, the girls pushing the pram, my Aunt Madge, Mr Hassett, the soccer players, all acquiesced in trying to spoil Jackie. But Timmie Droney never stopped the lorry at the end of the road to give him a jaunt up home. He didn't give Jackie a kiss or a fondle in public – or at home. Timmie Droney was involved in so much that there had to be so many attendant flashpoints. He brawled like a tinker outside Finucane's pub across the road from the coalyard and neither Mr Hassett nor his customers nor the soccer game noticed. Such was the power of the port wine stain.

Mr Spencer, though, on the way to one of his good works, might stop, shake his head in communion with Mr Hassett, and move on.

'How is your leg these days?' Mr Hassett said to Mr Spencer during rainy weather that didn't stop our soccer game.

'Inclined to act up, I'm afraid. Still,' Mr Spencer patted his crocked knee, 'can't complain. My blighty out of Passchendaele, eh?'

Any day that he was passing, Mr Spencer would stop on the footpath the far side of the game and watch a bit of the play. When the ball strayed near him he tamed it with his stick and gave it a kick with the good leg and if I didn't duck the shot would have taken my head off.

My aunt had his story. Mr Spencer had once been a likely lad of a soccer player. Mr Spencer was English. He was snapped up by his home town team, Gillingham, from where he used to take the train to his office job in Shepherd Neame's brewery in Faversham. He was spotted by a scout from the then second division Arsenal. And, since he was enlisting, invited back for another trial in a few months' time, after Christmas, when the war would be over.

The young man who would have been leaving it all behind for football glory was back in the brewery as the office gimp and the girls didn't chew their knuckles anymore wondering who he'd ask to the dinner dance. The Royal British Legion helped him escape the brewery pity by placing him in London as an audit clerk with the firm that years later sent him as part of their team to do the books for our own Ranks Flour Mill.

The auditors stayed over a weekend and were invited on a Ranks Social Club bus tour of the Ring of Kerry. Mr Spencer sat on an aisle seat opposite Dodo Wickham who was in charge of stationery and the labelling machine in Ranks. Dodo Wickham was thought to have been past it. She went around the houses on Friday nights with a slit box collecting for the Mill Hill Fathers Missionary Society. After four years of audits Mr Spencer and Dodo Wickham became engaged. Mr Spencer had to turn, but because of his war wound Protestant-dominated Ranks took him on as assistant general office manager.

Mr Spencer became the holy man of the neighbourhood. Ours had been a garrison city. Sassoon and Graves had been posted here. The people didn't have any of the 'Brits Out' nonsense about them. So Mr Spencer was not prominent as a sore thumb of an Englishman. Only his good works and gammy leg stuck out. He was a predictable convert who went the whole hog, gobbling up Catholicism like a lion who has tasted blood. His lay apostolate in its ubiquity embraced his being a secretary in the Arch-Confraternity of the Holy Family in the Redemptorists, a member of the Third Order of St Francis, administrator of the Pledge on behalf of the Pioneer Total Abstinence Society; he was in charge of acolyte recruitment in the Augustinians and figure of solidarity behind the St Vincent de Paul poor boxes. He was a knock-heads-together volunteer in the Marriage Guidance Counselling Service.

Jackie Droney had no hope of escaping such a man. Already the recruiting sergeant for the Christian Brothers used to sit on the desk in front of Jackie when he made his pitch. A word from Mr Spencer to Mr Hassett and from Mr Hassett to Mrs Droney and Jackie was shanghaied into the surplice at the Augustinians. Mr Hassett asked Jackie how he was getting on.

'I haven't the Latin learned yet. I only light the tall candles.'

'Only?' Mr Hassett said. 'Only?' He put his hand on Jackie's head and dug out the sweets. 'Ah, if I could only say that. I lit tall candles. St Peter would say, come in fast, what kept you.'

For ten months Jackie walked down the road carrying his altar boy bag watched through thinly parted curtains. Then Father Cletus walked up the road to see Mrs Droney and it seemed the neighbourhood could now bask in the accomplishment of watching Jackie flutter off the palm of its hand.

Father Cletus finessed through the tea and biscuits. He had a couple of Craven A cigarettes while Mrs Droney pretended she didn't smoke. Then Father Cletus asked Mrs Droney if she thought Jackie might perhaps have the seed of a vocation? Mrs Droney said that nothing had been said directly but that Jackie had never given her any trouble. But she hoped. Father Cletus said, of course. He

14

understood. Fingernails always immaculate, he said, no need to look behind Jackie's ears. A credit to you.

Father Cletus couldn't keep pawing the ground forever. There were certain times in life, Father Cletus said, when it was better to be cruel than to be kind. And this, he was sorry more than she could be expected to understand, was one of them. It was a matter of canon law and the impediments contained therein. Impediments that he had no doubt would not be seen as such in the enlightened future. For the moment, the best one could do was to think of the good company Jackie was keeping.

A judge, for instance, who has pronounced sentence of death.

Those who have held the office of executioner.

Unfortunates who have suffered the loss of a foot or a hand or a thumb or a forefinger or anything which would prevent a person from breaking the Host properly with the thumb and forefinger.

Those who were blind or dumb or who stammered excessively.

Those who have no nose.

Those who are genuine dwarfs or giants or excessively hunch-backed.

Those possessed of a deformity which causes a person to suffer from a form of external affliction which can be seen easily and gives rise to ridicule or abhorrence.

IGNATIUS VALELLY

I put the 'Back in five minutes' sign on the door of the bookshop and went for coffee. We'd begun with a nucleus of two, myself and Droney when I'd met him again for the first time in nearly thirty years. We used the Market Bar. One morning, while we were minding our own business, a voice said, 'Mind if I sit down, gentlemen?' He was holding his cup and had a parcel under his arm. He was a fine height of a man in his mid-sixties with a full mane of silver hair swept back and a co-respondent's silver tasher. His fawn suit had creased trousers. Cuffs and cufflinks shot out from the coatsleeves.

'What do ye think of my purchase?' He put the parcel on the table and opened the knot. He uncovered the wrapping. It was a picture frame. 'Guess how much?'

Myself and Droney knew this game well. Droney pitched the price at fifteen pounds, giving the man the scope to gloat out a derisory thirty bob. I said, 'A tenner?'

'Sixty pounds. Cheap means trouble is my motto. It's for my first communion photograph. Ignatius Valelly is my name by the way.' He didn't wait for our introductions. He had his wallet out. 'There I am. That's me. That was taken by Joseph Flood. Old Flood. It's a grandson that runs the business now. The whole town was going around with Provident cheques up to Sloans but my mother said no. Not Sloans for our Ignatius she said. Todds. Even now, even today, you can see it in the photograph, even in black and white, I mean,' Valelly laughed at the then prevailing absurdity, 'you can see that's a Todds' suit. That suit didn't come from Sloans!'

He rewrapped the frame. 'I'm going to get it blown up and hang it in the hall. The postman, anyone who comes to the door, will be able to see it.' I could see Droney was gripped even before Valelly went on, seamlessly for Valelly, 'I got my hair cut. Figaros. Eight-fifty. But I always leave the tenner.'

I walked into it. 'It's only two quid in Eddie Benson's.'

Valelly didn't say anything about my haircut. He looked at the ceiling, the length of the bar, consulted his coffee cup and then led me, a dumb beast with a ring on my nose. 'Did you look at his towels? Has he a steriliser? Has he an aquarium? If they can only charge two pounds, what types do you think sat in the seat before you? Would you pick up a magazine after them? They could have boils. What magazines does he have? What papers? Or has he any?'

'He has *Hello* magazines. And the *Sun*.'

Valelly waded in, knee-deep in blood. 'Figaros has *The Times* and the *Irish Times* and the *Sunday Times* and all the latest brand new motoring magazines. I mean, Jesus, Mary and Joseph, two pounds is a tip!'

Droney was at home here in a big way. Two madmen waltzing off, leaving me the victim of an excuse-me. I took out my Rothmans. Droney was on Gold Flake since childhood. I said to Valelly, 'Cigarette?'

'No, no. Put those away. Put those in your pocket. Try one of these.' Valelly took out his own packet – of Rothmans. I reached for my twenty-pence lighter. Valelly outdrew me from his inside pocket. A flip up and flick Zippo that he twirled between thumb and fingers, letting it sashay down the catwalk. Lighting his own fag Valelly saw his watch. 'Good God, look at the time. I have to go. Nice talking to ye.'

Before Valelly reached the street Droney caught my arm. 'You see? You see now what I mean? That's an example of what I'm always telling you. What the uptight world needs. People who are loose . . .'

'But who should be locked up.'

I left by giving Droney the limp 'Some of us have work to do.' I was only about thirty yards down the road when I heard the call: 'TOOTS.' I stopped, turned round. Droney was on the footpath

17

outside the pub. He cupped his lips with his hands. 'Toots . . . SING!'

Next morning we were at the coffee table, Droney drumming his fingers type of thing, my company not enough for him after the exotic Valelly. Today he was dressed like any off-duty postman, solicitor, doctor, drug dealer or accountant – jeans and a leather jacket. He was afraid Valelly might have been a once-off. So I lit a fag and stayed quiet, feeling jilted.

And then: 'Ah, my two friends are here.' Valelly was carrying a portfolio. He put it on the table while he got his coffee. I thought: guess how much. But the second Valelly's arse hit the seat he was off. 'I left school at fifteen and a half. But I got full honours in the intermediate certificate. Later in life I diagnosed it myself. Premature scholastic cabin fever.' He gave us a couple of raised eyebrows to see if we were capable of following him. Then he took a reference from the portfolio, put it on the table and stabbed it with his finger. 'That's from my second job.'

TO WHOM IT MAY CONCERN

For the past eleven months Ignatius Valelly has been employed by HENRY MCMAHON & COMPANY LIMITED in our TIMBER IMPORTING DIVISION as YARD/ERRAND BOY. During that time he has given the utmost satisfaction.

We unreservedly recommend Ignatius for any position of trust for which he may be deemed suitable.

However, we would be negligent in our duty to Ignatius did we not add that, in our opinion, Ignatius is superabundantly qualified academically, in demeanour, geniality, cleanliness and probity for work of a much higher calling than that of his present station here with HENRY MCMAHON & COMPANY. His expressed determination – made known to us when Mr Henry (Jnr) himself invited Ignatius to join the staff – is to continue to work with his hands. It was deemed that in all conscience we could not be an acquiescent party to such profligate stultification of the boy's growth. We have made every persuasion but, alas, to no effect.

We were, of course, willing to employ the filibuster of allowing

Ignatius remain in situ as it were until he would emerge from such a romantic chrysalis. But, again alas, Ignatius decided that he could not – in his own words – 'allow Henry McMahon & Company entertain such false hopes'!!

Accordingly we have no choice but to wish Ignatius well as he moves on and to nurse our loss with the consolation that Ignatius will be somebody else's gain.

Signed.
Miss Peacock,
Per Pro
John Young, BA,
Yard Office Manager.

Valelly put the testimonial back in its see-through pouch in the portfolio. 'They were bound to spot me no matter how much you don't flaunt it. Mr Henry Junior begged me. He said think of what Mr Tauber would say.'

I'd learned from the two-pound haircut. I took in Valelly's deprecatory pause and knew it was a version of Valelly hawing on his fingernails. I let Droney walk into it. 'Tauber? Not as in Richard Tauber?'

Valelly nodded while he fingered out the next exhibit. 'Richard Tauber I'm talking about. He was a great help to me getting the job in McMahon's. Anyway, I said no. I would not work in an office. I never once dirtied my brains for a living. Henry Junior even tried to blackmail me by dragging in what would John McCormack say. I said no. I was quite happy carrying planks on my shoulders around the yard. I'd do the bets for the men who didn't go home to their dinners and I'd make 'em up when anyone had a win but that didn't come in to using my head while at work. Miss Peacock was the first to cop onto me because I took pity on her and made an exception, helping her to balance the petty cash.'

' . . . *the* McCormack?'

'That was the second job gone. Here's me in the first before I grew out of the uniform. Wasn't I cute?'

The photograph was of Valelly in his capacity as a 'buttons' splendidly liveried and topped off with the chin-strapped pill-box hat.

'But look at the autographs first.' Valelly hauled out a type of teenybopper's book.

To Ignatius, Beef Supplier By Appointment to Yours Truly,

Jack Doyle & Movita.

You Are My Heart's Delight, Ignatius. Better tipster than Prince Monololu.

Richard Tauber.

Ever so grateful, Ignatius. And Bertie says Woof Woof.

Vic Loving.

Life saver, mate. Don't do anything I wouldn't do, Ignatius.

The Great Kusacki.

Valelly explained the encomiums so far:

He had run like the clappers to the butchers to get the steak for Movita's eye after Jack Doyle clocked her between the matinee and evening performances.

He stuck a pin in the winner of the Grand National for Tauber.

He brought Vic Loving's Pomeranian, Bertie, to the vet for a dose. The bitch was called after Burlington Bertie as befitted the pet of a male impersonator.

The Great Kusacki was a Cockney named Jack Nagle. He was supposed to be the 'Illusionist Extraordinaire Direct From Poland'. He wore exotic billowing silks and pantaloons and pointed slippers. He juggled, did acrobatics, card tricks. He hadn't a rib of hair. To go with his outfit he wore an elaborate wig in the fashion of one of the Three Musketeers. The Great Kusacki was on the bill that propped John McCormack in a one-night concert in aid of the foreign missions. On the night before there was a dress rehearsal for all – except, of course, McCormack.

Valelly gave the Great Kusacki the secret knock for getting

into Ma Hogan's after hours. Valelly gave the secret knock to everyone, but Jack Nagle *needed* it. In his theatrical dress, the Great Kusacki fell out of Ma Hogan's and tried to crawl on his hands and knees back to his flop in a Patrick Street tenement. He fell asleep in a gutter with the rain pelting down. After he did get to his room and woke the next morning, he sent a note to Valelly. Valelly brought the bazaar outfit to the cleaners, the pointed slippers to a shoemakers and the peruke to be teased by Alfredo Staedhli, the gents' hairdresser. Valelly was to explain that he was representing The Great Kusacki, who would personally call to convey his thanks and settle his accounts on the morning of the day of his departure. The cleaners, the shoemaker and Alfredo Staedhli were all shocked out of their pigeonholes when the Great Kusacki did call personally, convey his thanks and settle his accounts.

Ignatius, keeper of the Artistic Temperament. Go Raibh Míle Maith Agat.

McCormack.

Valelly dipped into his bag of tricks. 'Look at the playbill first.'

It was for the Grand Variety Concert in Aid of the Foreign Missions. McCormack was supported by:

BARTLEY MICHAELS, Baritone & Monologuist.
ANNIE HOBBINS, The Golden Vale Queen of Song.
THE GREAT KUSACKI, Illusionist Extraordinaire.
THE QUAY LANE MALE VOICE CHOIR, Conductor: DAN FITTON.
THE BOB NESBITT SCHOOL OF IRISH DANCING, featuring TOMMIE GILLIGAN, Holder of The Munster Belt.

AND MANY, MANY MORE...

Valelly then produced the concert programme and opened it at a page that included the dramatis personae of what was titled:

21

FULL COMPANY SKETCH

MAN DRINKING BOTTLE OF GUINNESS............ The Great Kusacki
WENCH... Annie Hobbins
MINE HOST.. Bartley Michaels
ENSEMBLE................ Members of the Quay Lane Male Voice
            Choir and the Bob Nesbitt School of Irish Dancing
OUR HERO.. Count John McCormack

The *Full Company Sketch* was by then the theatre tradition established by the manager Tom Norman when he came to the position from London eight years earlier. Tom Norman had a Drury Lane backstage apprenticeship. Involving the supporting acts with the star in a bit of business just before the finale was intended as entertainment in itself but it was also efficacious in having the entire cast together when the curtain fell and rose to applause. In Valelly's time alone OUR HERO had been played by Tauber, Vic Loving and Jack Doyle. The bones of the sketch never changed, Tom Norman adding flesh appropriate to OUR HERO's selection from his repertoire. McCormack was to close with 'La donna è mobile,' ''Tis a Charming Girl I Love' and 'I Hear You Calling Me' before the encores.

The drill hatched by Tom Norman entailed transforming the Great Kusacki into a churl. Valelly was to be sent to the pawnshops in the name of art to borrow a haul of wellingtons, potato digger's trousers and waistcoat, collarless shirt and a tinker's hanky to tie around the Great Kusacki's neck. Identifying the Great Kusacki in the programme as 'Man Drinking Bottle of Guinness' was superfluous since the Great Kusacki insisted in the name of vanity on retaining his peruke.

Annie Hobbins, the Golden Vale Queen of Song who earlier in the concert would sing 'Shall My Soul Pass Through Old Ireland' and 'One Day When We Were Young' was a local beauty dressed like an Irish Colleen and could play the wench without resort to any pawnshop.

Bartley Michaels, the baritone and monologuist ('Smilin' Through'/'The Touch of a Master's Hand') was to take part in the distraction as a statuesque factotum of a barman dusting a makeshift counter while McCormack sang 'La donna è mobile'.

Another curlicue of Tom Norman's demented creativity took the shape of the bottom of a cardboard box propped against the mock counter bearing the crayon-emblazoned authenticity: 'MA HOGAN'S'.

Eight conscripts from the Bob Nesbitt School of Irish Dancing and the Quay Lane Male Voice Choir – excluding Bob Nesbitt and conductor Dan Fitton who were both pioneers – were to be distributed in pairs at four scattered tables. Valelly was to be sent across the road for a pint bottle of Guinness and whatever the rest were having themselves.

While the rest were drinking whatever they were having themselves and talking rhubarb, and Bartley Michaels was dusting his counter, Annie Hobbins was to be down on one knee beseeching the Great Kusacki: 'Kusacki, I love you. Make love to me, Kusacki.' While the Great Kusacki pooh-poohed her away with one hand and glug-glugged from the bottle of Guinness. And Count John McCormack sang 'La donna è mobile'.

The idiotboard punchline of Tom Norman's sketch was that McCormack serenaded in vain. In preference to McCormack, Annie Hobbins was besotted by the Great Kusacki who spurned the wench for the bottle of Guinness.

The concert was to take place on Friday night. On Thursday afternoon, Tom Norman sent Valelly to Corrs' Printers to collect the programmes. Mr Corr always left a programme out for Valelly himself because Valelly was already a collector. Mr Corr was a beautifully spoken man with breeding leaking out of him. He loved the theatre, music and above all, singing. He was a member of a gramophone circle. Here you are, Ignatius, Mr Corr said with what Valelly took to be Mr Corr's habitual jauntiness, Here you are, Mr Corr repeated and then shocked Valelly by swearing: Oh my sweet Jesus, in this city, the home of song. Valelly said, What's wrong, Mr Corr? Mr Corr opened Valelly's own programme. OUR HERO, Mr Corr said, COUNT JOHN MCCORMACK. *McCormack*! It was the first Valelly knew of the intended McCormack involvement in a full company sketch. Valelly said, Maybe it's a mistake, Mr Corr? Mr Corr shook his head. He explained to Valelly that printers had a rule. Print the copy. You could be correcting spellings, dates, capital names for ever and you'd get no thanks for it. But if you once corrected what you thought was wrong for good reason – say, putting a capital letter at the beginning of every line of a poem – you could have the whole lot thrown back in your face by some ignoramus who thought upper case old-fashioned. So the rule was, print the copy. Even so, Mr Corr had telephoned Tom Norman.

Tom Norman said that it was all right, perfectly correct.

Good Christ, Mr Corr said to Valelly, if it happened to the ignorant cognoscenti of London, Paris, Milan, they would *deserve* it. But *here*, where the humblest messenger boy who would duck in and hang by his ankles from the rafters would have an ear beyond every kiss-blower on the continent. Take it away, Ignatius. Take it off the premises.

Valelly said: Mr Corr, why can't you take the staples off the programmes and lift out the page? Again Mr Corr shook his head: Ignatius, we only all have our place.

That night, after the dress rehearsal, Valelly had the full company sketch explained to him by the Great Kusacki while Valelly was giving him the secret knock. Valelly was only a year out of school, having left at fifteen and a half. He brought the problem home to his father who was just home from the pub. His father was still unhappy that Valelly had left school. But he was a great McCormack fan. Ignatius, he said, go in early in the morning, before it's too late, and talk to Tom Norman. Quote me if you must. Explain to him. And tell him after he's put his fucking sketch in the trashcan to send you to the nearest shop for a pin. So that we can hear it drop while McCormack is getting ready to sing.

Valelly lay awake in bed. The effort was extra-curricular. He tore tickets in half for a living. It was not his *job* to solve the problem.

First thing in the morning one of the cleaning ladies handed Valelly the Great Kusacki's *cri de coeur* and he had to deal with the pantaloons, silks, slippers and peruke. Then he ran up the town to the printers to ask Mr Corr how he should address the bishop but that it was all just in case because he was going to try the obvious first and talk to Tom Norman. Mr Corr was worried about Valelly's job and tried to stop him. Valelly said he had the backing of his father. Mr Corr said: God bless you, Ignatius, if anything happens I'll have a job for you here.

Tom Norman didn't like Valelly. Tom Norman was all right at first when Valelly started as buttons but then the manager saw them all mad about Valelly, all the stars. Valelly knew where to find Tom Norman which put Tom Norman's back up for a start. He went to Ma Hogan's where Tom Norman had his morning cure before opening time. Valelly had the secret knock so he was standing in front of Tom Norman before Tom Norman knew what was up.

Ma Hogan's was busy with an eclectic congregation of dockers, bank managers, shift workers and the predecessors of those who, in a pluralist future, would lie in the streets clutching bottles when that became acceptable. Valelly hesitated because of this audience. But Tom Norman showed no consideration in front of his cronies. Yes, Ignatius? Valelly said: I think we have a problem, Mr Norman. The manager said: *We*, Ignatius? and winked at the company.

Valelly tried to whisper: It's about the full company sketch, Mr Norman. The full company sketch, Ignatius? Tom Norman let his eyes take in Ma Hogan's full company, giving them permission to eavesdrop behind the scenes of show business. What about the sketch, Ignatius?

Valelly said that the Great Kusacki had been telling him about the sketch – this intimacy with the stars making Tom Norman frown – how the Great Kusacki was so much looking forward to it, and that Valelly had mentioned it to his own father who was counting the minutes waiting to hear McCormack and who said that Tom Norman was to be congratulated in getting McCormack to appear in the first place. Which Tom Norman did not contradict, even though the reason McCormack appeared was because the concert was in aid of the foreign missions and he was doing it as a favour to his friend, the bishop, Dr O'Neill. McCormack was in retirement.

Tom Norman's chest was sticking out, waiting to hear full company sketch compliments from Valelly's father. Go on, Ignatius, he prodded. My father was wondering about the sketch. Yes, Ignatius? He said to ask you, would the sketch on this occasion, would you not think it might be *infra dig*? It also used to bother

Tom Norman that Valelly could be a lord of language when he wanted to. Because of McCormack, Valelly finished.

Valelly was covered so far by the fiction that he was an emissary from his father. In the presence of a Sanhedrin with the delirium tremens Tom Norman was obliged to sit on his temper. Assure your pater, Ignatius, Tom Norman had a stab at the flourish, my humble sketches were good enough, if I may say so, for Mr Tauber, Jack Doyle, Vic Loving and another half dozen that Tom Norman rattled off. Then Tom Norman tried to bring the impertinence to a close: So we need not detain you any further.

But, as a representative of his father, Valelly could feel himself getting hot. He emerged from his father's shadow. Mr Norman, this is *McCormack*!

Tom Norman pushed Valelly's shoulder with his fist. Run along now, Valelly. Go on. Out. And don't let me see you here again.

McCormack was staying with the bishop, Dr O'Neill. Valelly ran back to the theatre and got his bike. He sped out to the bishop's palace. He rang the bell and took off his pillbox hat. A nun answered. Valelly asked to see Count McCormack. What business, the nun enquired. It was urgent, about the concert in the theatre, Valelly explained. The nun brought him in and told him to wait in the hall. She came back and led him in to their presences.

They were having coffee and cigars. There was McCormack and Dr O'Neill and Charles Foley, who was to accompany McCormack, and Michael O'Sullivan, the great public house singer of the time. Dr O'Neill was an aesthete handcuffed by his asceticism. He wasn't going to the concert. He never did. He did not believe clergy should be seen out and about, laughing and joking. But he loved singing. He was enraptured by Michael O'Sullivan. Dr O'Neill didn't drink but he used to get in a barrel of draught Guinness and sherry for a few priests who loved the singing, and invite Michael O'Sullivan to the palace to give an evening of Victorian ballads. Michael O'Sullivan knew Valelly from O'Sullivan's own appearances in the theatre.

Valelly was trying to nod to the four of them, saying Your Lordship, Count McCormack, Mr Foley, Mr O'Sullivan, when Michael O'Sullivan laughed, seeing Valelly nervous. Don't mind your mister, O'Sullivan said, Michael will do. What's up, Ignatius, we haven't burned down? That relaxed Valelly. All four had friendly faces but concerned in case Valelly had bad news. Somehow he got it out, told his story. He spared Tom Norman, pointed out that Tom Norman was not from the city, that it wasn't Tom Norman's fault, he wouldn't have been brought up on it. Michael O'Sullivan nodded at this exposition from the mouth of a babe and suckling and so did the bishop and Charles Foley.

But McCormack laughed. A great big happy stout man's laugh. McCormack said: Ignatius, well done. But don't worry. McCormack, McCormack said, is overdue a dose of humility. There will be no problem from McCormack. On with the motley. Your Mr Norman may proceed as planned. McCormack understands his feelings.

But Valelly said straight out, as bold as he could, because he could see Michael O'Sullivan was backing him up by the look on O'Sullivan's face, not to mention the bishop and Charles Foley, Valelly said straight out that he hadn't come worried about Tom Norman's feelings, that it was the city he was thinking about, that the people were never guilty in their entire lives of *lèse-majesté*, that the people wouldn't be able to hold their heads up, they'd be a laughing stock among themselves.

Michael O'Sullivan jumped up and and shook Valelly's hand and said: Good man, Ignatius. O'Sullivan turned to McCormack. My God, what did we nearly do. Ignatius is right, Count John, and 'twill be over my dead body too. It was a question then of what would have to be done.

Valelly was leaving them at it, starting to back out when the bishop shouted STOP. Dr O'Neill called a nun to get Valelly lemonade and chocolate biscuits. McCormack made another effort to try and say that, for the sake of peace, he would go along with the business, but he was hushed by Michael O'Sullivan who turned to the bishop: 'Your Lordship, this is a case for men of the world. Myself and Charles will handle this.'

Michael O'Sullivan told Valelly later that his strategy was to give Tom Norman a fong up the hole. But the bishop stepped in. Let it be an episcopal exercise, Dr O'Neill suggested, in seeing if my flock accepts guidance. So the bishop was driven in alone, ahead of Valelly on his bike. Valelly was still in time to have his ear to the keyhole outside Tom Norman's office.

McCormack was run down, the bishop told Tom Norman. He had noticed it himself when McCormack arrived at the palace. It was the bishop's personal opinion that McCormack should not appear at all. But Tom Norman knew what a trooper McCormack was? Everything was being done by the nuns to spare McCormack any exertion so that he would give of his best tonight. The bishop believed that Tom Norman had arranged one of his very popular divertissements? The bishop wondered, would it trouble the house unduly if on this singular occasion the public might be denied for the greater good? Thanking Tom Norman for his understanding, the bishop added a by the way: I'm told you employ a wonderful buttons. Another credit to you.

McCormack sang twelve encores. Valelly's father was five rows from the front, on his feet, whistling through his fingers.

When Valelly got home after the concert his father was waiting for him. Ignatius, you didn't leave school half early enough.

WALTER NIX

A few weeks after Toots Books opened I was lost in the racing page when I was handed *The Mysterious Affair at Styles*: 'Years since I read this. Walter Nix,' he put out his hand, 'you probably know me from the rank?' I said, 'Of course.' I *did* know Walter Nix the taxi driver to see him, yet I didn't recognise him now, even when he identified himself.

The second time he came in, seeing me smoking, Walter Nix asked if he could smoke. I told him fire away. He looked for an ashtray. I told him that was what the stone floor was for. I recognised him now as the man who had bought *The Mysterious Affair at Styles* but again I couldn't see him as the taxi driver – the taxi driver everyone in town, including myself, knew as a taxi driver. And I wasn't able to explain it as a case of mufti, the way one mightn't spot an international rugby player when he wasn't wearing his jersey.

Walter Nix was soon a regular. On top of a decent taste in literature generally he was mad for detective fiction, particularly anything by Agatha Christie or a Sherlock Holmes. Walter always let me know that he was at home with the genre, tapping the cover of Dorothy L. Sayers' *The Nine Tailors*: 'The most unlikely murderer in the history of crime.'

Walter might also mention as a gossipy item of news that a body had been taken out of the river or a shop robbed, what I took then to be the usual taxi driver lore – that is, after I had reminded myself that he was Walter Nix the taxi driver as well as Walter Nix the detective nut.

When I had the horses picked and the crossword done and

the shop was empty, I watched smoke curl from my fag and wondered why I could see Walter Nix the taxi driver but not Walter the book-buyer. I put up the 'Back in five minutes' sign and walked down town to the rank. Walter was sitting in his car out of the rain, reading. I could see he was Walter Nix the taxi driver but could not place him as my customer. I went back to the shop and, possibly deranged by my surroundings, deduced that he was 'The Invisible Man' or 'Dr Jekyll and Mr Hyde'.

Then one afternoon I heard him say: 'Detective Dan Mooney.' I looked up from my table thinking it was a fictional sleuth that I hadn't heard about but Walter was waving at a man outside on the footpath who was studying the books in the window. The man waved back and moved on.

'We go back a long way, Detective Dan Mooney and myself.'

'Back to when he failed his primary?'

'What's that?'

'They are all to a man one shower of thicks.'

'Oh. A bad experience?'

So I told him. It was a red Raleigh five-speed racer with the initials 'TB' carved on the saddle. I'd paid seventy pounds for it second-hand. A morning it was raining – and I didn't then have a peak cap – I cycled to the Market Bar for the coffee. I chained the bike to a railing outside the pub and looked out every few minutes. I cycled back to the shop and leaned the bike against the wall while I opened the door. I took down the 'Back in five minutes' sign and stepped inside to put it on the shelf. I shook the rain out of my hair and cleaned my glasses. That was all. Goodbye bike.

I wasn't simple enough to imagine that all leave should be cancelled and roadblocks set up at the four gates of the city. A guard at the Henry Street station counter doled out the blasé information that the bicycle theft division – a Guard Patrick Kirwan seconded from the warrants office – operated between three and four in the afternoon. When I called back I was directed down a corridor. I knocked. Guard Kirwan called out 'Come in.' His head was down over the paper work. He looked up. I trotted out my story, colour, make, initials on saddle. Guard Kirwan said: 'We'll go and have a look.' He took a big bunch of keys down from a hook and led the way. He clunked open the door into the bike morgue. 'Have a look around and see do you see it.'

It was a room full of crocks, bicycles ridden by district nurse types and the elderly who owned them unrobbed for years.

'D'you see it?'

'No.'

'What you should do is call in again any day you're passing. Between three and four. If I'm not here ask for Guard O'Carroll. He deals with it when I'm off. It might turn up.'

I called in again six times over six weeks. I got Guard O'Carroll the last time. He was an elderly guard and he gave me a stab of hope. 'Do you have the serial number?' I hadn't. I told him about the initials on the saddle. 'You should always take down the serial number. Have a look around and see do you see it.' And call in again it might turn up.

Walter Nix said, 'I understand.'

Next morning at ten o'clock he came in with Detective Dan Mooney. He introduced Dan Mooney. Just said his name. A cold nod from the detective and then Walter Nix said, 'We'd like you to accompany us to the station.' But he went on before I could get jiggy, 'We might have news about your bike.'

I thought going up the road: *we*? In past the counter and along the corridor. Dan Mooney opened the door to the warrants office without knocking. He ignored Guard Kirwan and took down the bunch of keys. Into the bike room. The detective hung back, a washing-his-hands stance. Walter Nix said, 'Have a look around and see do you see it.' The same gang of relics as before, except for a red Raleigh five-speed racer with the initials 'TB' carved on the saddle. I saw Walter slide his tongue across the upper lip. Detective Dan Mooney used his finger to test the dust quotient on a window ledge. I didn't need to be Flash Harry to cop on. Detective Dan Mooney looked at his watch, lifted the left cuff with his dusty finger, letting the world know that he was looking at his watch.

'It looks like mine,' I followed the scent, 'but it's so long since I've seen it.'

'It's yours, all right,' Walter Nix said, starting to wheel the bike out, 'it was down in Mary Street barracks all along. A clerical error, a simple omission in the cross-reference ledgers. My friend here,

Detective Mooney, sorted it all out,' imploring me with that cue to say, as I did, 'Thank you very much.' Detective Dan Mooney nodded. Just another miracle in the line of duty. And sort of jangled the keys to get us all the fuck out of there and back to work.

Walter Nix took charge of wheeling the bike back down the road.

'You do realise that you're a public figure. When people see you, they say that's the man who owns Toots Books. I'm the taxi driver. Barbers. Postmen. People in the public eye. Listening to the barber or the postman, people can believe they're going to get a good summer or that a thirteen-year-old will win the Grand National. The insurance man or the drummer collecting for the band on Friday nights – you won't hear the insurance man saying we'll get no summer this year. Or imagine the drummer talking to the woman at the door, whose young fella's bike was stolen out of the passage, imagine the drummer saying you can forget all about that bike, that bike will be in Dublin now, already resprayed on the way up in the back of a lorry. You understand? You can't take hope away from people. We all have to watch it. You and me, the two of us as well. Now, open up and I'll hold on here 'til we're safely inside and in future bike in first and sign in after.'

Walter Nix walked the bike the whole way in as far as my table. He slapped one hand off the other like a man finished changing the wheel of a car. 'And so. As we say in my debating society, to the motion that "This House Has Confidence in the Authorities", how does Toots Books speak?'

'It's not my bike.'

'What? What did you say?'

'The initials on the saddle are three times smaller than the ones I had on.'

'How can you be sure? It's so long you might be imagining.'

'I'm positive.'

'Wait. The guy who took it. The saddle might have got damaged and he had to get a new saddle and he put the initials back the wrong size.'

'Why would he want to put the initials back on?'

'Why . . . why, for luck. He might be superstitious.'

32

'My bike had butterfly handles. It's the reason I bought it. I can't use this racing type.'

'Exactly. It might be the other way round with whoever took it.' The sweat was running off him. He was still red since I said it wasn't my bike.

'I reported a red Raleigh and this is red – but mine in fact was more maroon than red.'

'That's the weather. The rain . . .'

'I had a saddle-bag for the puncture kit.'

'That could have got lost when he was putting on the new saddle. Or it must have been stolen. Bikes even safely locked – anything detachable walks . . .'

'You know the clerical error you mentioned. The simple omission in the cross-reference ledgers in Mary Street barracks?'

Walter nodded.

'Will you mind the shop here? I'll cycle down there now and ask them in Mary Street if they ever heard of a red Raleigh five-speed racer with the initials TB carved on the saddle.' I grabbed the awkward handlebars.

'Wait!'

Walter produced the *coup de grâce* from his inside pocket and held it like a crucifix wielded in front of a vampire. It was an invoice from the Bike Shop. 'To; One Red Raleigh Five-Speed Racer; Seventy pounds.' It was stamped PAID and addressed to Henry Street station.

One of Walter's eyebrows suggested we understood each other? I accepted the invoice and put the bike again at rest against my table. Walter snaked out as far as the door from where he delivered the afterthought: 'This is between the two of us. All the people need to know is that the guards are doing their job.'

Coming from the retired amateur detective himself, the Walter Nix letter of credence to our Market Bar coffee table consisted of the hardly Holmesian: 'If it isn't yourself,' indicating me. He was standing by the table with his tongue hanging out for an invitation to sit down. He didn't wait for us to roll out the red carpet. 'This retirement business, there's only so much DIY can occupy a man . . .'

'Do it yourself is my own motto,' Valelly was in through the crack, 'last week I painted my gates and a neighbour said I see you got new gates . . .'

Walter Nix's obituary would read: 'late of Thomas Street Taxi Rank'. His father had been a taxi driver when Thomas Street was the only stand and there were just six taxis in the rank. Walter succeeded him as another one-job man. The drivers did most of their waiting in McMahon's pub beside the rank except for Walter who had learned from his father's death being due to hardening of the arteries.

In fine weather Walter did his waiting walking up and down Thomas Street. He was slim and fit, an oddity in the trade. When it rained he sat in the car, reading. Walter was expecting to enter the civil service as a junior executive officer when his father died of the taxi man's disease. Walter accepted the car and the plate as his inheritance. He was a 'library hardback man' who developed a subtlety of observation denied to the 'fast, cheap, efficient' jockeys who screech around today trying to gobble up the custom – abdicating their responsibility as an adjunct of the Henry Street Garda Station.

As well as the car and the plate Walter inherited Guard Dan Mooney who had been the last to liaise with Walter's father. Only five weeks into the job, Guard Mooney approached Walter and tapped on the window at the driver's side. Walter did not roll down the window. He got out of the car to show respect. With elbows leaning on the bonnet their association began. It was about the hardchaw, Crick O'Neill, who had skipped the last time he was due up on a charge of slashing with a broken bottle. That had been ten months back. Now someone reported seeing Crick O'Neill on the Holyhead to Dun Laoghaire boat. The guards had the O'Neill house watched but there was no sign of Crick. Would Walter keep an eye out?

Now that he thought of it, Walter was able to tell Guard Mooney straight off, he'd noticed an extra half pint of milk on the Hannons' doorstep for the past few days. Wasn't Tojo Hannon some sort of cousin of Crick O'Neill's?

34

Walter had solved his first case.

During the next five years Walter Nix wasn't asked to the station to be thanked or invited to the guards' Christmas party. He knew that in a different line of business you couldn't come up trumps as often as he had without some recognition. A pull at the police cap when Dan Mooney was leaving Thomas Street was as much as Walter expected. Look at Sherlock Holmes and Lestrade. But one wet Monday morning the telephone on the taxi pole rang. Walter was third in the rank. The lead driver answered and came back to Walter: 'It's for you.'

'Tell them I'm third car. They have to take the first.'

'It's not a fare. It's Henry Street.'

Walter leapt out. 'Yes, Dan?'

'Mr Nix? This is Guard Mullins here in Henry Street. Dan Mooney said you might be able to help us.'

'At your service, Guard. Put him on.'

'It's about Mary Conway's the tobacconists, it was broken into last night. Or early in the morning. Now the position is, we were on to the maternity hospital in case anyone was out late last night and might have spotted anything. They had only one admission and we checked up and the father did use a taxi but he can't remember a thing. So was it yourself by any chance who took him or would you know who did or . . .'

'Guard Mullins, you said? Look, have you a window there near your phone? Right. What do you see outside? What do I mean? What I mean is, what's the weather like up there in Henry Street . . . yes, because it's lashing here too, you see. Down on top of my head. Anyway. It's Guard Dan Mooney I deal with. Like my father before me. What's that? Has he? Great stuff. Why didn't he tell me? Say I said congratulations. Sergeant Dan Mooney. I'm delighted for him. Tell him give me a shout and I'll see what I can do. As a matter of fact . . . pardon? Oh. I see. Well, if that's the way, if he won't then I won't either.'

Won't be dealing with cases like that anymore.

Twenty minutes later Sergeant Dan Mooney and Guard Mullins turned into Thomas Street. Walter got out of the car and put his hand out to the new sergeant. 'Congratulations.'

'Thank you, Walter. Walter, this is Guard Mullins. He'll be dealing with you from now on.'

Walter shook hands with Guard Mullins and said, 'Will you excuse us for a moment?' He indicated the passenger seat to Dan Mooney. When they were both in the car, Walter said, 'I got a bit of good news myself this morning.'

'Did you. That's good. What is it?'

'I've been promoted to taxi driver in charge of co-operating with the police in the matter of offences worthy of the attention of sergeant's rank.'

Sergeant Dan Mooney laughed at Walter's straight face. Walter looked out the window on his own side and whistled a non-tune. Dan Mooney put away the laugh. 'What are you saying, Walter?'

'Mary Conway's shop. That case is beneath you now.'

'No case is beneath me. It's just I have extra duties.'

'So. So have I.'

'Guard Mullins is a good man.'

'He's not. If you are interested in Mary Conway's shop, try a tall, thin, fair-haired man about fifty, stays in the Simon Community . . .'

When the red Raleigh five-speed racer was stolen Walter Nix had by then been promoted to taxi driver in charge of co-operation with the police in the matter of offences worthy of the attention of a detective's rank. But Walter had failed to keep up with the times. He hadn't evolved into the 'you should have kept all your windows closed even during the heatwave' school of detection where slipshod victims accounted for unsolved crimes. His case load had been dwindling for years before my bike was nicked. He would only deal with Dan Mooney and Dan Mooney was all the time trying to yank his last foot out of the swamp of petty crime. Dan Mooney looked the other way while the guards bypassed Walter and touted the other taxi drivers. More crime was reported by Walter to Dan Mooney in Henry Street than was brought by Dan Mooney to Walter in Thomas Street and less was solved unless Walter brought the solution with him.

Walter was promoted sideways after the case of the red Raleigh. Dan Mooney had come straight out with it. 'For Christ's sake, Walter, a fucking bicycle.'

Walter explained that it wasn't just any old bicycle theft. That Toots Books was by way of being a public figure. And here was a golden opportunity to disseminate positive propaganda through the influential conduit of the bookshop. Dan Mooney was accustomed to Walter's debating society language.

'So what can we do? We both know that bike was halfway up to Dublin resprayed in the back of a lorry before he could report it missing.'

Walter then told Dan Mooney the plan. The detective shook his head. He said, 'Walter, you must be off your game.'

The bureaucracy surrounding the petty cash department in the station would rear up on its hind legs at the idea of diverting seventy pounds to the Bike Shop.

'I know,' Walter said, 'what I meant is we'll cough it up between us.'

Walter saw the look on Dan Mooney's face so he quickly switched to: 'A better idea. Let it be my treat.'

Now that I had a full understanding of the Case of the Red Raleigh, I put Walter Nix down as off his rocker the way an American Express is slotted in to a melodeon of credit cards. There was Droney, no argument about Droney. And there was Valelly, who copper-fastened his scroll halfway through Walter's biography.

A man from the asylum used to come into the pub once a week and sit at the next table, just within my peripheral vision. He was known affectionately – in that droll way the *compos mentis*, viz., Droney, Valelly and Walter, are wont to baptise – as Mad Martin. Like all the harmless let out around town, Martin's trousers were at half mast and his coat sleeves only reached midway between the elbows and wrists. He was over forty years locked up and the talk was that his epilepsy was the crime used to diddle him out of a farm. That was how the madhouse got most of its early recruits.

I had only once seen Martin have a fit. Andrew, the experienced barman, ordered everybody to back off and let Martin thrash out on the floor. Outside of that Martin was accepted and ignored and let be to drink his whiskey and stare straight ahead at nothing.

One morning, while Walter and myself waited for Droney and Valelly to come in so that we could proceed with Walter's story, we heard Martin's glass rattle on the table. We turned around and saw Martin slide off his seat. Andrew vaulted the counter. 'Everybody stay back.' He pulled the tables and chairs clear. 'It's just a fit. Let him alone.'

'That's no fit,' Walter said, experienced in heart attacks. As Walter knelt to give the kiss of life he said, 'Ring an ambulance.' Andrew filched that job. I squatted down beside Walter to give him moral support. My back was to the front door so the first I saw of Valelly was the shoe.

Walter was half a minute into the business when I saw the brand new Blackthorn brown brogue poised about six inches from the ground and an inch from Walter's nose.

'Guess how much?'

Detective Dan Mooney did not go to the rank again. When Walter called to Henry Street he was told that the detective was at a meeting/not in his office/on leave/up the country at a funeral. Walter had to learn about Dan Mooney's retirement from the local newspaper, a full page of photographs, Dan Mooney and his wife with the Waterford cut glass presented by the Chief Superintendent; barristers holding brandy glasses with their heads thrown back, laughing; the presidents from the Licensed Vintners Federation, Rotary, Chamber of Commerce; a group captioned 'Colleagues and Friends' where Walter could surely so easily have been fitted in. The speeches were given, including Dan Mooney's in which he did not mention Walter or Walter's father. An enjoyable social followed, the paper said. The detective was returning to his roots to live out his retirement where he looked forward to resuming his great love of hare coursing – giving a sub-editor his cue: 'POPULAR DETECTIVE TO REMAIN IN HOT PURSUIT'. Ho ho ho.

Walter flogged the cab and plate for fifty thousand. When he handed over the keys he watched the buyer put a bat with nails sticking out of it under the driver's seat. Walter hadn't had the nerve for the night shift in years. As a totem, the bat of nails was as eloquent as any Waterford cut glass in telling Walter that his time was up.

MADELEINE BROWN

My name's Jimmy Imbusch. I was called Toots all over a toy bugle in a Christmas stocking. When I met Droney again for the first time in nearly thirty years we traded histories. He remembered me as part of the warm neighbourhood conspiracy that nurtured him. He had to agree that I was entitled to have lost my sense of humour but he insisted, 'It's my turn to help you now.'

Droney was with me the day I signed the lease for Toots Books. It was the ground floor of a three-storey building down the road from Henry Street station. It had just been a shoe shop. I was impressed by the carpet and shelving and storage heaters and cash register all left behind in a hurry, along with a floorful of harp-stamped brown window envelopes. I needed only bring in the books. For myself I thought: dicky-bow, gambler's waistcoat, beige cords, arm garters and a strap to let the glasses fall on my chest. But Droney said: 'All that will have to come down.' He turned up a corner of carpet and pointed to the stone floor. 'Exactly.' He peeled off a strip of wallpaper, knocked on the hardboard with his knuckle and then attacked the wood with a hammer. 'There you are. Stone walls. What more could we ask.' So we stripped the shop of everything but the stone floor and the stone walls. 'A drawer for a start. Come on. I know a guy in the market.'

In exchange for the carpet, storage heaters and cash register, we got a drawer, tables and shelving planks all made entirely of woodworm. Thrown in for good luck was a smelly oil contraption to battle the hypothermia.

'Now to yourself. You go back to the shop, give me a half an hour.'

Droney splurged a whole pound on the old overcoat and twine in which he was seen out on peak cap day. They became his own when I told him to go and fuck himself.

'But these aren't the same without that coat,' producing a pair of fingerless knitted gloves. 'The miser's look is the thing. People must think you have thousands stashed away.'

I held out for my own clothes.

'All right. But one thing I insist. You have to put the ball through the taxman's legs who might suspect thousands stashed away. You must sign the dole three days a week.'

'Can I do that?'

'That's what the drawer is for, instead of the cash register.'

To establish the float Droney added his library to mine.

As part of what he considered my therapy Droney hunted me off on holidays a few times a year. When I came home he put his head in the door of the bookshop and said, Well? He meant Operation Shipboard Romance. He saw me landing a widowed, childless guesthouse owner with a button undone who would knock at my door at two in the morning to ask if I needed a hotwater bottle. He didn't think I was right to fight the flesh.

The shop stayed open while I was away with Droney in charge, wearing the old coat and twine and miser's gloves. He took the shade off the bulb in the interest of what he called verisimilitude. He took in stuff I wouldn't touch: comics, *National Geographic*s, *True Detective*s, old soccer programmes. Droney made sure to have at least the same turnover as I had. Some of the books he donated to the start-up were always sold while I was away. I guessed he bought them himself. Also, you couldn't go into a second-hand bookshop and walk out again without buying something from a man with a port wine stain.

While I was on holiday Droney begrudged every minute that he was away from the shop. He maintained the tradition of the 'Back in five minutes' hour's coffee break. He believed that the customers must never be able to depend on you. Don't open until ten. Close sometimes at five, sometimes at four. Disappear to watch a state funeral on television. That was his prescription for Toots Books. But on his own – outside of lunch and the coffee break – Droney was in the shop from eight in the morning until eight at night.

I went to London for my first trip away since we'd been infiltrated by Valelly and Walter. Mine was a Sunday morning to Sunday afternoon flight. I hadn't intended ringing Droney from London. The only reason I had a phone in the shop in the first place was, according to Droney, in case of an accident outside the door when somebody would rush in to call an ambulance. And the number had to be ex-directory in keeping with the exotica of the stone floor/naked bulb motif.

On the Tuesday morning I was in a Paddington pub across the road from Ladbroke's with the coffee, fag and the racing page. My bet was three cross doubles and a treble. The first horse to leap out at me was called Jack Doyle. I went hunting in that direction and let the cigarette burn my fingers at the sight of Inspector Clouseau. All I needed was a nag connected to Droney.

There wasn't one. I was about to fall back on the form book when I noticed Dead as a Dodo and I remembered the woman with the slit box collecting for the missions in Droney's neighbourhood, married to the English gaffer with the gammy leg who had the shot like a rocket. On Wednesday morning I slid my flat palm down the results page. Jack Doyle 7/2. Inspector Clouseau 6/4. Dead as a Dodo 5/1. One hundred and twenty pounds and seventy-five pence.

I got a fistful of change at the bar and rang Droney. There was no answer. It was a quarter to eleven. Odd. He must have gone for coffee early. I waited until twelve and then rang every ten minutes up to one o'clock. I didn't get him until ten past three. He answered a suspicious 'Yes?' in accordance with the principle of keeping customers thwarted. Droney wasn't a punter but that shouldn't have diluted his reception of my click.

He said, 'Go way. That's good, isn't it?' I'd have got more enthusiasm from Mr Ladbroke.

I went on, 'I tried to ring you earlier a few times but there was no answer.'

'What time was that?'

I told him and had to feed the slot fifty pences while he was thinking. 'I know what it was. They were digging up the road outside the door – you wouldn't hear a bomb drop.'

'I'm running out of coin.'

'OK. See you soon.'

Not Droney at all. Didn't say, give me your number, I'll ring you back so that he could ask: 'Well?' I rang again at half ten and quarter to three on Thursday, Friday and Saturday and didn't get an answer. I couldn't sleep Saturday night even after a gallon of London beer. What was going on?

At four on Sunday I was standing on the stone floor of the shop. The *Dandy*s and the *Beano*s and *National Geographic*s and *True Detective*s were down a bit. In a few sections of the shelves and tables books were leaning on each other as though three or four had been grabbed in a hurry at the last minute to show a busy week. The drawer had too many tell-tale ten-pound notes and fivers.

I looked out the front window. There was no sign of where the road might have been dug up.

I opened at half-nine on Monday and waited for Droney to appear with the lascivious 'Well?' He hadn't turned up by coffee time. Only Walter and Valelly were in session. My welcome home was subsumed by Valelly's 'Himself is across the road with the wino.'

I sat down with my coffee. 'Droney? What wino?'

'She's a woman wino. The day I got the brochures for my new shed, Tuesday, she staggered in here and fell up against my new suit. I'm going to get it cleaned and give it to St Vincent de Paul. Droney put her arm around his neck and they went across the road. They're there every day since.'

I walked my cup to the front door. I could see them on the high stools at the counter, Droney's face, her back. Across the road was a respectable O'Brien's but it had a reputation: theatrical posters and photographs – the owner, Dolly O'Brien as Lady Bracknell – marked the card. It was the usual arty pub – a cauldron of hospitality for dockers, prostitutes, homosexuals and businessmen. Droney used it as a downtown local at night but it wasn't for me. Too much of an inclination over there to celebrate life.

While I was at the door Valelly passed me. 'I have to go.' He said it as though he had done his best for an ungrateful world. He was magnanimous enough to offer the consolation, 'But I'll see ye tomorrow.'

I went back to Walter. He said, 'She's not a wino.'

'No?'

'Her name is Madeleine Brown. Her husband . . .'

Bobby Brown, Financial Consultant, ended up at the old robbing Peter to pay Paul scam. They were knocking at his door for nearly two hundred thousand. He got eighteen months suspended in response to the plea of never having been in trouble before, now ruined, never be able to hold a position of trust again, willing to undergo counselling.

Bobby Brown wasn't rumbled for stuff like having a fifth share in a horse that came fourth in the Grand National or his wife Madeleine always togged out by Madame Dillons. Pointers. But not taboo. Nation of punters and we all knew women. What did him was a hawkeye who had invested fourteen thousand spotting Brown on the early morning businessman's special to Dublin coughing up a tenner for the Irish Rail breakfast at a time when even stately home owners were giving it away for one ninety. Begrudgery gnawed the investor. He called in to Brown and demanded to put his fingers in the wounds. He wouldn't give Brown time to buy time. He shot his mouth off. There was a run.

Before the crash Bobby Brown and his wife came across to the sheltered, such as myself, as a jet set couple. I used to see them at the races on St Stephen's Day, Bobby Brown looking into the distance, getting cheek-to-cheek whispered tips from the cognoscenti, his head nodding under a trilby, binoculars dormant on the chest of his fawn crombie, wine scarf knotted around the throat any old way; Madeleine Brown in boots and tucked-in cords, polo jumper and Princess Anne hat; both of them waving race cards at friends and none of my own vulgar resort to the torn half-page from the news-paper.

They were a couple who knew Lanzarote in winter long before the stampede of the poor and the sight of Pound Shop clients under the neighbouring poolside umbrella. The Browns were photographed at masked balls, hunt balls, Strauss balls, all the beautiful people's annual dinners, the fashion shows before the rugby clubs invaded that territory. You'd have to guess it had been holy week if they weren't smiling at you from the local paper.

All this was there to be gleaned by any half hermit. And you didn't have to be a Walter Nix or Sherlock Holmes to pick up that Madeleine Brown was a ride.

I'd once wangled tickets for a Richard Harris première. During the interval I was fighting at the bar to try and get the attention of a barman who had a Diploma in Catering. I couldn't even see over the shoulders of a couple of rugby jocks. But I overheard 'Did the business there once, could she fuck, thought my arse was going to go through the ceiling.' I looked around and saw her in a group talking to Harris himself. The jock went on, 'Old Charlie Smirke's horse only trotting after her.' I remembered that Derby winner: Hard Ridden.

That was as much as I knew of the Browns until the court case. Then they dropped out of the local paper, weren't even faces in the crowd anymore. By then I'd become Toots Books. Bobby Brown turned up at the labour exchange on the three-day week lark like myself. His briefcase was now bucket and sponge, squeegee and step-ladder. I'd sit in the shop and wonder how they do it, some people, bounce back. And would I be fucked up for the rest of my life.

I told Walter: 'I see him going around cleaning windows like he's just won the pools.'

'That's true.'

'What's Valelly calling her a wino for? Didn't you tell him who she was?'

'I was about to that morning after Droney took her across the road. But Ignatius had just ordered a new shed for his back garden. He started showing me the brochures. I've noticed something about him. He's not inclined to pay attention unless he's the subject of the discussion himself.'

'You've lost none of your old powers.' Walter took it straight-faced.

'Then I let it go. I know Madeleine. She's John O'Kane's daughter.'

I'd heard of him. John and Marian O'Kane were the doyen and doyenne of the Old County Debating Society in the days when the local paper used to attend and report who spoke for and against, contributions from the floor, who chaired the meeting, the result of the vote.

'Hard to imagine her as John O'Kane's daughter.'

'Why not?'

'It's not exactly the third secret of Fatima that she's a bit of a . . .'

'Stop!' Walter held up his hand. 'She didn't start out like that.'

'Walter, I do understand she wouldn't have been at it before her first communion.'

'Madeleine O'Kane was a bluestocking.'

'Yeah?'

Madeleine O'Kane used to attend the debates when she was only seventeen, Walter said. And she had it all then: humour, vocabulary, when to give the rostrum a thump. Then she went to University College, Galway, to do arts. They'd only see her first or last debate of the season. The summer she graduated she met Bobby Brown in a pub in Salthill. Women had only just emerged from the snugs. There was probably drink involved. A swept-off-her-feet story accounted for the fast wedding. Bobby Brown was eight years older. He'd been pulled into the insurance business by his old school tie. He was only ever up against competition like himself, except the competition didn't have his looks. Now, in the Golden Pages, outside of the computer listings, the biggest section was under 'Financial Consultants'. Throw in the recession. Bobby Brown's good looks and charm could only carry him so far. He was never used to a rat race.

All of that was in the future when Madeleine met him in Salthill. She brought him to one debate. Walter himself was chairman that night. The motion was that 'The tea break is here to stay'.

Walter threw the debate open and looked around for a hand up. He saw Madeleine nudge her husband. The Old County Debating Society used to meet in the technical institute, partition pulled apart to give them two big classrooms. They had an average of a hundred to a hundred and forty every week and even that was down on what it had been.

Walter wasn't surprised to see Bobby Brown shaking his head and keeping his eyes focused on the inkwell. Walter had known the first-time-out terror himself. So he moved on and gave the nod to a regular. After each of the next three contributions from the floor Madeleine continued to give Bobby Brown the elbow. Walter leaned forward, ignored a hand at the back of the hall. There were over a hundred present but the Old County was past its great days even though the plague that was to prove impervious to cultural pesticide – television – was yet to come. The society panted for new blood. When Bobby Brown's hand inched to the half-mast position Walter pointed quickly: the gentleman on my left in the second row. People had seen Bobby come in with Madeleine. They knew he was her husband. Son-in-law of John and Marian O'Kane. The hall gave him the hush. He was willed on.

Bobby Brown stepped out into the aisle and turned his back on Walter. He put his foot on the seat of the desk, his right elbow on his right knee and thrust the left hand into his trouser pocket. Walter was outraged by this show of confidence. It belonged some place else. Bobby Brown was tall and slim with jet black hair then and the Clark Gable moustache. He could have said the 'Our Father' in Irish and he'd still have been the prodigal son.

Walter let him off not addressing the chair. Bobby didn't even say 'ladies and gentlemen'. Walter saw Madeleine frown at the foot on the seat of the desk. And Walter knew then. Everybody in the damn room knew. But Walter was the only one who could see Madeleine's face. He was the only one who knew that she knew. Turn his back on the chair. Not bother with ladies and gentlemen. Put his foot on the seat of the desk. Salesman stuff. With the peculiar stance that he'd affected Bobby Brown began

47

to chat to the audience. Chat. He told a story in support of the motion that 'The tea break is here to stay' of how one morning he buzzed for one of his clerks who, according to his secretary, had stepped out. So he said send someone else in. His second choice was not in the office either. And the third was supposedly out on some errand. He grilled his secretary. They were all out for coffee. Brown Consultants didn't have tea breaks. So – 'what we done was we bought a kettle and made a present of it to the three clerks next morning'.

Down the hall John and Marian O'Kane both held their foreheads, trying to hide themselves. Walter saw Madeleine's face redden. Bobby got a few thin smiles for his kettle anecdote from the less pedantically grammatical. But he'd opened with his high point and then limped on to a lame conclusion, managing to squeeze in 'we could have went down a different road'.

Madeleine was having her face rubbed in it. And this, Walter elucidated, was long before managers of soccer clubs reformed the English language. Walter didn't know whether Madeleine had already realised that she had married a shell. Probably not or she wouldn't have brought him to the debate. But she knew now.

The Old County Debating Society were serious people. They knew a dud penny ever before it failed to clink off the ground. To make it worse for Madeleine they gave Bobby exaggerated applause. She didn't bring him again. She didn't bring herself again.

From there she went on to try and make the best of it, acting the Mrs Bobby Brown rather than have him as Mister Madeleine O'Kane. Walter would see her photograph at some meretricious function and scratch his head: what is she doing there? Cultured people don't go to hunt balls.

Late in the day, when the Browns' son and daughter were reared and at university, Walter heard talk in the rank that he didn't want to believe. Even though rank talk was usually gospel. Then Walter saw it for himself. Madeleine would bundle into a taxi with one of their crowd, but without Bobby. She was always edgy in Walter's car. Walter stood for a better world. She'd ask how the debating society was going and say she must go again soon. She didn't know Walter beyond the debating society. When she was with somebody she shouldn't have been with, Walter would be given an address and then transparent talk for Walter's benefit when they were getting out of the car about how they must have arrived before the others. Walter knew there were no others.

Walter deduced that she must have justified it to herself by thinking it was all part of making the best of it. Walter never once heard of Bobby Brown screwing around. And Bobby must have known. But buried it. Like he couldn't figure out how he had landed her in the first place. And this was the price. Like the money to tog her out at Madame Dillons was part of the territory.

I knew the rest, Walter finished. After Bobby was caught John and Marian O'Kane stopped going to the debating society. But Madeleine stood by her husband. She cut out the messing. They had to sell the house and trade down. Bobby cleaned the windows of some of the people he caught for money. They drank in places like across the road now.

'So what's she doing with Droney?'

Walter hunched. 'He took her out of here Tuesday. Last Friday I saw them come out of O'Brien's after Ignatius left. Like you I went to the door to have a gander. When Droney moved off she stayed outside O'Brien's until he was a good bit down the road. Then the way he does it to you, she shouted after him "Jackie, SING!" I think she's found intellectual stimulation again with Droney. That's just my own observations you understand,' Walter concluded, *ex cathedra*.

The head appeared just after two. 'Well?'

'No luck apart from the horses. Well, yourself. I hear you've been holding court across the road with a lady. Bobby Brown's wife.'

'Toots, she sings. I used to see her in O'Brien's. Then, when I helped her across the road, she'd been hitting it hard, started that morning at one of the market bars at six, a day her husband had to clean some place early. I just fed her coffee and tomato juice for a couple of hours . . .'

'Two hours? What about my shop?'

49

'Queue of fools looking at watches when I went back. Toots, listen to me. I was able to help her. She was down. Burying it all in the drink. I began to explain to her. I showed her that Bobby Brown cleaning windows was actually singing. Fuck the few shillings he did away with. Wasn't there two robbers on the cross with Our Lord . . .'

'For fuck sake.'

'You're not listening. You never listen. Look.' Droney closed the front door. I said, 'What are you doing?' He pulled down the blind. Then he turned his back to me and opened his belt. He dropped his trousers and underpants and arched his arse.

'Jesus. Somebody might look in the keyhole, you fucking headcase . . .'

'I'm as worried about the keyhole as you are. Quick. Read it.'

The letters were divided, a buttock apiece. 'Si' and 'ng'.

'You see it?'

'Cover yourself, you lunatic. Get out of my shop.'

Droney zipped up. 'Follow me.' He opened the back door that led to a passage past the jacks to a small room where I had a convertible couch that I used when I was too drunk or too lazy to go home.

'Yesterday, when you were up in the air in your aeroplane, I was lying down there on my belly and Madeleine Brown was sitting on my back with her biro and she was writing on my arse. And when she was finished, she said, you can turn round now, Jackie my love. Until I ride you.'

I led the way back out. I pulled up the blind and opened the front door. 'Out. Out of my shop please.'

'But can't you see? It's singing.'

'Out.'

I thought of her the night of the Harris première. Blind bollixes of barmen ignoring me while the whole town seemed to have ridden her except me. I let the temptation rise up my loins, the one that comes to even a good man when he thinks he isn't living at all. I saw myself and Madeleine banging on the stairs because we were too impatient to reach the bedroom.

Droney with a real woman. Not a wino. Droney and his port

wine stain. Writing on his arse in our sleepy hamlet while I was lonely in London. I leaned on one of those 'there's hope for us all' canes. Take her off him. Should be no trouble to me with my unblemished face. Then I woke up because I'd come from a line ivied with decency.

So had my wife.

NELLIE

Gravel will always bring it back to me. Or a Harlequins jersey. We had just sacrificed part of the front lawn to accommodate Nellie's Mini. The first image by which I'm ambushed is out of sequence. It is that of the unfamiliar crunch under my feet as I try to make it to the door, fumbling with the key. Nellie was ironing in the kitchen. She could see me in the hall. She said, Well, did ye have a nice . . . before she noticed I had closed the front door. She said, puzzled, Where's . . . and I burst out: Nellie . . . She said, What . . . Nellie . . . Jesus above in Heaven . . . Nellie . . . Johnny's dead . . . he's been drowned.

The only way I had been able to get her to believe me was to explain how it happened. I forgot to back a horse. I was sitting with Johnny on the grass at Sandy after our first dip, enjoying my fag, when I remembered that Alittleofwhatyoufancy was running again that afternoon in the four-thirty at Mallow. The tip had been for Gowran Park a month before where he was beaten by a short head in the bumper after being boxed in and changing his legs. I said to Johnny, I'll be back in a few minutes.

I didn't have to go far. The outer suburbs now had food markets, video shops and a bookie's. But there was a level crossing between Sandy and the suburbs and the gates just closed on my way back. I smoked a full cigarette in the hot car while the train passed.

Down below on the overgrown bank I saw a man pulling at the branches of a tree to look across the river. I stopped. He answered my unasked question, Looks like somebody's after been drowned.

I ran on, praying please Jesus . . .

I saw fifty or sixty people all standing up. They were mostly women and children and a few skinheads with an Alsatian. The Harlequins jersey was folded on top of Johnny's shorts with the runners underneath, hiding his watch. A woman saw my face search the water's edge and across the river. I said, 'There was a little boy sitting here . . .' and already I could see she was sorry for me. She said, 'Are you his father?'

Then I had a crowd around me. A girl said she saw him swim across and heard him shout 'Help!' and go under as the current took him. A man said, 'See the boat, there's a man diving over there I think.' He was looking about three hundred yards down river opposite where I'd come back to the bank. I saw the boat. A man came up from under and climbed in. He was in a shirt and trousers. He stripped and dived in again. He'd once been a member of the old Blue Star Swimming Club. He stayed under a long time. When he came up again he shouted something, and the word came across the river and back to us along the bank. They think they've found him.

While I was backing the horse somebody had gone to telephone. The crowd moved down the bank when they heard the ambulance siren. The driver did point duty, holding back the crowd to allow his mates to run with the stretcher to a slipway while the boat was rowed across the river with the Blue Star man holding Johnny across his lap. The three ambulance men and the Blue Star man ran with Johnny on the stretcher across the field to the ambulance.

Nellie felt her way out of the kitchen, touching the wall like a blind woman. I had my arm around the bannisters. No, Nellie shook her head. No, no. It's not true. No. She slid down and sat on the floor with her legs stretched and her arms folded holding herself together. No no. My Johnny, no. No no. And then the first tentative aaagh. Aaagghhh. And the scream that brought in the neighbours. The type of scream we'd been brought up on in Christian doctrine class that was supposed to be the signature tune of the sinners in Hell.

Mr Johnson and his wife Mona from next door took charge. Mr Johnson telephoned to find out what hospital. He wouldn't let me drive. Mona would come and sit in the back with Nellie. Mr Johnson appointed another neighbour to ring my brother Maurice who would know what other calls to make.

We were a group recognisable to the matron who came towards us as we reached Casualty and asked, Are you the parents? She said we could wait in her office. They're still working on him, she said, but nothing yet. I didn't understand. It had taken me five minutes to go from Sandy to the bookie's and twenty to go back because of the train. Say another fifteen minutes before they took Johnny out of the water. Forty-five minutes to drive home. Five minutes before the scream. Fifteen for Mr Johnson to get us organised and make the hospital. Yes, after nearly two hours they were still trying to save Johnny. It was possible.

The women knelt. Mona started the rosary. I went outside and walked up and down. I gripped and pressed my forehead to a drainpipe. Jesus, Mary and Joseph. I'll go to Mass every day of my life. I'll do anything. Please . . . please Jesus . . .

The doctors worked on Johnny for another hour and a half while the rosary went on with Nellie and Mona reinforced by two nuns. I went in and out and in and out from the matron's office to the drainpipe and my fags and my prayers. Oh Jesus please. My brother Maurice arrived with his wife. He'd telephoned Nellie's father and sister.

Maurice and his wife and Mr Johnson and Mona and the two nuns were all in the office when the matron came in and said the doctor was coming and would they mind he wanted to talk to the parents alone. I stood beside Nellie with my hand resting on her shoulder. I'm sorry, the doctor said, we did everything we could.

The matron and the other two nuns and everybody came back in and the nuns and Mona and Maurice's wife took charge of Nellie while Maurice and Mr Johnson led me out, holding an arm each.

At home it was soft crying now and no screams, with Mona holding Nellie's hands and Maurice's wife with her arms around Nellie's neck. Somebody was full-time at the kettle. People arrived with sliced loaves, cold meat, apple tarts. Maurice and Mr Johnson stayed close to me, maybe to have something to do if I tried to collapse. Mr Johnson always had to be a schemer to get to the pub. He was inspired to ask Maurice 'Would Jimmy need a drink?' By way of clearance, Mr Johnson told Mona they were taking me down the road for a minute.

I was helped by the distraction of the pub liturgy, watching Maurice fight off Mr Johnson for the right to buy the first round. Mr Johnson took such gulps out of the pint that even in my state I had to admire the marvellous consistency to his swallow.

None of the three of us had ever been down this road before. I can't believe it, Maurice said, to happen to you of all people. He meant that I had once done the Kilkee Bay swim in twenty-eight minutes. Then there was no escaping the How exactly . . .

I told them how only last Sunday we had gone to Kilkee for the day and how Johnny met a school pal on the beach. They asked could they go to the Pollock Holes. I checked that the pal could swim. Johnny said that the pal was a better swimmer than himself. So I said yes. The thirty-feet-deep Pollock Holes. I wasn't worried about Johnny. He knew the business. He'd learned at nine. I'd taught him myself to tread water once he'd conquered his first breast stroke. He was swimming a full year and a half.

Maurice and Mr Johnson were with me all the way so far. Then I said, 'A month ago I got a tip for a horse at Gowran Park.'

Maurice doesn't back horses. He's Chief Officer in the Medical Card Department of the Health Authority. He's an older brother type, a man who frowns on 'characters' running in local elections. He waited now, antennae suspicious.

Mr Johnson was a retired electricity meter reader. I thought of him as Mr Johnson because I lived in what was once my parents' house and Mr Johnson was their next-door neighbour. In his job he would have come across tips for horses but I didn't know of him to bet either. Mona was the boss. Mr Johnson was never in a pub at closing time, always looking at the clock, saying 'I'll be killed.' He had to make the best of occasions, even this one. He powered his way to the end of the glass and held up three fingers to the barman.

I backtracked to tell them how Johnny had already swum across, no bother. But I had to admit what they would have known, that there's ten yards at the far side where there isn't ground, where the current is. Maurice said, 'What are you saying about a horse?'

Maurice doesn't smoke either but I'd have been better off saying I went to get fags, even with the whole world out on the pavements puffing like lepers. I finished my story as Mr Johnson acknowledged the barman and went to the counter. Maurice looked at his watch. When Mr Johnson came back I said, 'If the train hadn't come along, if I'd only been there, I'd have saved him.' I had to put a knuckle between my teeth to fight the tears. Mr Johnson squeezed my arm: 'It wasn't your fault, you're not to blame yourself.'

Maurice didn't echo the absolution. It was in the air: a man leaves his son to drown while he goes to back a horse. It would carry. The bona fides I'd established of Johnny's swimming talent wouldn't travel.

Maurice put his palms on his knees and looked around the pub decor, searching for something to say. Mr Johnson attacked the Guinness. I had sneaked shamed sups from the first pint. The head of the second was already sinking. 'Try and get that down you,' Mr Johnson said.

Then Nellie's father came in and saved them. Tom McAllistrim was a retired teacher. His wife, Molly, had also been a teacher. She'd died before Johnny was born. Tom McAllistrim was protected from the desiccated lust for life that chokes those in his profession by the Rabelaisian carapace of his being a Kerry man. In a pub his stance was that of one elbow on the counter while he sang, recited poetry and dipped into his erudition to make the party go. He was huge – six feet four. People saw a gentle giant. The elaborate courtliness with which he seated ladies communicated an artificially high standard to the men in the company. The swear box didn't get a shilling while he was in town.

In newspaper interviews or on *The Late Late Show* or *Sunday Miscellany* his successful past pupils all attributed their prominence to Tom McAllistrim's early influence. He was at his best where he had the courage to lack impartiality. For example, when he saw a young fellow – or a young fellow's father – in a Manchester United jersey or any jersey of that ilk, he would first sigh 'We died at Kinsale.' Then he would thunder 'Victory – love, passion, our own King.' And then, with a grandiloquent sweep of his arm across the bar, 'Defeat – Coca Cola!' This was my last father figure come in now to relieve Maurice and Mr Johnson and help me down off the cross.

Maurice got him a large whiskey. He sat down beside Mr Johnson, keeping Mr Johnson between himself and me. He took a mouthful of the Paddy. 'A sad business,' he said to Mr Johnson, 'I jumped straight into the car.' It can't have been half a minute but it seemed longer before he looked at me. He said, 'Nellie said . . .' And then he cut himself off as though what Nellie said couldn't possibly add up. He tried it a different way: 'How exactly . . .'

So I repeated what a great swimmer Johnny was and he nodded, nodded to show that he knew there was no doubt about that. But he stopped nodding when I came to the horse. It was only my third time of telling, first to Nellie, then Maurice and Mr Johnson, yet already I could feel myself slipping into cornered rat armour. Why did he keep Mr Johnson between us? Why didn't he come over and put his arms around me? Say, You're not to blame yourself. And we could both weep together. Why didn't this folk hero of the summer schools do better than just stop nodding after I mentioned the horse? This intellectual legend who could filch from Shaw, Shelley, Shakespeare at a morning session, rant against the Virgin Queen in the afternoon and in the pub later move from 'Now Sleeps the Crimson Petal' to 'I've Got a Lovely Bunch of Coconuts' – what was he doing clutching his crutch of a whiskey as though he had the better title to being the cripple?

He went on with another sentence plucked from the mourning manual to pierce the silence when nobody can think of anything to say: 'This will kill Nellie.' I slumped my head onto my arms on top of the table and gave in, forgot about manliness. I cried. Then there were two hands on my shoulders. Maurice said, 'I'll take him back.'

Neighbours had come with offerings of brandy, gin and vodka. Tom McAllistrim and Mr Johnson stayed another hour in the pub and brought back a few bottles of whiskey and a couple of slabs of draught Guinness cans. All that ammunition and the protocol of neighbourly condolences spurred the hands of the clock. Maurice was on the phone, making the arrangements, giving people the news to pass on: Griffin's to St Joseph's. Mass twelve o'clock Tuesday, funeral immediately afterwards to Mount St Laurence. All else that I can remember was the oddity of a male neighbour helping with the washing up and Mr Johnson giving a bit of a stagger when he and Mona were the last to leave.

It was half-past three when we lay beside each other on the bed, both of us clothed. I squeezed her hand. She answered. I started to say that it was all my fault but she pushed her leg against mine. 'No. Don't say that. Don't think that.' She turned her head and kissed me.

I woke up alone and was hit with the shame that I had slept. Nellie was downstairs with Mona.

She had written to me using the majesty of my full title: James M. Imbusch, Advertising and Sponsorship Manager, E. M. Hamilton & Company Limited, Tea Merchants. The appeal was typed on Gas Company stationery where she was secretary to the engineer whose daughter was a spastic. Would I sponsor a foursome for the Cerebral Palsy Association Golf Classic.

I had a problem with the event but not with the cause. No matter whom I invited to participate I'd put the back up of some other big customer. It was the end of July and I hadn't yet passed halfway in my budget. Two hundred pounds wouldn't hurt for a deserving charity and there was the attendant publicity.

I wrote to Miss Nellie McAllistrim, explaining why it was not company policy to patronise golf classics but assuring her of our future support in the event of their next fundraiser being in harmony with the company's objectives.

I was at a meeting next morning in Eddie Hamilton's office. We'd been at college together. He head-hunted me when Hamilton's began to nibble at the national market. We were now up to eight and a quarter per cent. When I went back to my office reception rang. There was a Miss Nellie McAllistrim waiting downstairs to 'follow up' her letter.

I was thirty-four and eleven months to her twenty-eight. To go with the miss I didn't see a wedding ring.

She began: 'Do you know Bernard Luttrell, Mr Imbusch?'

I did. He was a brand manager with Guinness.

'Bernard told me that most of the sponsorship appeals go straight into the bin.'

'I can imagine.'

'I learned to do the same myself with rejections.'

I was desperate. Thirty-four years and eleven months and little experience due to a strict religious upbringing and a lack of opportunity. Already I was going to first nights of exhibitions. There were five paintings in my office. Poetry readings, plays, public meetings, any event where an 'oops, sorry' might lead to a wife.

'Aren't you hard on us, Miss McAllistrim? It is Miss?'

'Yes . . .'

'Seeing it as a rejection?'

'You could invite the owner of the smallest shop in town that stocks Hamiltons . . .'

'You may have hit it. Tommy Sullivan's kiosk snug between the railings of the park. Tommy Sullivan is about eighty-four. He has a son sixty-two. Maybe the grandchildren. And who can be jealous. Good idea. Except it leaves me with a different problem.'

'What's that, Mr Imbusch?'

'If I sponsor the fourball you might then feel obliged to say yes when I ask you for a date.'

It wasn't Cary Grant. It was thirty-four years and eleven months.

'Might I, indeed.' She was cool while I did the blushing. I ploughed on. 'Damn. Miss Lenihan.'

'Pardon?'

'I forgot about the kiosk outside the Lyric. Miss Lenihan might get the hump when she reads about Tommy Sullivan's. Wait a minute. The obvious way out there is to sponsor two foursomes. What do you think?'

'That would be terrific, Mr Imbusch. That's very decent . . .'

'Except that leaves us with a bigger problem.'

'And what's that, Mr Imbusch?'

'If I sponsor two foursomes you might then feel obliged to say yes when I ask you to marry me.'

The feeling when your horse begins to quicken in the straight and you suspect you're going to win. I thought I saw her heft the proposal.

'What might I be obliged to say yes to if there's three kiosks?'

'No. Only two. Let me get you the cheque.'

Nellie introduced me and Tom McAllistrim brought out the whiskey. I said, 'Please. Not for me.' He looked at Nellie. Horrified that she had brought home a pioneer. 'It's just I can't drink spirits.'

'You drink a pint?'

'Of course.'

'To horse.'

In the pub I matched his whiskey and medium with my pint over seven rounds. He set in straightaway. 'Tell me. I'm no believer in long courtships, young man, but seven days?'

Nellie's younger sister was already married off. Tom McAllistrim's face was indoctrinated with crinkles in anticipation that I would come up trumps. Eliding my repartee I explained how we met.

'Sounds an interesting job,' he probed.

I fed him Hamilton's eight and a quarter per cent. 'We drink it ourselves sometimes. Drink nothing else from now on, you can be sure.'

We went to the Lyric where *How Green was my Valley* had turned up again. Courting in the back seat had died out. No more need for it when couples took to the streets with their hands shoved down the jeans of each other's backsides. Nellie, too, had had a strict religious upbringing. The pubs closed early then on Sunday nights. I walked her home. Outside her flat I didn't know what to do. She said: 'Thank you for a lovely evening.' She opened her bag and took the key out of her purse.

'Marry me before I'm thirty-five.'

She stood a foot away, leaned forward and pecked me a kiss.

I said to Tom McAllistrim, 'We just hit it off first date.'

Tom McAllistrim was a Nelson Eddy buff. He slapped his leg. He sang: 'I'm sure I could love someone madly if someone would only love me.' And said, 'Tell me, your own parents approve?'

As he did of them. My father was a bank manager. My late

mother had been a nurse. No matchmaker in Kerry could have done a better job.

Going downstairs I looked over the bannister and saw Tom McAllistrim inspecting the framed photographs. Johnny at nine, taken at a school pal's party, the only one not too shy to sing solo, 'Stout Hearted Men', learned at his grandfather's knee.

He stopped in front of his favourite: Johnny standing on the table in the Kerry kitchen, shaking his fist, declaiming from 'The March to Kinsale':

> O'er many a river bridged with ice,
> Through many a vale with snow-drifts dumb,
> Past quacking fen and precipice
> The Princes of the North are come!
> Lo, these are they that, year by year
> Rolled back the tide of England's war;
> Rejoice, Kinsale! Thy help is near!
> That wondrous winter march is o'er.

Tom had taught him while he had Johnny under house arrest during our Kerry holidays.

Nellie in her wedding dress with Sister Mary Monica in the convent of the Faithful Companions of Jesus where Nellie had gone to secondary.

Nellie in our holiday group when she was seven months pregnant, just before her second miscarriage. Then, slim again, looking drawn.

Nellie, radiant at last, with Johnny in the cot.

Me and Nellie holding Johnny on the steps of the maternity hospital. It was an induced birth, fourteen days over her time. She told her visitors, 'He didn't want to leave me.'

The word was out before the death notice appeared. Eddie Hamilton came early on Sunday morning. I was to stay out as long as I liked. Anything the firm could do . . . Sunday had been knocked about a bit for so long that the shopping centres were open. The women took Nellie to buy black. They would eat out.

Mona left a salad for the men. I wasn't a day drinker. Mr Johnson took Tom McAllistrim to the pub.

Sister Mary Monica came in the afternoon while Nellie was still shopping. She said one decade of the rosary. She gave me a blessing. She didn't ask: how exactly. She looked at the photograph of Nellie visiting the convent on our wedding day. She sighed. She said: God called.

In the evening Tom said he hadn't gone to Mass yet. Nellie wouldn't be up to going and by extension neither would I. But I was passed fit enough to go to the pub with Tom, Maurice and Mr Johnson. I drank hard. Tom McAllistrim picked up a bit on his pub persona. We brought home more booze and some strays out of all the people who helped make the pub hours pass by sympathising with us.

We lay on the bed and held hands until sleep came. We didn't touch, kiss or fondle. Inappropriate, as it had been after both miscarriages for a while.

Next morning Maurice was impatient for action. Nellie's sister, Joan, was married to a Kerry engineer on a six-month contract in London. They could only get a flight into Dublin. Tom McAllistrim would meet them off the train. Maurice was taking me to Griffin's the undertakers. He nodded me out to the hall.

'We have to face what Johnny will be laid out in.'

'I can't ask Nellie. Say it to Mona.'

Mona and Nellie went upstairs and came down with a gear bag. We collected Sister Mary Monica at the convent. She left us with Mr Griffin in the office while she went on in with the bag. There was the question of the grave. Did we want to open a new one or put Johnny down with my mother and father. Maurice had bought a plot for his own family. I funked out again. Maurice rang home. Nellie would be happy with whatever I decided. But she said he'd have company with my parents. The school principal had been onto Griffin's. Although it was holiday time he'd contacted some parents. He could provide a guard of honour in the school uniform.

All day the house was Clapham Junction. Mona brought Nellie next door to get something hot inside her. Tom and his daughter

Joan had lunch in the railway hotel. I smoked and drank coffee. Then it was time to be getting ready.

It took two and a half hours for the sympathisers to shuffle through the mortuary. Another large crowd waited outside the church. The priest swung his censer and blessed us in. Maurice moved around the crowd telling anyone who was interested that we were going back to the pub where he'd ordered sandwiches and sausages on sticks. The women went back to the house.

In the pub our circle of Tom McAllistrim, Maurice, Mr Johnson and myself were augmented by Joan's husband, Joe Quill. I'd always been at ease with him. But now I noticed a change. The Kerry football team's prospects came up as it always did. They were clannish, Tom and the engineer, as all Kerry men are on the subject. I'd always managed a half-intelligent question that would elicit a crumb of arcana from the Kerry football lore, because I was family, where a normal outsider would get the chill they believed all the other, lesser counties deserved. They would drip-feed understanding to the non-native simpleton who had married Nellie. They did it with kindness the way Tom taught Johnny Nelson Eddy and 'The March to Kinsale'.

Tonight they were cold. I said to Joe Quill, the engineer, 'Will you hold the Cork forwards?' He said, 'Hard to know.' And turned away. He and Tom talked around me. I tried once more with the engineer: 'I see it's a first championship game for your centre back.' He shrugged, 'Haven't seen him.'

More people accepted an invitation back to the house than we expected, the delay in the mortuary having baulked their quota in the pub. I was grateful for them because they helped smother the frost from Nellie's sister Joan. She sat with Nellie captured on the sofa. She had been all about me in the beginning when I was unveiled as not just someone Nellie had fallen for to take her off the shelf, but Mr Right. Now, when I put my hand on Nellie's shoulder, I saw that Joan couldn't hide it: *her* husband would not have gone off and left a child to drown.

I clung to the fuck-'em-all raft to keep me going. We were clear of the house by half two. Nellie's sister and her husband had booked into a hotel. That was a statement. Tom McAllistrim stayed with Maurice.

While Johnny was lying in his coffin on the altar of St Joseph's, I thought of myself. I said it to Nellie, 'People are blaming me. Joan and Joe.' Nellie said, 'Jimmy, that's nonsense.' I showed her how Tom sat with Mr Johnson between us. She turned over and put her arms around me. I was in the raw, Nellie in a camisole. She drew me into her chest and made a rocking motion. 'Jimmy, Jimmy, don't feel like that. They're all shattered. You're imagining. They love you.'

Next day I was seduced by everybody's indifference into believing Nellie was right. Under the hats the women fluffed the ends of their hair in front of the sitting-room mirror. I told myself, of course, Nellie is right. Nellie is the rock through all this. She's the only one who matters. We're still us. We'll come through.

In the church I concentrated on living off her strength. I held her hand. 'Nearer My God To Thee . . . where Lazarus is poor no more . . . Come Home'.

We buried him.

Maurice organised lunch in a hotel. I didn't drink, I'd had more than I was used to in the previous two days. Once I had met Nellie I'd stopped being one of the boys, went out only with her. Happy to sit at home reading or listening to Nelson Eddy, thinking only of switching on the television the way another couple might suddenly remember to take the dog for a walk.

I asserted myself after the lunch. I told Maurice we wanted to be alone now. We were going home to be by ourselves. To face up to it. Maurice nodded, relieved.

I opened the front door and let Nellie walk in before me. She went into the kitchen. She sat down. She switched on a manic smile, like she used to do after taking off her clothes. She began with sniffling. I went to her. She said, 'I'll be all right. You have a cigarette. I'll be grand in a minute. Put your feet up in the sitting room.'

I sat in the armchair and smoked three cigarettes one after the other while I listened to her crying in the kitchen. I looked up at the ceiling, up where God is supposed to be. Why, I let myself think. Why? What did we ever do, either of us? We were good parents. Johnny was a fine boy. Tom McAllistrim and his wife Molly, from what I'd heard, my own mam and dad, they

64

were all good people. What the fuck did we ever do to deserve this? Do you exist at all? Nellie was getting worse. Oooohhh. Oooohhh Gaawwwddd. I went back into her. I put my hands on her shoulders but she kept her head down, shaking me away. I said, 'Nellie, go upstairs and lie down.' She let me lead her.

I made coffee to see would it help with more cigarettes. Other people have suffered besides you, a thought said. I trawled through man's inhumanity to man. The survivors of grief. My mind wandered. Cot deaths. Car accidents. The Welsh village where the coal tip fell on a school full of children.

Two hours passed. I went upstairs. Nellie was asleep.

Later I heard her in the bathroom. She changed out of the black. She came down with her face done. She wasn't crying any more. I thought: we're going to start fighting back. I brought her into the sitting room and sat us down side by side on the sofa.

'Nellie. I've been trying to think. People have survived worse than us. Think of the Holocaust. How did they do it? The people who had to live after it. But they did it. Maybe they felt they owed it to those who died. Just to carry on . . .' I thought she was with me. She was looking into my face. She was my same Nellie. 'We have to fight it, Nellie. The two of us. We can do it. We . . .'

There was someone at the door. Through the frosted glass I could see the silhouette of a woman. When I opened the door I didn't recognise her. Across the road a man sat in a car with the engine running.

'I saw your address in the paper,' she said. 'I said I'd wait until after the funeral. I minded these for you. I'm sorry, I hope I did the right thing.'

The woman who had said, 'Are you his father?' The shorts, the runners, the watch, the Harlequins jersey in a department store bag.

'That's very good of you. Won't you come in?'

'No, no. My husband is waiting in the car. I'm so sorry. I had a Mass said for your boy. I'll always pray for him.'

I took the bag. 'Thank you. Are you sure . . . my wife . . .'

'No. I'll leave you. You'll want to be alone.'

How grateful I was to that woman then. Nellie sat up for hours, hugging the Harlequins jersey. Her face was bathed in a serenity

I'd never seen before. I didn't speak because she seemed so happy in the silence. She spoke herself just once. She said, 'He didn't want to leave me.' She smiled as though it had been a comical aspect of Johnny's birth.

THE CONVENT

I walk up the gravel of the Faithful Companions of Jesus convent. In the early days Sister Mary Monica was still swathed in starch and would receive me with her fingers entwined inside the loose sleeves of her habit. I sit at the top of the long mahogany table and accept the lunch, afternoon tea or evening meal set off by the best in napery, delft, cutlery. Sister Mary Monica waits in the armchair by the fire until I finish.

This afternoon I'm given tea, biscuits and buns. I eat one biscuit and one bun and then sit in the armchair opposite Sister Mary Monica and put my cup beside the ashtray on the coffee table.

'How is she?' I ask but the hope in the question is all but dead. Though now Reverend Mother, Sister Mary Monica has accepted sartorial emancipation but only as far as what appears to be a conundrum of cardigans.

'During meditation, Jimmy, from matins to vespers, I never stop praying that God's will be done. That his will be to send her home.'

I nod. The prayers didn't work when she wore the full habit. Now, take away her veil, in that rig-out she might be a spinster hogging the porch in a cold seaside hotel. I remember my early forbearance until I cracked and said: 'Sister Mary Monica, do you realise, does *anybody* realise, it's been eight *weeks*?'

After five years I nod to hide the dead scepticism that has replaced my patience. I see her mufti prayers as a gambler throwing good money after bad.

'Tell me about yourself, Jimmy. How is your little group? I believe they're good for you.'

'We have a lady now.'

'Oh wonderful!' Sister Mary Monica claps her hands, hands free of the habit, hands maybe breaking some old rule that has fallen into desuetude. 'And who is she?'

'Ah, ah. Wait for Nellie.'

'I'll get her.'

I'd come rehearsed. Try Madeleine Brown on her. See if it would awaken something. Sister Mary Monica comes back with Nellie.

'Jimmy!' She rushes to me with two hands stretched in front of her to meet mine, 'let me look at you' style. She turns her head so that my kiss touches her cheek. 'How *are* you. What news have you?'

She wears a long black dress with a narrow white ruff. I take an odd comfort from the dress in so far as it is symbolic of the horror. We sit down. Nellie pulls over a chair from the mahogany table. I light up. 'Tell us everything,' Nellie says.

I buck myself up. 'We have a new member at the coffee table. A lady.' I look to see will Nellie frown. No. She is innocent and eager, a child with an ear for the bedtime story.

I motor on to try and prod Nellie. 'Do you remember a Bobby Brown. He had an insurance business . . .'

'I do, yes. Didn't he get into trouble?'

'He's a window cleaner now. His wife, Madeleine . . .'

'. . . we saw her at the Dickie Harris première . . .'

'That's the lady. She's now a member of our coffee table.'

'But she was beautiful. How did ye . . .'

'A gang of misfits like us capture a stunner? She still is. Beautiful.' No bite. 'Droney found her while I was in London. She has her problems. Droney showed her how to look on the bright side. Don't ask me how.' Or I'll have to tell you that she rides the fuck out of him and inscribes tomorrow's diary on his arse.

Sister Mary Monica says: 'Oh Droney' and rubs her hands. She's seen him in action in the streets. Sister Mary Monica wasn't allowed out to our wedding but now she is exposed to madmen and her sanctity towards the touched helps her to pray:

there but for the grace of God go I. Droney is her favourite in my soap opera.

Leaving out Droney and Madeleine screwing, I go bald-headed and tell them everything else about loose Madeleine as I heard it from Walter, using polite language, in deference to Sister Mary Monica, and more euphemisms than you'd find necessary in *Coronation Street*, Sister Mary Monica's favourite programme after missing out on forty years of public-service broadcasting. Madeleine's appearance maintains the TV ratings in the convent. But there are so many characters and all must get a slot centre-stage. Sister Mary Monica says: 'Ignatius. How is Ignatius?'

Introducing Madeleine didn't work with Nellie. I watched her. No artifice. Just the same wide-eyed interest, as always, in anything to do with Jimmy. In the hope that Jimmy might be happy. Like it was Jimmy who was sick.

'Ignatius is Ignatius. No more news there. To Be Continued.' This I aim at Sister Mary Monica, who takes it that I wish to be alone with Nellie.

A holiday relief housekeeper once answered the door and was puzzled when I asked to see Mrs Imbusch. She put a question mark after the name. I described Nellie in her black dress and white ruff. 'Oh, you mean Sister Mary Francis. Come in. I'll get her.'

They could have baulked at letting her play at taking a name in religion. It encouraged a finality that was not in anyone's interest. But to deny her the name they might as well not have allowed her to kneel and kiss the floor after matins. It was a necessary consistency.

I am alone now with my wife who is five years in this convent. While I'm snorting the sleep of the drunk she is up at half-five meditating before matins. After Mass and breakfast she helps the lay sisters to do the laundry and cook dinner. Sister Mary Monica once let me see the room while Nellie was doing her scrubbing. It was as much of a cell as one might expect, with pictures on the wall of Our Lady, the Holy Family, Padre Pio, Maria Goretti, Blessed Martin, Pope John, the Sacred Heart, John F. Kennedy. A statue of the Child of Prague. A holy water font. It was a job lot inheritance that came with the room. The linoleum floor was covered at one side of the bed by a thin rug that was almost threadbare in two knobbly spots where Nellie knelt when she talked to Johnny and prayed for me. With the sleeves folded, as you might see on a shop dummy, the Harlequins jersey reposed on her pillow.

'Jimmy,' Nellie says, immediately Sister Mary Monica closes the door, 'how *are* you?'

I shoot back with a supposedly jaunty thought with which I've been suddenly inspired: 'Nellie, would you like to come home?'

I've hurt her. She's pained that I'm still clinging to such a delusion. I have prayed and prayed and prayed that one day she will blink out from whatever derangement it is that controls her and say, 'Oh Jimmy', and fall into my arms. It's not going to be today. She is sad that I ask again but patient with me because she believes that I know no better. It hasn't been given to me as it has been given to her. But she can step outside her ecstasy to deal with the intrusion of the world: 'You must tell me how you are. Do you eat properly? You mustn't neglect yourself.'

No son. No wife. No sex. People a hundred yards off, fading into department stores, in case they'd have to say hello.

I mustn't neglect myself.

THE WHOLE COASTGUARD

Nellie did not believe in crockery or saucepans that hid the dirt. She wouldn't have any of those brown or dark green cups in the house. The interiors had to be white so that the first hint of teabag scum could be detected and destroyed. She had six willow-pattern mugs hanging from hooks attached to the overhead cupboard.

Eddie Hamilton's wife called one afternoon. She had stayed away until 'it would have all blown over'. I went for a drive to let them at it, woman to woman. When I came back my throat was dry from the cigarettes. I made coffee. That was when I first noticed a stained mug.

Spatters of grease began to nest on the cooker. The bed was made with less and less precision until the covers thrown up any old way became the norm. She let her hair stay mussed after sleep, didn't bother with lipstick. The bathroom grew dirty. The vacuum cleaner stayed under the stairs. When I'd come home from work I'd find Nellie in a beatific state clutching the Harlequins jersey. I resurrected the pep talk that had been interrupted by the woman who brought Johnny's stuff. Nellie smiled agreement with everything I said. The way she might humour baby talk.

I told myself the neglect fitted. I would know that true recovery had set in when Nellie resumed the housewife of the year act. I mopped up the backlog of cooker, crockery and incipient cobwebs in preparation for the month's mind Mass. Nellie picked up for that activity. We had a busy house: Tom McAllistrim, Maurice and his wife, Mr Johnson and Mona, Nellie's sister Joan. Mr Johnson made hay again in the pub. I saw Mona in the kitchen. She had to clean the glasses before she served the drink. She emptied and dusted each unit of the fitted cupboards.

Sometimes I'd ring from work and get no answer. Nellie explained, 'I thought I'd take a run and see Sister Mary Monica.' Then, one night after I had to present a sponsored under-fourteen basketball trophy, Nellie wasn't in when I got home. I tried Mona's. She wasn't there. At half-past ten Sister Mary Monica rang. 'Hello, Jimmy? Nellie said, would you mind if she stayed here tonight?'

'Why would she want to do that? Put her on.'

She was already in bed. Already asleep. I had to drag it out of Sister Mary Monica. Nellie wanted to be near Johnny.

She came home at seven, sparky in remission. She shouted up: 'Jimmy, I'll get your breakfast.' When I came down she stopped nursing the fry to put her arms around me. She gave me the first unequivocal kiss since Johnny drowned. She drew her knee up between my legs. 'I had the most wonderful, wonderful night.'

'In a convent?'

'Sit down and have your breakfast. I had mine with Sister Mary Monica.'

She sat beside me. She looked fresh, the inert rapture diluted. 'Jimmy?'

'Yes, Nellie.'

'Johnny is all right. No, don't ask me. Just believe me. Our Johnny is fine. I had such a wonderful sleep. He was so near me.'

'I know,' I said, not knowing, worried as much now by her animation. I put my hand on her thigh. She said, 'Can you take a half day?'

That afternoon we did it on the floor of the sitting room like we used to do when Johnny was in Kerry. We'd learned together. Nellie got up on top and let herself go. I gave thanks to Sister Mary Monica.

Our domesticity fought for its growth again. We went out on Saturday nights. I noticed people were edgy with me and nobody mentioned children. No matter. We came home. We fucked goodo. We had each other.

But then the listlessness would encroach. Dirty cup. Matted hair. A slip strap off the shoulder. Until I heard myself say, 'Have you seen Sister Mary Monica lately?'

A pattern evolved. She'd stay a night at the convent and come home transfigured. I wasn't bothered. Nellie made love with less reticence than ever. It was second honeymoon stuff. When she'd go and stay a night at the convent I thought of her going for a shot. That was the drill up to Christmas.

Tom McAllistrim used to come up for Christmas and St Stephen's Day for the races, and we'd go to Kerry for New Year's Eve to be part of a gathering that included Nellie's sister and her husband, Joe Quill. Tom wasn't coming this time. The races weren't mentioned. We had Mona and Mr Johnson in Christmas morning. Then we had a dinner as a couple who miss the jollity of having a child around. I brought up New Year's Eve. I dreaded seeing her brother-in-law. Viciously I had salivated over Cork beating the shite out of Kerry. I said, 'Nellie, I don't think I can handle it.' She was slipping back into her rapture. 'We'll stay at home,' she said, and sank into a foolish smile.

We went to Mona's on Christmas night. Mr Johnson organised a dispenser and barrel of draught Guinness. The neighbours beat a path to his door. It was a night when Mona let Mr Johnson rip. Since it was Guinness on tap he got full before he got foolish.

I didn't know how to handle St Stephen's Day without the races. I was warned off by my conscience. Alittleofwhatyoufancy was beaten by a head. Nellie said after the cold lunch, 'I think I'll go and lie down.' She didn't clean up.

I stayed in the kitchen over coffee and fags. I studied the leg of turkey that would have been Johnny's. The races on less than a mile away. The plates not washed. Nellie upstairs. Me in the kitchen. Was this coping?

She hadn't come down by tea time. I went up. She was resting, the Harlequins jersey under her chin. I said, 'Will I get you a cuppa?' She smiled at me, shook her head as though she was so happy now a cup of tea would be doing the dog on it and we'd been brought up to be frugal.

She was asleep when I went back up at ten. She didn't wake while I nursed her under the covers. It was a relief when she shook me in the morning and said, 'I think I'll call on Sister Mary Monica.' Sister Mary Monica rang as early as six that evening to say Nellie would like to sleep in the convent. I went to the pub and gave Mr Johnson an excuse to stay out beyond his time.

I didn't wake until nine. I listened but couldn't hear Nellie downstairs. At half-ten the bell rang. It was Mona. Was Nellie coming to the sales? I asked her in. She'd watched me grow up. I confided in her. She was on the ball.

'Ring Sister Mary Monica. The paths are frosty. She could have left already, she could have fallen. Anything might have happened.'

I rang. 'Jimmy, she's still here. Jimmy, I want you to come and collect her.'

Sister Mary Monica brought me into the waiting room. 'Jimmy, she wants to stay here.'

'Another night?'

Her hands were hidden. She remained standing, magisterial in her habit then. 'I said everything to her as you might expect from someone in my position, as well as that of a family friend. In effect: go home to your husband. Jimmy, I'm very worried. I don't believe Nellie is . . . right. I think she is very ill.'

I gave Sister Mary Monica my own evidence. I said, 'What can I do?'

'Take her home. Keep her at home. If she needs to see me I'll go and see her.'

We went to the parlour. Outside Sister Mary Monica composed her entrance. To a child being collected from a party: 'Now Nellie, here's Jimmy to take you home.'

Nellie tried to climb further back into the armchair. 'No. Please no. Jimmy don't. Please Jimmy.'

I gave the nod to Sister Mary Monica to leave us. I knelt down beside Nellie. She was hugging the Harlequins jersey. I had to coax her hand free so that I could kiss it.

'Nellie. Nellie, what's happening to us?'

'Jimmy, promise me something.'

'Anything. Anything Nellie.'

'Promise me. Promise me you won't let anybody . . .'

'Anybody what, Nellie?'

'You won't let anybody . . . come to look at me. Any doctors or people. I'm fine, Jimmy. There's nothing wrong with me.

Johnny's in Heaven. He wants me to be near him. That's all. You understand that, don't you, Jimmy?'

I was seeing her like doctors or people who might come to look at her. I tried: 'Won't you come home?'

'Don't make me, Jimmy. Please.'

'I won't make you, Nellie. If you want to stay, stay. But for how long?'

I was still kneeling. She put her hand on my hair. 'Until we see.' I stood up and kissed her. 'Let me talk to Sister Mary Monica.'

Sister Mary Monica was impatient with me. 'Couldn't you talk sense into her?'

'I can't pull her out by the leg. She didn't listen to you.'

Sister Mary Monica wasn't used to a lack of obedience. The impotence jarred. But she was a woman of God. She had charity, love. 'All right, Jimmy. She's welcome as long as you say so.'

Until we see. I poked the open-ended ramifications. I got a surge of leadership. I said, 'I have an idea.'

I went back to the parlour. Nellie froze into the armchair again. I said straightaway, 'No problem with Sister Mary Monica, Nellie. You stay here. I'll go off for a few days some place and we'll put it all behind us on New Year's Day. You wouldn't mind? Staying until then?'

She saw through it. Behind the motherly bemusement at the daft things little Jimmy says her eyes were awake to take on anybody who might come to look at her. 'I'll stay, Jimmy. You go off and enjoy yourself. You're to have a good time. And we'll see.'

So much for a nailed-down release date. I went home. Mona was at the door while I packed a bag. I told her the score. Tom McAllistrim was likely to ring and not getting an answer would try Mona. Our story was that Nellie and Jimmy had gone off to the west for a few days.

I drove to Dublin and booked into the Gresham. I launched myself on Leopardstown. I didn't win or lose outside of the entrance fee. I tooled around at night, a pint here, a pint there, and finished in the hotel bar with a book of blurred writing supposedly as companion. On New Year's Eve I was able to go to sleep early, having got drunk earlier.

It was over.

I shortened the journey with that mantra: it's over. It's a new day. A new year. We're beginning again. Foot down. I went home to shower and look my fresh best. Tom McAllistrim and Nellie's sister Joan had telephoned. I said to Mona: 'We'll see you later, just going to collect Nellie now,' shoring up my own 'act masterful' approach.

'All right?' I asked Sister Mary Monica.

'I don't know. She's inside sitting down with that jersey. I said Jimmy will be here soon. I don't think she heard me. She looks in a trance. But she smiled. The awful thing is that she looks so happy.'

I went to the parlour, let the door open so that Sister Mary Monica could see the man of action.

'Right, Nellie?'

I spoke as I breasted the side of the armchair. 'Jimmy!' Nellie pursed her lips to accept a kiss. 'Sit down and tell us,' she noticed Sister Mary Monica, 'how have you *been*?'

'How I have been, Nellie, is spoilt rotten. Living like a lord in the Gresham. I should be ashamed of myself. Anyway, here we go. New Year's Day. Bounce back time. You and me, Nellie . . .'

'Please . . .'

It was worse than a scream. I was expecting it, dreading it and now I couldn't handle it. 'Please don't make me. Please Jimmy . . .'

I had to face it. My wife was sick. 'Nellie, I love you. I wouldn't ever make you do anything.'

'Oh Jimmy.'

I called out the whole coastguard: fast forward to the psychotherapist.

Our own doctor recommended a man who operated from Wellington Road, Dublin 4. The address and enough letters after his name to impress California gave me hope. I went up on the early morning train and rang his bell at a quarter to ten. He wore a cravat. 'I delayed breakfast in anticipation that you might be hungry.' A gent. As we set into the fry he said, 'Tell me about yourself.'

Before I moved to E. M. Hamilton & Company I had been nine years with Regional Development where my brief incorporated making presentations to American multinational pathfinders. I learned to respect their time and give them what they needed to know in bullet points. University, infrastructure, quality of life, educated workforce, bankers and politicians who were practical, understood the world didn't consist only of altar boys.

So by the time there was only the rind of the rasher left the psychotherapist knew me.

'Now. Let's sit over here and tell me about your wife. Is it too early for you to smoke?'

'I had five coming up on the train.'

He didn't have any kick-the-English-language-in-the-bollix smoke-free-zone signs. Nor an ashtray. He handed me a saucer. 'Light up. Tell me about your wife from day one since the accident.'

I brought him to New Year's Day. I said, 'I couldn't handle it on my own anymore. I sent for her father.'

I rang Tom McAllistrim the next day from work. He thought we'd just returned from the west. I told him I didn't think Nellie was herself. I wanted him to see her but I'd fill him in first. He said he'd leave now. I cried off work and met him at the house. I explained; we weren't in any west.

He couldn't hide it: his daughter nuts in a convent. He wasn't buying that. He'd go there straightaway and get to the bottom of this. More than likely she just couldn't stand being in the same house as this man who went to back a horse and let her child drown. That was how I interpreted his concentration on my story and his immediate hurry to go and see Nellie.

I stayed in the waiting room and let Sister Mary Monica show him in. Our scam was that I hadn't sent for him. He thought he'd surprise us since we hadn't gone down for New Year and he hadn't been up for Christmas. Sister Mary Monica came back to the waiting room and reported hearing as she left the parlour: 'Daddy, how *are* you? I hope you're looking after yourself.'

'Nellie, why are you here in the convent?'

'Jimmy says I can.'

We waited. Sister Mary Monica sent for tea and sandwiches. I still hoped that Tom would come in with Nellie and say: young man, take my daughter home. But he came back alone. The tea was hot under the cosy. Sister Mary Monica poured him a cup. His giant hand shook. 'All she wants to know is how *I* am.' He looked at me with a softer respect. 'She says you're letting her stay here.'

'I won't force her home.'

'But how long? How long will this last?' he put it to Sister Mary Monica. She had no answer. I said, 'You asked her to come home? What did she say?'

'Just as you told me. She wants to be near Johnny. She's the same. She's my own girl. But this . . . this nonsense, why didn't you tell me sooner?'

'I wasn't sure sooner. What about Joan? Sisters . . . she might be able to get closer.'

Joan and the engineer were back from London. Joe Quill was about to start his own consultancy in Dublin. I landed Tom with the job of making the call.

Next day was the soonest Joan could come. I insisted Tom McAllistrim stay with me. I rang Maurice. It was time to bring him in. Mona gave us our tea in her house so we were able to drag Mr Johnson along to the pub. Mr Johnson knew his place. He didn't contribute except to hold up four fingers when his turn came. Maurice summed up: 'She needs professional help.'

'I told you. She won't have it. No doctors or people coming to look at her. I gave my word.'

'I can talk to Dr Chrichton.'

'No.'

Chrichton was the chief psychiatrist in charge of the madhouse. He was responsible for everyone from the hardchaws to the daytrippers in with nerves and the booze mob. He'd tablet Nellie into a fool. I thought of Mad Martin. The clarity of my reaction helped me inside Nellie's soul. Fuck them. No people coming to look at her.

'I only said I can talk to Dr Chrichton. He knows this territory. He might have a suggestion.'

'I said no.'

It wasn't the best night's drinking the four of us ever had.

Maurice was sullen: as a clerical officer in the health authority he was overruled by a layman. Tom McAllistrim said, 'Maybe Joan . . .' We hung on to that. Sisterhood was a science beyond us, above doctors, psychiatry and people who would come to look at her.

We picked Joan up from the early train. Joan asked the questions of her father. I was a chauffeur. She saw Nellie. Tom and I sat rattled in the waiting room with Sister Mary Monica and the tea pot. Joan came back. 'She needs help.'

I gave her Nellie's position. She said, 'Nellie isn't in the best state of mind to decide.' She snapped at me, 'somebody', charging the word, 'somebody has to act'.

I acted. I asked Sister Mary Monica to come with me. I knelt down and held Nellie's hand. 'Joan thinks you should see . . .' I groped for a euphemism.

'Jimmy, you promised me.'

'You don't have to see anybody. Whoever visits will have to do so through Sister Mary Monica. If you want to see them, see them. It you don't, you're not available.'

'Jimmy.'

I finished my story to the psychotherapist. 'She's almost nine weeks in there now.'

He said, 'It's a delusional disorder hiding under the flag of religious mania. While she shows resistance there is no good in my seeing her even though it is possible she needs to see somebody. But I even doubt that. She knows, sorry, she *believes* in society's likelihood to inflict professional care. Hence her obsession with how her husband is faring, her father, her sister. It's a defence mechanism, but a pathetic effort that you've seen through yourself. She *believes* she may need help so she sets up a diversion to make it appear that you need help to cope with the death of your son. Because she's happy in her withdrawal. It is part of the fundamental denial, her way of not facing up to his death. He is not dead while she is in touch with him beyond death. So I deduce from what you have told me. But now, tell me more. Tell me about yourself this past nine weeks.'

'I go to work. Eddie Hamilton knows. I had to tell him. But anybody else at work who asks, I just say she's fine. With the neighbours it's different. I don't know who knows or how much they know. Mona and Mr Johnson and Eddie Hamilton are the only ones outside the family who officially know. I go to our nearest shop for fags and milk and stuff and the woman there asks, how's Nellie, we haven't seen her in a while. I've told some people she's in Kerry and others that she's resting in a nursing home, that Christmas affected her badly. Some ask what nursing home, so that they can go and visit and I have to say she's not allowed visitors for the moment. The truth is, I don't know who I've told what. And some aren't asking anymore. When friends ring, I give out the same old ding-dong. Maybe Mr Johnson let something slip to someone in the pub. Mona herself even. Or one of the cleaners or somebody like that in the convent. I notice people are getting more and more uncomfortable with me. I know Eddie Hamilton is worried. We're in trouble there. We stuck our neck out too far in the national market. Lyons hit back and knocked the hell out of us with promotions and giveaways and cut-pricing. We've had redundancies and it looks like we're going to have more. I'm lost at meetings. My mind is everywhere. I'm beginning to skip the corner shop because I can read it in the faces now that they believe Nellie is off her head some place. I come home and I sit around after banana sandwiches or something and I go mad until I force myself out to meet Mr Johnson in the pub where neighbours don't breeze into our company like they used to. I can see it in Mr Johnson and Mona, they're getting old from it. At weekends I drive all over the place just to keep moving. I cry a lot. I sit on the floor the way Nellie did when I brought home the news and I cry. I say things like, Jesus have mercy on me. I beg him. I say I'm not able for this. I say, do anything to me. Give me pain that I can bear. But not this. I pray to my mother. I say, talk to God for me. I cry and I cry and I cry . . .'

I was crying telling him. He let me break down. Then he fingered my cigarette packet towards me.

He said, 'Stay away from the convent.'

I thought I was ahead of him. I had tried that. Eddie Hamilton dragged me to our Dublin office just for the company. I had no function. We were there for two days and one night. I forced myself not to visit the convent on the third day. But all I got from

Nellie was the same: Jimmy. I told this to the psychotherapist but he shook his head.

'Stay away from the convent for your own sake. You must find a life for yourself. Let me be brutal. She may recover. But she may not. That is, recover by our lights. She's found her *modus vivendi*. You find yours as fast as you can in case – in case you're going to need it. At least, to use Nellie's deadline, until we see.'

He was treating me with respect. I knew that. He didn't insult me by trying to cushion the desolate prognosis. But I couldn't meet his confidence in my strength. I was broken. I wanted more. I wanted him to give me hope.

'I'm sorry,' he said, reading me. 'Any time you feel the need, by all means come back to me.'

I wanted to lash out. Lump him in with the amorphous quack community sneered at by all commonsensical laymen. Fat fees feeding off the post-religious age. I'll cure her myself with the help of God. I was in a delirium of emptiness.

He said, 'I'll get you a taxi.'

I got my chequebook ready. 'What do I owe you?' I blustered, to hide the hope gone groggy.

'Let it be my pleasure. I'm sorry I can't be of more help, but please don't hesitate if I can do anything. Whenever you're in Dublin . . .'

At Heuston, I asked the driver, 'How much?'

'That's taken care of.'

I tipped him a fiver. Shame shortened the journey.

Part Two

THE COFFEE TABLE

Droney slipped Madeleine Brown in by having her arrive late so that he could stand up and say, 'Madeleine Brown, a friend of mine from across the road. Ignatius Valelly, Toots Books. And you know Walter.'

Valelly made much of her immediately. 'Here. You must sit in my chair.' As though all the other fucking chairs were defective. 'I'll get you a coffee. Cream? I always have cream in mine.'

'How are the debates, Walter?' she asked while Valelly got the coffee.

'Twenty-four at the last meeting. You'll have to come back.'

'Now,' Valelly put the cup in front of her. 'Try that. You'll like that coffee.'

'Thank you. Jackie told me how you saved McCormack.'

'Oh that. I must show you my references.'

'And you're the man with the bookshop?'

'Yes,' I said, awkward, like I was thirty-four years and eleven months again. But she'd already moved back to Walter. 'Only twenty-four? What was the motion?'

The debating society gossip gobbled up fifteen minutes. She was so unknowing of me that I copped on: Droney had told her. Everything. Then Madeleine indicated Droney with her thumb: 'Guess what I saw him getting up to last night?'

Valelly, Walter and now Madeleine Brown had discovered Droney when he was on top of all inhibitions as a madman about town. 'Two muscles with scars on their faces,' Madeleine Brown told us, 'outside that nightclub, Wiseguys. Jackie says,

85

excuse me, gentlemen, do you have any good fights inside? The bouncers saying, no, we don't have any rows in here. Jackie says, I'll try someplace else so. Gas.'

Walter and Valelly agreeing, no sense of humour around. While I sat surly on my hands.

I wanted to say to them: try this for a sense of humour. My telephone rang. My ex-directory number. A woman's voice.

'I'm enquiring about the plot?'

'Pardon?'

'The plot advertised in the weekend paper.'

I told the lady she had the wrong number. She apologised. And rang back, seconds later. I had fifteen calls that morning. And had to let the phone off the hook for a week.

Burial Plot For Sale. Mount St Laurence. Owner Emigrating. And the ex-directory number. Droney – singing.

I didn't give him the satisfaction of fucking him out of it. I sang dumb. It was wasted. He caught me by shouting into the shop. 'Toots. Toots, don't go. The economists say things will improve.'

I stayed long enough at the coffee table to observe the decorum attendant on Madeleine Brown's introduction. Then I left, weary of the Droney non-stop diet of the piquant. Let him have the coffee-table chorus of approval. I sat on my hands. Not that that wasn't noticed. He called in to the shop.

'The lads asked me after you left. They said how come he never laughs.'

'The lads. The lads, my arse. What did you tell them?'

'I didn't. I didn't think you'd want me to.'

'Don't even tell those two lunatics my name. Is your friend with us to stay?'

'Would you mind?'

'It should be an improvement on guess how much.'

They didn't know my name. I was just Toots. Valelly brought the guillotine down on his CV after his buttons. Walter was the red Raleigh taxi-driver detective. I didn't know if he was married or had a family. Officially, outside of Walter, myself and Valelly didn't know Madeleine Brown from Mao Tse-tung. Yet we were now a coffee table. We might have been five hoboes under a bridge who only gave as much of themselves as was necessary to get at the stockpot.

No matter how much Droney worked at being himself a coffee table is a coffee table and when its DNA asserted itself I allowed myself to be sucked in. One morning we might be a star chamber of malcontents grousing about the bollixed state of the world like any other group over thirty. Another day we might deliberate on possible developments beneficial to mankind – such as the cure for stress.

Here Droney produced his rainmaker's bottle of singing in the streets and shouting out loud when making love. Valelly prescribed three free pints a day, a snack box and access to a brothel for everybody with a medical card instead of the butter vouchers with which they bought fags anyway. Walter thought: if a man could only walk behind a brass band once a day. Madeleine Brown showed that all Walter had said about her in her debating days must have been true. She probed deeper into the psyche to imagine, if it could be arranged, a department store burned to the ground and all the people cordoned off watching, and a few looters arrested. If we were to examine our conscience, wouldn't that take anyone out of himself?

Odd, Madeleine Brown didn't ask me for a contribution there. Then again, Droney knew and I suspected he'd told her.

I had gone into the convent so often, thinking this will be the day, and come out again hardly able to drag one leg after the other. I always took the long way out of the convent down the pathway under the trees past the basketball pavilion and the tennis courts and the hockey pitch. The long way out could not be long enough for me. I had nothing left to hold onto anymore except the endless tears that I would try to camouflage when I passed a stray strolling nun dispensing a smile. I often had to go around the convent perimeter twice or three times to cry myself out before I was able to exit onto the back road and blend with the public.

Stress?

THE LETTER

Madeleine Brown was just over a week with us when Andrew the barman delivered the letter addressed:

TOOTS BOOKS COFFEE TABLE – TO BE OPENED
IN THE PRESENCE OF THE FULL MEMBERSHIP

I'd come in last and sat in my usual seat in the circle with Walter and Valelly to my right and Droney and Madeleine on my left. Andrew put the letter on the middle of the table facing myself, Madeleine and Droney. I fingered the envelope for Walter and Valelly to read. We all gave it a bemused respect until Walter said, 'Where did this come from, Andrew?'

'It must have been hand-delivered. I found it with this morning's post.'

Andrew was inclined to hang around. We waited until he caught the consensus that he should fuck off and mind his own business. Then Walter plucked one from his debating society bag of tricks. 'Toots, since the coffee table is designated under your suzerainty, you should have the honour of opening it.'

I slit the envelope with my thumb. It contained a single sheet with ten words.

ONE OF YOU IS ABOUT TO COMMIT
A HEINOUS CRIME

I handed the page to Valelly, an act of deference inspired by the fact that he had his hand out waiting for it. Valelly let the sheet flutter dismissively onto the table. 'Some crank.' Droney picked it up. He and Madeleine Brown read it together. Droney used his shoulders to say, search me. Madeleine Brown said, 'I should hope it's some crank.'

Walter held the paper up to the light. 'No watermark,' showing the rest of us up as amateurs. He examined the envelope. 'No brand name. Looks like done on one of those word processors,' narrowing the field to only about thirty thousand if the provenance was confined to our own city.

I was indulging such amusing thoughts when I began to notice our group dynamic changing. In so far as a nutty confederation such as our coffee table could have a head, I had never thought of myself in that eminence. Let Valelly add that to his portfolio, I would have shrugged. Yet here were Droney and Madeleine and Valelly looking to Walter for leadership, Valelly asking, 'What do you think of it, Walter?' Especially puzzling since Valelly had dismissed the warning as having come from some crank.

'I don't know yet,' Walter said, holding the A4 sheet at arm's length, studying the evidence now with long sight, the scrutiny an inch from his nose having yielded no solution.

Madeleine Brown almost begged him, 'Walter, surely it must be a crank?'

Valelly revived, 'That's what I said.'

Droney, Madeleine and Valelly looked at Walter with their chins in their hands – an Our Gang backing group. I couldn't help the mischievous: 'A job for Henry Street, Walter?'

Walter ignored the mention of Henry Street. 'I can see two scenarios. First: crank as Ignatius says. Second: somebody at this table sent it.'

'Whose surname begins with D,' I said.

'Hey. I swear. It's not me.'

'Somebody at this table sent it. We'll call him – or her – A. A sent it to let B know that A knows that B is about to commit a crime.' Walter folded the sheet and put it in the envelope. He handed it back to me. 'Let's go once round the table. Beginning with you, Toots. Did you send it?' Walter looked at me as if he was a lie detector. I gave him a bald 'No'.

89

Droney volunteered: 'I didn't send it. But I wish I had.'

'Madeleine?'

'No. It wasn't me, Walter.'

'I just told you, Walter,' Valelly said. 'It's a crank.'

'If it's a crank, it's a crank. Fine. But just in case it is one of us, I have a suggestion. I'm not saying it's much of a suggestion but it's all I can come up with. I'll put it to you this way. If anyone wants to bring it to Henry Street that's OK by me but I'm not going near the place. I've had enough without this. And I'm retired. But what I do suggest is, I propose that we keep an eye on each other.'

We observed about a half a minute's silence in honour of Walter's suggestion which settled on us like lethargy on lotus-eaters.

From the incident of the red Raleigh and Walter's own subsequent delineation of himself as an adjunct to Henry Street Garda station I'd thought of him starkly as a burlesque of the wannabe detective. I didn't now all of a sudden see him as the real McCoy. But I would give him this: I agreed with him. It wasn't the work of some crank, at least not the work of some crank outside the coffee table. Even if it was Droney who did send the message, it wasn't Droney *singing*. It was Droney *sick*.

As Toots Books I lived through a long drab day every day. Mad women came into the shop and brought a Barbara Cartland to my table and asked me, 'Have I read this one before?' Suppose we could take the letter as true. A crime yet to be committed was as good as the circus come to town to deflect me from the agony in the convent. So I stood up and backed Walter: 'I go along with Walter. It's his territory. It's not from some crank.' Though I'd not been in the bar long enough to get halfway through the coffee or light a second fag nobody asked, what's your hurry. I figured they had their hands full accepting that the letter had come from one of us.

There were three browsers in the shop when Droney came in. He put his knuckles on the table and kept his voice down. 'It's not me. You know who did send it?'

'Who?'

'Walter.'

I weighed the candidacy. 'Walter? Not Madeleine Brown who

parachutes in out of nowhere? Not Valelly? Walter is out there in the open on a leash to Henry Street all his life.'

'He could be cracking up for want of a crime.'

'Spoken like Walter himself.'

'Ignatius and Madeleine both said straightaway that it was a crank. My first reaction was that it was a joke but I'm the only one who comes up with jokes like that. Then I started thinking after you left. Walter was too sure of himself too quickly. That business of A sent it to let B know that A knows B is about to commit a crime. No matter how much of a Sherlock Holmes you are, you couldn't come up with that in ten seconds flat.'

'So what do you think he's up to? He proposes we keep an eye on each other.'

'That's what we will do. Humour him. But I'm not going to cramp my style just because I'm being watched. How is . . . how is Nellie?'

'What?'

'Your wife. How is she, how are things in general with you?'

'I told you I don't want to talk about it. Why do you bring it up now?'

'Sorry. It's just . . . in case you ever want to talk. If the pressure or, you know, if things are getting to you . . .'

'And I start thinking of committing a heinous crime and Walter is onto me. For fuck sake . . .'

One of the customers had settled on a Jeffrey Archer. I reached under the table for a recycled paper bag. Droney remembered himself. He tapped the book and told the man: 'I read that one. Wonderful metaphor for the human condition.'

I had finished *The Times* crossword in the morning before the coffee break, a two-fag problem. I used the rest of the afternoon to think about the letter. It had come from one of four people. Why? I wasn't in a position to grill them under a naked bulb. But I could question myself. What do I know of them? I began with Droney.

AFTER FATHER CLETUS

When Father Cletus called to see Mrs Droney I was six weeks into my third year at boarding school. My father was a Dubliner who had never read *Ulysses* yet he was more Joycean than John Stanislaus Joyce himself in the matter of the Christian Brothers. Not for either of their Jimmys.

A supermarket had opened around the corner from my aunt's. My mother said it would hit Madge. Nonsense, my father claimed, hadn't she carried the neighbourhood on the book during the emergency and for years after the war. They wouldn't desert her.

When I came home at Christmas my Aunt Madge had sold out to Finucane's who also bought the house between the shop and the pub.

I had no reason to go to the neighbourhood again. I wouldn't speak to Droney again for the best part of thirty years.

When I did meet him I was wandering demented through side streets, hiding from the world. I had seen him: the poor misfortunate young fellow with the puce thing down the side of his face making an exhibition of himself in the streets.

I walked into him coming around a corner. 'Jimmy Imbusch?' he sang, 'I have the right man?' I was disarmed that anybody was happy to see me. 'God be with the days. Let me buy you a coffee.'

We cobbled together how we had not met for so many years. I hadn't seen him because he'd been in London since he left school. I said, 'London must have suited you. You seem a happy man about town.'

'You've seen me in action? Why didn't you talk to me?'

'I'm not good company these days. I have my own troubles.'

'Do you need money? Can I help you?'

'My problems aren't money. I'd prefer not to talk about them. What about Mr Hassett and his whistle?'

'And old Spencer. He ended up in a Protestant home for bewildered gentlemen and scholars after Dodo died. He was never the same man after Father Cletus. Neither was Mr Hassett.'

'Who's Father Cletus?'

'Father Cletus over the altar in the Augustinians. That time he came to see my mother.'

'Sorry. I'm lost here. What are you talking about?'

'Didn't your aunt tell you?'

'Tell me what?'

He gave me the story. He came home from school. His mother was sitting on the couch in the kitchen holding a damp handkerchief. She pulled him to her chest and told him what Father Cletus had said and about the dwarfs, stammerers, judges, executioners and the people with no noses all in the same boat. He could have told her then how happy he was. That he never had the faintest notion of wanting to be a priest. But he didn't.

Mrs Droney said, 'How will we tell your father?'

She gave Droney a cup of tea and a Marietta biscuit and ran out next door to Mrs O'Donoghue. Mrs O'Donoghue went to my aunt's for the evening can of milk. From there the fuse flamed in the door of Finucane's. A loose tongue crossed the road to Mr Hassett. On his way from Ranks Mr Spencer rested his leg outside the coalyard. Then he went home to Dodo.

''Twas the same as if some Indian was waving his blanket on the Hill of Tara. Now let me ask you a question. Did a scream go up from the neighbourhood?'

I shrugged.

'Did Mr Spencer have to use all his strength to push open the unlocked door of the Augustinian sacristy because Father Cletus had used the cincture of his soutane to hang himself?'

I copped on that Droney didn't expect answers.

'Dodo Wickham. Did Dodo pull down her drawers in the street and piss on the Mill Hill Fathers collection box?' And the girls around the road who used to fight to take him out in his pram, did they grow up to go on the game?

'No.'

Timmie Droney pushed the fry away half-eaten. He poured water into the basin, shook himself out of the top of his overalls. He waved the shaving brush: 'Jackie, go upstairs and bring down my new suit.'

Mr O'Donoghue was sent down to Finucane's to protect Timmie Droney from himself. They were afraid he would get into a fight with someone. Anyone. But Timmie Droney didn't take his usual seat at the angle of the counter where he used to lord it. He sat by himself in an out-of-the-limelight martyr's corner. He sat thoughtful and quiet, nursing his drink and taking afflicted draws of his Players Medium. Everybody knew his sorrow but they couldn't mention it because they weren't supposed to know. The port wine stain had come up trumps at last. Timmie Droney now had a cross to carry with enough tits on it to be milked until the cows came home.

He stopped fighting. He didn't whistle anymore when he hopped down off the Holo truck. He bought a blackthorn stick to go with a long Sunday morning walk so that the whole world would know that he was going for a walk instead of going to Mass.

All the things that ordinary fathers used to do with ordinary sons overtook him. The first manifestation took the shape of his decision to bring Jackie to a rugby match. He stopped outside the gate of the house with his hand held out from his side. Jackie thought he was pointing to something on the ground. Then Jackie realised, Timmie Droney wanted to hold his hand. They went down the road and around the corner. Timmie Droney said, 'I spy with my little eye something beginning with C.' The C was the clock in a butcher's window. Before they got to the match he switched to O'Grady Says. 'O'Grady says count to three.' Jackie went along. 'One two three.' 'Count to six.' 'Four five six.' Ha! O'Grady didn't say it.

He brought Jackie to Kilkee, not now on a Finucane's excursion when Jackie wouldn't see his father all day because of the pubs. Timmie Droney borrowed the Holo truck. Mrs Droney stayed at home. It was a day out for the men of the family, they would swim in the nude in the men-only Pollock Holes.

At Christmas Jackie was forced to draw a line under his co-operation when his father said *à la* Mr Hassett: 'Jackie, I'll take you down to Woolworth's to get your photo taken with Santa.' The last photo Jackie had with Santa was four years earlier and there was a smell of porter off that Santa.

Jackie's father mentioned the circus. Jackie thought: trapeze. But it was only clowns and star-spangled ladies on ponies and old elephants.

Timmie Droney brought him to see De Valera at the O'Connell Monument. He lifted Jackie over the railings of a Georgian building so that Jackie could stand on the window ledge and see over the crowd. He took Jackie to the championship hurling matches. Jackie saw the legendary Christy Ring play.

Timmie Droney joined the library. He encouraged Jackie to take out books that he would read himself. He taught Jackie how to handle a cue in Burton's.

All this time Timmie Droney put on the Oberammergau in Finucane's. Mr O'Donoghue was the William Howard Russell on the spot. Timmie Droney didn't go to the pub now until half-nine instead of seven. He was a model customer. With Timmie retired from all offices the Finucanes had to run their own pub. At home while reading his library book waiting for the new pub departure time Timmie Droney would look up at Jackie doing his homework: 'If there's anything you don't understand ask me.'

Little Blackie McDonald made his first communion. He had his photograph taken outside the house with the whole road gawking. Mrs McDonald asked Jackie and his mother and Timmie Droney to stand in. Timmie Droney put his arm around Jackie and pulled him close.

That Saturday night Jackie was up late listening to Radio Luxemburg. Timmie Droney came home from the pub while Jackie was having his cocoa. When Jackie stood up to go to bed Timmie Droney put his arm around him again. And kissed Jackie on the forehead. Taking aim so that he would miss the port wine stain. But he did that as though the port wine stain was something he didn't want to hurt. Something he respected.

Every Thursday, on his half-day, Timmie Droney gave Jackie the money to go to the pictures after school because Mrs Droney would be having visitors and Jackie might only be in the way. Jackie had to grow older to understand that Timmie Droney had rediscovered his wife and the Thursday half-day was when they made love and not just when Timmie Droney came home from the pub on Saturday nights.

The benefits of the port wine stain began to gallop in all directions. In primary school Jackie had only been given token slaps. Now in secondary, with exams and the Brothers wanting to maintain their reputation, Jackie's face alone would not have saved him. But the visit of Father Cletus had reached the school. Jackie was seen as a sort of Joseph of Cupertino. He was never picked on except to go on messages.

Jackie – and his mother – were still obliged to go to Mass. Women and children could not share in this burden. But Jackie no longer had to serve. Mr Spencer knocked on the doors of those who thought they had outgrown the altar. Mr Spencer stopped children in the street and gave them an inspection and told them to be sure and stay out of trouble. But now when Mr Spencer saw Jackie he discovered a reason to cross the road and if he didn't see Jackie in time he said hello Jackie with fondness.

Timmie Droney had given everyone a lead.

Mr Hassett stood stricken outside the coalyard. He tried the game on Jackie just once more. Jackie, will we go to Dublin and see the GPO. Jackie said, I can't, I haven't time, I have to do my exercise. Mr Hassett said, pity. He didn't say he had a magic carpet. Jackie already had his hawk eye for seeing inside people's souls. He saw a defeated Mr Hassett. Mr Hassett was a bachelor just like my aunt was a spinster. Mr Hassett was a spare father to all the children with his whistle and his sweets.

All of them, Mr Hassett, Mr Spencer, Dodo, my aunt, the neighbours, the Brothers and the other boys around the road, they all took what happened to Jackie as part of their lot the way they had been instructed from pulpits all their lives. So nothing cataclysmic happened that you could point your finger at. It was a drip-drip process, Droney the adult philosophied, today everyone is free but you can't leave the key in the front door anymore.

For three and a half years after Father Cletus called to the house Jackie was smothered by the man trying to be his father. Timmie Droney tried hard. But it didn't work. It couldn't work. He'd started too late.

Gone With The Wind came back. Timmie Droney began his rounds early so that he would be finished early enough to have his tea and get dolled up and be on time for the seven o'clock start since the picture was four hours long.

Timmie Droney and Mrs Droney and Jackie joined the huge queue. Once they had their place Timmie Droney left to go to the shop. He was gone a long time. Jackie and his mother moved on with the queue until they reached the box office. They couldn't get the tickets because Timmie Droney had the money. Mrs Droney sent Jackie out of the cinema to find his father.

Jackie saw the crowd gathered outside Daly's shop.

Jackie and his mother were not allowed in to see him while he was in intensive care. When they were admitted they saw a man with his face all twisted. He couldn't talk. He managed a grunt in the direction of the bedside locker. It was the stuff he had had in his pockets when he collapsed in Daly's. A small box of chocolates for Mrs Droney, twenty Churchmen for himself, a holiday from the Players Medium, a packet of Rolos, a Cadbury's Dairy Milk and a Turkish Delight for Jackie.

The bed was brought downstairs into the parlour. Mr Spencer came with a man in a van and they brought in a type of chair with a hinge on it that had a po inside. A fire was only ever lit in the parlour on Christmas Day. It was part of the big treat. Now the parlour stank all the time of shit. Jackie would gag when he had to bring a meal into his father and when he collected the tray afterwards.

When the weather was fine Mr O'Donoghue would help lift Timmie Droney outside the door. Jackie had to stay near the house. One of the other boys would say: I think your father is trying to call you. It might be no more than an open shoelace. Timmie Droney tried to talk by moving his head like the MGM lion but all that he could say was 'Yackie.'

Timmie Droney had had good wages with the Holo. Now the family was reduced to a disability pittance. Mrs Droney worked on the sewing machine for some of the neighbours to make a few bob. Mr Spencer made mysterious visits. Mr Hassett stopped Jackie and said, 'Why don't you go to the pictures for yourself with that, Jackie,' slipping him a half crown.

For two more years Jackie went to school and was on hand all the time to help his father and there was the smell in the parlour and the cry of Yackie and the shame of the twisted man in the chair outside the door with everyone stopping to say hello and listen to the grunts.

At last the leaving cert. was over and the bottle of ink and ruler fucked into the docks straight after the last exam. It was look-for-a-job time. Further to your recent interview I regret to inform you.

The Castle advertised for a guide. Good knowledge of history. Outgoing and pleasant personality. Neat appearance. Jackie was called for an interview with a Mr Queally.

When Jackie was shown into the office Mr Queally stood up from behind his desk and the first thing Jackie noticed was that Mr Queally had a hump. And Jackie also saw that the first thing Mr Queally noticed was the port wine stain on Jackie's face.

Mr Queally had Jackie's letter of application and leaving cert. results laid out on his desk. There was none of the usual bollix about tell me about yourself or why would you like to join us. 'Excellent results,' Mr Queally said and read out Jackie's hobbies: 'Reading, Walking in the country, Attending the theatre, Travelling, Sports, the Cinema.'

Mr Queally chuckled. He said, 'I must be the only one in the city who plays snooker.' Then he told Jackie about the job. Jackie would have to learn the history of the castle and get to know the exhibits in the folk park so that he would know what he was talking about showing the tourists around. They would be interviewing all that week, Mr Queally and his boss, who was seeing half the candidates and who had the final say.

'But if you don't mind my saying so I think you're overqualified for the job.' Mr Queally tapped Jackie's results. 'If you could wait a month one of the clerks in the office is leaving. It will be advertised in the papers. I'll get you on the shortlist. You might think now you want to be a guide but there isn't any way up. You'd be promoted faster from the office. I came here myself in response to an ad for a guide and was offered the office. I'm damn glad I took it.'

Mr Queally wrote to Jackie, addressing him as 'Dear John'. 'Further to your recent interview, I regret . . .' But there was a codicil: a few words on a 'with compliments' slip. 'Don't forget to keep your eye out for the clerical vacancy.'

Jackie hid the 'with compliments' from his mother, didn't mention that Mr Queally had a hump or that Mr Queally wanted Jackie in the office. He had stumbled upon an inspiration that he was to canonise: Queally's Theorem. He reasoned that if he applied for the position of Commissionaire with the Ritz the personnel officer would feel obliged to offer him a job in the alley loading a skip with bottles destined for recycling.

He could use the theorem to escape from his father.

LONDON

Jackie asked his mother not to tell Timmie Droney that he was going until after he had gone. He didn't want an emotional scene. He left at seven in the morning to get the boat train after an emotional scene – with his mother. He walked down the road and turned the corner. There was Mr Hassett outside the gate of his coalyard.

'Hah, Jackie,' Mr Hassett said, as though on that mild September morning Mr Hassett was expecting a mob with boxcars at the ungodly hour. 'You're off, Jackie. Now here's a little something to speed you on your way.' The envelope was closed. Jackie opened it on the train. Ten English fivers. Money for a man. For a Droney.

Courtesy of Mr Spencer, Droney had the address of a Kilburn landlord and an introduction to the Marian Employment Agency. He was sent to Harrods as part of the autumn recruitment in preparation for Christmas. He sat in a crowded waiting room with the seasonal Sloane Rangers and fledgling Hooray Henrys. The cream of the home counties had to back off when they caught his eye.

Droney was seen by Mrs Willis. Mrs Willis put Mr Queally in the ha'penny place. She might have been sitting across the desk from Rock Hudson. For something to do, Droney observed, while she was thinking fast, Mrs Willis hmmmed as she read the leaving cert. results, the hobbies, the references from a Peace Commissioner and the Superior of the Christian Brothers.

Mrs Willis summed up. 'Well now, you come highly recommended. What would you like us to do for you?'

'I'm here about the job as shop assistant.'

'Shop assistant. You're much much much too good. Let me have a word with our Mr Snelling in wages.'

It took Droney six months to discover that he was not cut out to be a pen-pusher. I was fagged and coffeed out when he told me and was unsympathetic to that cliché. I could sniff what was coming. Trading down. In all he had seventeen jobs. The Harlesden and Willesden factory saltmines. A dental laboratory gofer collecting impressions and bringing the finished sets back to the dentists. The job with a Mr Jones who recruited in a hired hotel room those who were 'tired of the same old routine and who wanted unlimited income'. A mob driven in Mr Jones's van to sell sentimental landscapes to susceptible housewives.

I twisted my watch to the underside of my wrist to steal a look. I was weary of idiot romanticism. But I had to hear him out . . . He had asked me if I needed money. I owed him an audience for that. Then he came to his last job where he stayed eight years. It was with the André Deutsch publishing company.

His position with André Deutsch was that of book-lifter. He did act as tea lady and messenger boy and anything else in the dogsbody stakes such as running to the nearest pub with the off-licence-purchased whiskey bottle to have it topped up from the optics to accommodate the unexpected visit of an Irish author. But otherwise he was full-time as a book-lifter.

The house specialised in publishing quality literature. Print runs were small but remainders were high. The building in Great Russell Street was incommodious. There were books in the hall, books on the steps of the stairs, books on the landing, books in the lavatory, books on window ledges, books on tables, chairs, floors, books on top of bookshelves, books under desks, books on top of typewriters and books under typewriters, books used as cushions by typists, books cluttering the cupboard that contained the whiskey bottle, the vodka bottle, the gin bottle, the milk, teabags, coffee, sugar, kettle and spam.

Droney had to lift the books off the typewriters so that the typists could type and off the floor so that the typists could walk. He had to move the books temporarily out of the hall in case an indigent visiting writer might stumble on riches in the form of a compensation claim.

Every other week André Deutsch himself would attempt to bring his fine mind to the problem. 'Jackie, suppose we moved Mrs Whitby's desk to face the other wall . . . or if we put V.S. Naipaul's Booker Prize into that corner . . . if we shifted the books on the stairs to one side only in a higher pile . . . Sheila Murphy really doesn't need an office, she's out so much entertaining, if Sheila moved in with Mrs Whitby . . .'

'That's when I learned to sing,' Droney said.

I thought it was another job coming up. 'You became a singer?'

Droney might have his tea break with the receptionist, the typists, Mrs Whitby, if she was not at an editors' meeting, or Sheila Murphy the publicist, who might call back having forgotten her hat on the way to stroke a magazine or newspaper fiction editor. But sometimes, so as not to wear out his welcome, he had his cup alone on the landing, sitting on a chair of books.

Sitting on the literary throne he began to think. What's it all about? He considered the sea of books at his feet. That's probably what they are trying to find out, he thought of the writers. He knew every book that was in the house. He knew that he was sitting on a tome on philosophy. Being alone on the landing he couldn't stop asking himself the question: what's it all about? Is this it? He had always seen himself as others saw him but now the introspection led him to step over the footlights and join the audience. Now he could see the hairline defect in his mosaic. He could see the guilt.

His landlord was a decent Mayo builder. Droney paid his rent and sent home a third of his wages after that. Forty-five of Mr Hassett's fifty pounds was lodged in the post office that first Christmas. He could have gone home. But he didn't. Your father sends his love, Mrs Droney put at the end of every letter. Droney would go home when he was better established, Droney wrote. That was the trick. It was time-honoured. When he could make a splash. But it was the smell of the commode and his own hoof fettered to the summons 'Yackie' that made him stay and send money and excuses.

All nine of Droney's fellow lodgers worked for the landlord and they used a communal kitchen that stank of steak and onions. Droney was too shy to muck in. He had a kettle in his room. Otherwise he ate out. On the first Christmas Day the landlord invited Droney to dinner because of the port wine stain, Droney figured, even though the landlord coated the charade by inviting Droney on the grounds that everyone else was going home. Droney said he was going to an uncle. Three of the labourers stayed in the lodgings and had T-bones on the pan.

On the nineteenth of December of his third Christmas in London Droney got a telegram: Dad had had another turn. Droney couldn't get a flight. He was lucky to book the ferry sailing on the twenty-first. Six hours to Holyhead, three on the boat, another three on the train. He didn't think of the smell from the commode or the cry of Yackie. He became stomach sick at last with love and longing to see his father.

He got a taxi to the hospital where he met his mother being led out by Mrs O'Donoghue, Mr Spencer and Dodo.

He went home every Christmas after that and his mother always asked: when are you coming home for good? He knew that she thought: how are strangers treating my boy with his poor face? He did say how kind the English were but he didn't tell her that he was at home in London. And the English were kind. Even if they did see him as a comic figure, a come-up-trumps character like Frankenstein's Igor, who would always emerge from the rubble after the explosion, covered in mortar and dust.

Droney was happy at André Deutsch until the great thoughts began to invade his tea break on the landing. Something was missing. What's it all about? Is this it? He began to skip the solitary cup. When he couldn't join Mrs Whitby or Sheila Murphy and the typists and receptionist were having a giggle he continued working. But André Deutsch himself, a great believer in English traditions, was shocked. He looked at his watch. He tapped the face. 'Elevenses, Jackie.'

Droney had to say, 'I'm off it for the holy souls, Mr Deutsch.'

Then the 'what's it all about' conundrum began to follow Droney around no matter what he was doing. It even crept into Mrs Whitby's office when he was having his cup there. A penny for them, Jackie, she'd ask when he was far away, thinking something was missing.

The *Eureka* came to him one morning while he was on the way for the carton of milk and the typists' KitKats. He was held up at a traffic island. Something is missing, his mouth said and the lady standing next to him smiled. An English rose of a vintage you would expect to hit you over the head with an umbrella. But she smiled. So this time he spoke, knowing he was speaking. He went on, 'I mean, what's it all about?' The lady maintained her smile and nodded in some form of agreement.

The lights changed but Droney forgot to step off the island. He had spoken to a stranger and she had smiled at him. In London.

A new crowd joined him. 'Vroom, vroom,' Droney said to the man on the left, using his thumb to indicate the traffic. 'Vroom vroom vroom.' The man nodded but with a much thinner smile than the earlier lady. Droney upped the stakes. 'Vroom, vroom vroom vroom vroom.' He was in the company of about eight people all of whom had to acknowledge that he was in their midst. As he searched for their eyes they eluded him and smiled at each other. The lights changed and everybody crossed at what Droney suspected was a faster pace than usual in case any one of them alone might land on the pavement beside him. They needn't have worried because he crossed at a slower pace than usual but with his brain racing. Is this it? It is. What's it all about? This is what it's all about. For half a minute on a traffic island he had brought strangers together.

When Droney went back to the office both Mrs Whitby and Sheila Murphy were available as coffee companions but Droney went to the landing. He wanted to play with his thoughts. The English: they were a fun people. Didn't they like nothing better than to get home and put the feet up and listen to a comedian telling dirty jokes? They loved the knees up. They had given the world Vera Lynn and Gracie Fields and Flanagan and Allen. They had it once. But now if you marched through the streets, singing 'I'm getting married in the morning', people would shake their heads instead of joining in. A great people with a natural love of life had lost it. Something was missing. And Droney had found it.

Droney went to Harrods and walked around the men's department with his hands behind his back until he found a victim. When he used to wander around the shop as an employee all the patrons in the men's department would have at one time shot a grouse. Today the people trying on the two-thousand-pound leather jackets looked like they were drug dealers or armed robbers. So he settled on a shop assistant near the tie rack. An Indian gentleman. 'Seventy-nine pounds for a tie?' Droney said, 'you'd get ten shirts for that in Tipperary.' The man didn't smile or nod. But that was as it should be. This was Harrods.

Droney started to write on the backs of his hands. GBPW. Go to Buckingham Palace and move among the crowd. They say she smokes one Woodbine before she goes to bed every night. An American told him, geddoudeddawayyacreep. But a Japanese gentleman was so happy with the secret that he insisted on taking Droney's photograph.

In the tube itself, half a minute before his Tottenham Court Road stop, Droney said, 'Why can't people celebrate anything without fireworks?' Back on the landing at André Deutsch he reflected on the fruits of his ministry. The man who lifted his nose behind the *Financial Times*. The girl with the Walkman. She'd stopped shaking her head for a second. The Rastafarian with the 'hey man I'm with you' look in his eyes. The hungover brickie who blinked awake. And they were only the few whose reactions he could monitor. To a cyclist resting his foot at the traffic lights, who had to lift the headphones to hear him: 'Excuse me, young man, would that be called a Walkperson today?'

News from home came in the letters hidden in the local paper that Mrs Droney folded and tied with twine and ceiling wax. Mr Spencer had died in the Protestant home for bewildered gentlemen and scholars. Mr Hassett was slowing up. He was in and out of hospital. The coalyard was closed. Mr Hassett went to a place called the Cedars of the Lebanon Nursing Home. Mrs Droney visited him. Mr Hassett had Alzheimer's. Half the time Mr Hassett did not know who she was. Once he said to her, 'I know, we'll drive to Killarney and have a ride on a jaunting car. Run up and ask your mother.'

Mrs Droney had taken to going to bingo to get out of the house.

A woman in a hurry to get at the slot machines after the last check of the night excused herself to Mrs Droney but Mrs Droney was dead. Droney let the house to two post office workers.

Coming out of the shop where he bought the milk and the typists' KitKats Droney was faced by Sheila Murphy standing in the doorway. 'Jackie, what are you doing? Do you know her, the old dear?'

'Not really.'

'But I heard you ask her, where would we be without the wrestling. What did you mean?'

'Only being chatty.'

Luckily Sheila Murphy was in her usual hurry.

He was having his cup with Mrs Whitby. The editor said: 'Is that true about Mrs Thatcher? I heard you telling the postman. I thought, funny, André didn't ever mention that and he would surely have known. Who told you she keeps pigeons?'

A man in a pub.

Back to the landing. Mrs Whitby and Sheila Murphy and André Deutsch were all nice people. They had been good to him. Even so, why should he have to answer for himself? A man shouldn't have to look over his shoulder when he was about his business. They were nice people but they were human. It would be natural to say: guess what I saw our Jackie up to today.

He would have to lie low or look over his shoulder and that would be a pity because in the shop where he bought the milk and the Kitkats the girls seemed to accept that he was entitled to address strangers with mad remarks.

Then he got the letter from Donworth Breen Cahill. Eleven thousand pounds in saving certificates. The coalyard. And a three-storey derelict building two blocks down the road from Henry Street Garda station. He didn't even know that Mr Hassett had died.

Now he could go home and make a splash. But who'd hear it? Everybody was dead. He hadn't kept up with anyone. Then again it could work the other way. There wouldn't be a Mrs Whitby or Sheila Murphy catching him in the act. And home was in as much need of a Messiah as England: when he had gone into Finucane's – under new ownership and now called the Crow's Nest – after his mother's funeral a hired young man with a beard was playing a guitar.

He sold the coalyard with full planning permission in a deal that allowed him to own three of the fifty-two houses that were built there. The houses were designed to have only two bedrooms and no gardens yet they sold for the price of a three-bedroom suburban semi-detached. The auctioneers called them 'town houses' even though the town was a ten-minute walk away.

A couple of the developer's men worked on the side for Droney. They made the top floor of the three-storey building habitable so that Droney could move the two post office workers in and out of his own house. He let the second floor to a hairdresser. And downstairs the man selling the cheap shoes had just done his flit owing three months' rent.

'What about yourself, Toots? I'm sorry to hear you've problems.'

I hadn't kept up with anybody either. Outside of Sister Mary Monica I didn't talk to anyone without my guard up. Tom McAllistrim, Mr Johnson and Mona were all dead. I didn't even know the name of my new next-door neighbour. Droney calling me Toots again was a comfort. I didn't realise what I had bottled up. There was no blink of disapproval out of Droney when I came to the bit about backing the horse. I had his sympathy all the way. I cried in the telling.

Droney said. 'Are you *sure* you don't need money? I have buckets of it.'

When Eddie Hamilton had head-hunted me from Regional Development he'd put a golden handshake into the contract. He called me into his office once he knew Hamilton's would not survive. He told me to grab mine now. He wanted to get out while he could still give the men a decent slice of redundancy on top of the statutory. I sold the lump sum for a pension.

Tom McAllistrim left Nellie the house. Nellie hadn't gone to the funeral. Neither had I. Her sister Joan hadn't spoken to me since the day I wouldn't let anybody come to see Nellie. Doctors or people. I didn't want to sell the house. I asked Sister Mary Monica to be with me when I asked Nellie. I thought of the house as Nellie's womb. I might be giving away the cure. But

all I could get was: 'Jimmy, you must do what you think best.'
So the holiday home was still there, rotting. Until we'd see.

'I'm not short of money. Thanks all the same. I'm short of
my wife.'

'We have to get you on your feet. First, you must find something
to do. And I have it. My shop. To become your shop. Toots
Books.'

THE DROP OUT

I used the five-nights-a-week soccer on television as my life-support machine in a downtown pub called the Drop Out. The original licensee had been a rugby man. Successive owners, who purchased on the audited figures, saw no reason to disestablish sport as the religion of the customers. It was a great place to be anonymous among the crowd while they shouted 'Yes' or 'Fuckit' after Manchester United scored.

I drank seven pints there every night between half-eight and twelve and then went for a takeaway in the Chicken Hut. 'A thigh and superchip,' the girl at the till called out once I approached the glass door. I was that regular. I got a cab home.

Sometimes, in a fit of petulance at the hand I'd been dealt, I'd slum on, fall asleep on the couch with my head by the chicken box. Waking up hung over in crumpled clothes and looking at the bones in the box was just one way of crossing off the date on a calendar, notching a reminder to whoever had flung me into the pit.

No breakfast. Up on the bike when the neighbours had already left for work or sometimes I'd take Nellie's Mini to keep it exercised. Coffee and fags in the Market Bar. Lunch in the Drop Out. Soup and a roll. I had tried to keep up a fry at tea-time but that had degenerated to a salad, then corned beef, and finally a banana sandwich until I became too listless for that operation and just buttered the bread and had the banana like a monkey.

Monday to Friday I drove fourteen miles to the leisure centre in a hotel after my banana and swam eight hundred metres to avoid becoming gross in appearance as well as habit.

On Saturday after work I forced myself to the pictures to hang on to some sort of culture. Sundays weren't so easily whipped. I drove sixty miles in any direction that pushed its way to the head of the queue and ate a roast some place and hung around with the Sunday papers. On the way home to the half-eight start in the Drop Out I went to Mass. I prayed in the back of the church the way I'd never prayed before I lost her. I paraphrased two thousand years of liturgy into three words: Oh Jesus please.

The Drop Out counter was partitioned into cubicles, the first of which, just inside the door, only accommodated two high stools. I sat on the stool that took in the front door and the television behind the counter. There were three other televisions around the pub so that no matter where you were on a big night you couldn't miss the action. My space was only ever invaded by loners or oddballs rushing in from bingo at half-time.

Skinny Mitchell, a mature third-year arts student, had become a Toots Books regular. He'd come in on a quiet morning and looked around at the stone floor, the spurting oil heater, at the naked bulb, at me. He said, 'Fuck me pink.' I looked up. He went on, 'I like it. I like it. Tell me, you haven't *The Hunchback of Notre Dame* with a torn cover and a few pages missing that I could buy for half fuck all?'

'Look around.'

I watched him getting lost. John Dos Passos between a Mills & Boon and M. G. Eberhardt. Droney's anti-filing system. I'd once taken in a lot that included six Richard Condon novels and put them together on a shelf. Droney was offended. In his redistribution, *The Manchurian Candidate* found a home between *The ABC Murders* and *Dr Zhivago*.

But this Skinny Mitchell was able for us. After a minute squinting over his equally skinny glasses, Skinny Mitchell said, 'You wouldn't know where it might be? I need it for two months' time.'

He called in once a week. 'Any sign of my Quasimodo?' He

seemed more interested in the floor, the heater, the naked bulb, my bicycle. I picked up *The Hunchback* at a book fair.

'Good man. What do I owe you?'

'One fifty-seven.'

'One fifty-*seven*? I love it. I love it. Tell me, you wouldn't have a job going here around next September by any chance?'

'Sorry.'

'It's co-op year. Work experience they call it. I went in as a mature student to get away from work and now they're hunting me out for a year. I'm doing the Romantics. I ask you, is that a nice thing to do to a romantic. Fuck him out to work. I could tidy up in here. Oil the bike? No? Have you Aids or Aids-related diseases? They have that down on the forms now. Is there any insanity in the family? Yes, me. For applying for the fucking job in the first place.'

The next time I saw him I was sitting on my stool in the Drop Out. He came in out of the rain, his long hair plastered. He took his glasses off and didn't notice me until he had dried them with his shirt. 'My friend, how are you? I've just come from the happy hour. Six until nine. A pound for everything but you couldn't drink the Guinness. I'm up to here in lager and my mate's gone on up the road, wondering how I got lost. May as well have a decent pint.'

I paid for the pint over protests that he couldn't buy back. He was twenty-seven. He did a year of Business Studies at university because he had high points and high points were needed for Business Studies. 'I was showing off my high points.' He dropped out and went to a factory in Amsterdam. He busked in Munich. Pot nearly killed him because he was so thin. 'That's why they call me Skinny, the cunts.' He came home to drift on the dole. Then he solved the aptitude test – 'I had two arms and two legs' – to become a Manufacturing Team Member in Dell. Now it was shit or get off the pot time. He was going to become a teacher.

He took to dropping into the Drop Out on nights when he could pay his way. I'd bought him three pints the first night. I was glad to see him. I was lonely and he was company but no threat to my loneliness.

He was here now while I was thinking about the letter Andrew the barman had put on the table that morning. 'No co-op job yet. My oul fella thinks he might be able to get me into the Civic Trust for six months. A chain gang, going around cleaning up the canal . . . *the sun is warm, the sky is clear*. Written in dejection near the fucking canal. It's when the sun isn't warm that bothers me. *Season of mists and mellow fruitfulness*. Get through that all right. But: *In a drear-nighted December*. Bollocks frozen off. *Happy Insensibility*. That's the only boy. Get pissed.'

I had an idea. I put it to Skinny: 'Would you be interested in a temporary part-time job?'

'Yes? In Toots Books?'

'No. As a detective.'

'A detective? Do you mean a detective as in Sherlock Holmes or is it quality control where I'd spot if there wasn't enough currants in the scones?'

'I want you to follow someone. You don't have to do anything except tell me what you see.'

'Are you serious?'

'Yes.'

'Who? Who do I follow?'

'If you're interested I'll tell you tomorrow night. I'm talking about possibly one hour a day and I'd pay you ten pounds into your hand for every hour. Plus any expenses like buses or taxis.'

'Fuckit. Ten quid.'

'Think about it. If you're on I'll talk to you tomorrow night.'

I went to the market first next day and then put the purchase on the coffee table. 'Guess how much?' It was a disposable camera.

Valelly examined it, puzzled that it didn't seem to be a trick water pistol. 'What does it do?'

'It takes pictures or else I've been robbed.'

'Are they giving them away in the bank?'

'I bought it in the market.'

'Two for a fiver?'

'Eight pounds. I got a mad figairy: we should have our photo taken.'

112

'With that? I could have brought in my Olympus . . .'

I got them to say cheese then I sat down and let Valelly do the snapping. Andrew took one of us all together. Valelly said, 'The one I took will definitely come out.'

I left them without having coffee or a cigarette. I didn't know how long it would take to get the film developed. I didn't realise there was such a thing as a one-hour shop. When I used to take photographs . . . I had to blot that out.

I showed Skinny the photograph taken by Andrew so that he could see me in the group.

'There's his nibs, the mad guy. Mad Droney?'

'That's right. It's a game. I meet these people for coffee. You don't need to know the reason but we're sort of keeping an eye on each other. I'm too busy with the shop so you can be my spy. Are you on?'

Skinny pointed to the photograph. 'Who's the lucky victim?'

'It could be any of them. But Droney in particular.'

'Jesus, he doesn't do anything that isn't strange.'

'Well? Yes or no?'

'Ten quid. Fuck the canal. Let the other guy rescue the supermarket trolleys. So when do I start?'

I SPY

I introduced Skinny Mitchell to Nellie and Sister Mary Monica. I'd come up with a new scheme to hit Nellie's knee with the little mallet and see if I'd get a reaction. Up to now I'd hidden my lifestyle from Nellie and Sister Mary Monica. When Nellie would ask: Jimmy, how *are* you, I'd filibuster and try to turn the spotlight back onto herself. It would have been a waste of time complaining anyway, counter-productive, Nellie seeing me as a man of petty grievances beside her quest to join the soul of our son. Now, through Skinny Mitchell and the other coffee-table detectives I could unveil a glimpse of my existence in supposedly throwaway fashion.

The Drop Out was the pub I used at night to help pass away the time, I told them. Not a flicker of sympathy from Nellie or Sister Mary Monica, that a man who never went anywhere without his wife, who was not a pub man at the best of times, was now a controlled alcoholic. The Drop Out was a television-ridden pub, I told them, where everyone seemed to know the name of the golfer eighty-seventh in the world rankings. An easy place for someone like me to lose myself in, I pushed home.

Now there's this hotel that I go to five nights a week, that has a leisure centre. I go there to swim eight hundred metres to keep in shape and work off the tea – which is hardly necessary since I usually only bother with a cup of tea, a couple of slices of bread and a banana.

Oh, I was a crafty little cunt and wasting my breath. The only blinks I got signified yes, yes, get on with it.

Anyway, I went on, I'm halfway through my eight hundred metres when I have to stop for a second to clear my goggles. I just happened to look towards the exercise room which is separated from the pool by a wall of glass. Beyond the tableau of pumping iron disciples, stationary cyclists, walking-machine merchants and push-up freaks I saw a face that quickly withdrew from peering around the door. Even without my glasses I recognised Walter. I abandoned the swim, skipped the jacuzzi and steam room, had a cat's lick of a shower. I scoured the hotel and reached the Mini just in time to see a car reverse like mad and roar out the gates in first gear. I didn't have the horsepower to catch up. No disrespect to the Mini, which is in great nick because I keep it serviced and waxed and give it a run every day.

I might as well have been waving a hand across two blind eyes. Her very own Mini.

I was in the queue for my usual thigh and superchip when I got a tap on the shoulder, I told them. Madeleine Brown with her husband. Hi. I went down the block to a cab. Coming back up town I spotted them pulling out in a rust-bucket as I passed the Chicken Hut. I could see them all the way in the side mirror. They followed me home, slowed down until they saw me get out and go towards the door.

If you ask me, everybody in town must go to the market on Saturday mornings. I never used to go myself. Saturday had been my time with Johnny, I reminded them . . . letting it trail off. But, I told them, since I became Toots Books I often found myself twiddling the thumbs early on Saturday morning. I didn't open the shop until half-ten in honour of the customers' lie-in. But the day I bought the camera I got a taste for the market. Now I go there on Saturdays until it's Toots Books's opening time.

On the three Saturdays that I went to the market, since we got the letter, I saw Valelly, Walter, Droney and Madeleine there. OK, everybody in town went to the market. But the whole point of the market was that there you could ignore everybody in town. My brother Maurice called into the shop maybe once a month with the sad question: any developments? But when he saw me across the stalls in the market he no more saluted me than he would in the middle of Mass. But take Valelly. I was dreamily transfixed by a hawker smearing candle-grease on good trousers preparatory to giving it a dab of a miracle cleanser when from a dozen stalls away at the motor accessories stand Valelly yoo-hooed: 'Hello there, Toots.' That wasn't market form. That wasn't Valelly form. And Walter and Madeleine and even Droney, they were on their toes in the crowd in case I'd miss them waving at me. When in an hour we'd all be at the coffee table anyway.

I mean, I said to Nellie and Sister Mary Monica, trying to rub Nellie's nose in it, what can they expect, following me around? My life is an open book of non-stop routine. Droney could tell them. There's the shop, my swim, the Drop Out, the Chicken Hut and straight home to bed. I go to the pictures on Saturday before the Drop Out and Sunday I go for a long drive for the sake of the exhaust in the Mini and maybe stop and have a proper dinner for once and then Mass and the Drop Out. Where do they imagine there's a heinous crime going to pop up out of all that?

A waste.

Even Sister Mary Monica wasn't listening between the lines. She said, 'And your friend, Skinny, has he found any clues yet?'

Droney had two haunts. He used the Crow's Nest, formerly Finucane's, to keep in touch with a few of the old neighbours. He'd call in there for a glass before going on downtown to O'Brien's. He was only technically a drinker, a few half-pints man.

Skinny and his mates were pub crawlers. Skinny could say: 'Let's try O'Brien's.' In that way he could camouflage himself among his *domestiques*. Once established as a crowd who came in an odd time, Skinny could graduate to going in alone as a guy who came in an odd time. Skinny took exaggerated care to make sure Droney didn't spot him wearing his deerstalker and cape. He ignored Droney, didn't turn his head when one of his mates said, 'There's your man who goes around town roaring at everyone.'

Skinny reported: 'Fair amount of shirt-lifters going in there?'

I could imagine how Skinny saw my proposition in the Drop Out. This Toots character, oil contraption, naked bulb, stone floor, one fifty-*seven* for a book, putting up a tenner an hour, what next? One day, bring me to the back of the shop. He has something to show me. His mickey. Hasn't happened yet. Only he sends me after Mad Droney into a pub where guys mince past on the way to the jacks with their hands growing up from their elbows like they're carrying little tea cups.

'It's an arty pub,' I conceded.

Droney sat at a table with the lady in my photograph and another guy that Skinny often saw around cleaning windows. Droney was quiet in the pub, not at all like the madman about town. And Mrs O'Brien was a genius: she was able to conjure a lunar sea of bubbles on the head of the pint despite the best efforts of the Guinness boffins.

This was lame stuff and Skinny knew it. Still he had the neck to risk: 'I had four pints. The drink wouldn't come under expenses? No?'

Yes. I gave him his tenner and the price of the drink.

With every night that he had nothing to report, Skinny was more nervous that the well might dry up. He came in once excited with a local free newspaper.

Russell, Jack. 13 Mount Pleasant Avenue.
Peacefully after a short illness.
Deeply regretted by his great friend John Droney,
neighbours and postmen.
Internment tomorrow at 3.30 in Droney's Backyard. No flowers
please. Bones, if desired, to City Pound.

We'd already had the cutting at the coffee table that morning. No, Walter and Valelly were delighted by my assurance, Droney didn't have a dog. They were on their feet and in on the act to shake Droney's hand and say, I'm sorry for your trouble.

'I like it. I like it. Must be a gas bunch. Is there anything I should be looking out for in particular?'

'I don't know what I'm looking for myself. Just stay with it.'

Skinny charged into the Drop Out. He had chanced the Crow's Nest. He went in with one of his mates. Nets hanging from false timber ceilings. Ship's bell and steering wheel. Sea shells. An anchor in a glass case. A skull and crossbones. The gents identifiable by *The Captain* and the ladies by *The First Mate*. The usual shite. Currency notes from all over the world sellotaped to the fascia over the bar counter.

Droney was there in the company of three old ladies. Skinny's mate said, 'There's Mad Droney from O'Brien's.' Skinny affected a rigid lack of interest. He had his back to Droney. Then Skinny heard, 'I'll leave ye girls.' One of the old dears pleaded, 'Ah you're not going, Jackie.' Skinny's risky glance saw that Droney was already on his feet. 'I have to. I have to sing.'

Skinny said to his mate, 'Fuckit. I forgot I have to meet my sister. I'll see you later in O'Brien's.'

Skinny followed him.

I knew the terrain from my days playing soccer outside the coalyard. Droney took a left out of the pub, then left again into an avenue for about twenty yards before he turned right into a sheltered community for the elderly that had once been the collection of lanes from where the poor used to emerge with the prams and handcarts to get the coal from Mr Hassett. The new development retained the topography of the old lanes and was all corners where Skinny could wait at one until Droney disappeared around another.

Skinny was able to follow him through the sheltered community into St Joseph's Street and St Joseph's Place and into the park. Skinny was lucky that Droney took the perimeter path through the park where every twenty yards there were huge trees where Skinny could hide. But once Droney was out of the park Skinny had no more cover.

Droney went straight across the road into Collins Avenue, once slums but now a cul de sac of about forty houses in crescent shape. Skinny stayed behind the last tree near the park railings.

I could see what was coming. Droney had told me about this lark in other parts of the city.

Skinny saw Droney stop at the first house in Collins Avenue. Droney took out his notebook and made an entry. He moved on to the next house and did the same. And so on around the entire crescent until it looked to Skinny that Droney was coming out of Collins Avenue and back to the park. Skinny hid in a pile of bushes at the back of the greenhouse where Droney wouldn't see him but where Skinny could still look out through the railings.

But Droney didn't come back across the road. He went to the fifth or sixth house from where he'd started, stopped, and as far as

Skinny could make out, Droney took out his fags. Skinny thought Droney had put something on the wall of the house and then Droney stood back and saluted like a soldier. Droney came away from Collins Avenue and headed past the railway on his way to O'Brien's, Skinny figured.

Skinny investigated. The Collins Avenue residents were house-proud except for the inhabitant where Droney made his award. A Mr Whippy van stood inside the gate on concrete and the rest of the garden was a jungle of weeds. On top of the wall, Droney had put the cup made from silver cigarette paper. He'd put two stones on either side of the base of the cup to stop it blowing away.

Oh Droney, Sister Mary Monica said. She was delighted he'd stayed in character. Soap opera rules OK. I didn't always stay on to be alone with Nellie and I didn't today. I'd come in full of cuteness and hope. I had to go around the convent three times to kill the thought: she'll never come out.

MADNESS

Mad Martin died (peacefully) in the loving care of the nurses and staff of St Joseph's Psychiatric Hospital. Greatly missed by a wide circle of friends.

Andrew the barman showed us the death notice as his credentials while he went from table to table collecting fifty pence a skull to send a wreath from the Market Bar.

The notice did not mention a relative. We did such a good job explaining to Madeleine Brown the sad circumstances of poor epileptic Martin that she asked, 'Will you go to the funeral?' Group indignation set in. None of us would have had the remotest notion of going within an ass's roar of Mad Martin's funeral but because of Madeleine's innocent enquiry we were now going to show that the world wasn't full of unfeeling bastards.

The removal to the church from Griffin's took place that night at half-seven. When I arrived at quarter past, Valelly, Walter, Droney and Madeleine were waiting outside so that we could all go in together. 'Andrew was here already,' Valelly greeted me, 'we said we'd wait for you.'

Gerry Griffin and one of his men framed the door in their black suits. I saw a priest in the background looking at his watch. Three men stood in the mourners' position. So we shuffled around the coffin towards them. Dr Chrichton from the psychiatric hospital I recognised. We shook hands with him. He introduced the other two nurses.

Nobody else came. We were the wide circle of friends. We stayed on while the priest dashed off a decade of the rosary. Gerry Griffin gripped my arm: 'Would your friends help with the coffin?' Gerry Griffin and his man, myself, Droney, Walter and Valelly carried the coffin out to the hearse and the four of us walked in the funeral as far as the church. Dr Chrichton and his two nurses went by car. Madeleine travelled with the priest. We carried the coffin up the church and we were all thinking: this means we'll have to do the business again tomorrow.

Prayers were not flown in from Rome for Mad Martin's funeral. Even though the priest raced through a reading from the Gospel and one decade of the rosary I still had time to think in the church: is this it? How did I end up here with only mad people for company at the funeral of a madman whom I didn't even know? I thought of how things might have been. Johnny would now be in his leaving cert. year. Nellie and I had decided: not boarding school for our Johnny. He had been accepted by the local Jesuits. I saw him now as scrum-half on the school's cup team, maybe captain, Nellie, as was the tradition, presenting him with the cup. We had conventional parental ambitions. I carried gloom heavier than any coffin walking back down the church.

Skinny was in the Drop Out before me. News was written all over him. 'Stroke of luck today. Plod and a stroke of luck. The mark of the great detectives. There's this mate of mine – his oul fella has a hackney, see. He went back to uni same time as me and for co-op he does the cab by day. I was chattin' away to him when who comes along but our friend and he gets one of the taxis next door to the hackney place. Just as they were getting into the car the guy at the base runs out and asks the taxi guy will he be long, that there's someone after ringing who uses him regular. The taxi guy says, I just have this run to Clarina Woods. So I said to my mate: follow that car. He thought I was off my game. He knows Droney to see him, like everyone else, so I could say, c'mon for the laugh. But the problem is he has to tell his base where he's going which means I had to pay him. Anyway, since our car is unmarked we could keep up with the taxi, no bother. Droney gets out at the woods and pays your man off. Me and my mate give him an headstart and then we follow him. Talk about gas.

'Droney went through the woods until he came to a field of cows. He rested his hands on the bar of a gate leading to the field.

He said, "My dear men. It is most edifying to see you here in such large numbers tonight." Then Droney frightened the nearer cows by shouting, "BE YE PERFECT EVEN AS I AM PERFECT. Words, my dear men, spoken by Our Divine Lord Jesus Himself." At the mention of Jesus, Droney briefly lifted an imaginary biretta from his head. "And Jesus", again raising the hat, "was, as we all know, the perfect man. He was six feet tall. My dear men he was not five feet and eleven and three-quarter inches. He was not six feet and one thousandth of an inch. He was exactly six feet. The only man in the history of the world who was exactly six feet. No man before or since was ever that perfect height. He was the height of perfection. If there is any one of you listening to me here tonight who is six feet and one inch, then I would say to you, strive for perfection. Walk with a stoop. And he who is under six feet, I would recommend that he take up basketball. In the name of the father and of the son and of the holy ghost amen."

'That was it. He went back through the woods to a pub across the road where he must have rung for a taxi. We fucked off pronto. Does it make sense to you?'

'Does Droney make sense full stop?' I answered Skinny. But it didn't make sense to me. If that was Droney *singing* then he was singing off key. It sounded, in so far as I could interpret parables, that Droney was cursing his port wine stain. It sounded sour.

I was sour myself. I had to make an effort in the morning to clean myself for the funeral. I clanked around the house in self-pity. Fucking madmen. I tried to turn back the clock. If I had managed to pull my weight in Hamilton's. If the company hadn't gone to the wall. Nellie might be still in there but I'd have the company of peers. Instead of misfits. I'd gone from Jimmy Imbusch to Toots Books overnight. Maurice said, 'Why didn't you consult me?' To make a decision like that without going to your older brother. He used to come in often to the shop in the early days, solicitous, in case the shop might be a stepping stone to tying a rope around my neck. He'd mention jobs in my line that he'd seen advertised in the local paper. Second-hand bookshops were always run by odd people. 'Characters'. There was no one ever odd in our family. I stayed away from his house. I didn't want to embarrass him. Here's Uncle Jimmy he used to say when I'd visit. I could reason on Maurice's behalf. A person couldn't be going around as Toots Books if he hadn't done something to deserve it. If God decided to take a hand . . . God helped those who helped themselves. He helped them to be totally fucked up if they fucked up by drowning a child. Maurice couldn't stand out against that.

I had to rage alone going to Mad Martin's funeral. Couldn't you have one small bit of fucking mercy on me? Are you fucking blind and deaf that you can't see and hear that I am in so much fucking pain that I can't bear it anymore? And I've tried and I've tried and I've tried to carry it. But I can't do it anymore.

The funeral Mass was at ten o'clock. Outside of the few old people who normally went to that Mass the funeral party consisted of our coffee table and one of the two nurses from the night before. The gravediggers were shovelling lumps onto the coffin by ten past eleven.

Walter hadn't brought his car so he came with me in the Mini. We hadn't been alone together since the morning he had told me about Madeleine Brown. We had our own rapport because of the red Raleigh and Walter's being a customer of the bookshop. Walter was at ease, opening with 'Well, Toots, how are our investigations progressing?'

'You tell me, Walter. I'm in the bookshop six days a week.'

'I have to ask you, Toots. I hope you won't take offence. I asked Ignatius. I asked Madeleine. I asked Droney. Are you in any trouble? Can I help you? It can be between you and me. No word to the rest.'

'No offence. Let me put it to you this way, Walter. That letter, right?'

'Yes, Toots.'

'I'm clean. Anyone thinking of me and that letter is wasting shoe leather. I have nothing, absolutely nothing to do with it.'

'That's what Ignatius said. He showed me his references. And I got the McCormack story that he'd told yourself and Droney. You know he's a widower?'

'I don't. I don't know anything about him that he didn't tell us himself.'

'His wife is dead five years. She was a teacher but she always

123

kept her own name. Miss Edmunds. I'd heard the name. She used to teach in the Salesians. He has three children, two daughters and one son. He made them all stay at school. They're graduates. He says they're married to good people. He has lovely grandchildren. He worked in London and New York on buildings, bar work, garages. There's nothing he doesn't know about cars. His wife fell for him because he was so good-looking and then she discovered he had a super brain. That's why she didn't mind him working with his hands. Then when he was fifty he got a job driving Ned Toomey the solicitor.'

I knew Ned Toomey from reading about him in the paper. Past captain and president of golf and rowing clubs. *Mens sana in corpore sano* after-dinner speaker. Founder of St Munchin's Boys' Club. Provider of holiday home at the seaside for the poorer children. A decent man.

'Mr Toomey had multiple sclerosis for the last twenty years of his life. Ignatius drove him everywhere. Ignatius got a pension out of him, plus a lump sum that he didn't say how much, but with his wife's insurance he's comfortable. That's why he can pay over the odds for everything. He's had a good life but he has one problem, the problem he always had. His problem is he thinks like lightning. He's there and back before the other fella even thinks of setting off. He says he's been there and back with this one. It isn't any of us. It's a crank.'

'You asked Madeleine?'

'It's not Madeleine.'

'How are you so sure?'

'I just know. But it brings me to the point. Droney and yourself. You're good friends? Go back to when you were children?'

'Yeah, we're good friends. Why?'

'I'm worried about him.'

'Worried, why?'

'Can I talk to you in confidence? You're his friend. What I say won't go back to him?'

'If you're worried that way don't tell me then. But for what it's worth I give you my word. If you think I can help.'

'I don't know that I've a right to say this, even to you, Toots. I could be totally wrong. I could be a million miles out of order.

No. I won't say it. I'll wait until . . . but then again, if anything happened . . .'

'Walter, for fuck sake, say what you have to say. It won't go past me. You have my word.'

'All right. Do you know the Model School?'

'I went there.'

'It's co-educational now.'

'I know. My . . .' I caught myself. Almost told Walter my son went there. I substituted Maurice's daughter. 'My niece was there.'

'Droney hangs around the bus stop outside the school. I saw him once by accident. I just happened to be passing in the car. He gives sweets to little girls.'

The Model School was a long way from Droney's neighbourhood. There was a perfectly good school near him if he wanted to dole out sweets.

'You're saying, Walter . . .'

'I'm not saying anything.'

'It's a thing he'd do, isn't it? There used to be a man had a coalyard in Droney's area, a Mr Hassett, that's the man who left him all the money. Mr Hassett was all the time giving sweets to children. He gave them to me. My aunt had a shop across the road from his coalyard. I was often there on messages. I used to play soccer on the road. Droney might be just, you know, sort of carrying on the tradition?'

'I hope you're right. But it's the same two girls in the few times I've seen him. If he was giving all the children sweets . . . They're probably no more than eight or seven. They hold hands like they were taught to mind each other. Probably being collected off the bus.'

Martin was buried in the paupers' plot. Gerry Griffin thanked me for bringing the crowd.

While Martin was going down I watched Droney. He looked himself except that, like the rest of us, he had his chest stuck out that we were such good Samaritans. I said to Walter going back in the car, 'It's probably part of his overall . . . You know, his *singing* business. There's probably nothing to worry about.'

'I know. It's just . . . three days in a row. I used to get a feeling.

When I was doing my best for that ingrate Dan Mooney, I'd sense things. No. You're right. I'm letting that letter get to me. But . . . in case we'd be kicking ourselves afterwards, would you kind of keep an eye out yourself?'

'Of course.'

'Poor Martin' was the natural topic at the coffee table. 'It wasn't right', Madeleine Brown said, after we elaborated on Martin's history, 'to keep a man locked up for forty years.'

'There's no such thing as madness,' Valelly claimed. 'It's like alcoholism. An alcoholic is a man who drinks more than his doctor. *Great wits are sure to madness soon allied and thin partitions do their bounds divide.* I learned that at school. I can still rattle it off. Martin might have been a genius and no one spotted it.'

I understood Valelly to be referring to himself.

Droney observed: 'Don't they say a madman is the last to know he's mad?'

It hurt. Forced me to think of Nellie in conjunction with that word – mad. Droney couldn't have realised what he was saying. He was more sensitive than most people. I forced myself to be breezy. 'Some of us have to work.'

I was low all day in the shop. Droney was all I had in the world whom I could think of as a friend. He'd been good to me. He insisted on giving me the shop on a ninety-nine-year lease at five pence per annum. With Martin buried another diversion had come and gone. My thoughts were like the low grey wintry clouds and the east wind that you want to hurry home from and be by the fire with your wife and family. I looked this way and I saw Nellie. I looked away and there was Droney with the two little girls and to look beyond that was unbearable. No. To lose Droney, it wasn't on. Walter had misread the situation. Or invented it. Was that possible?

When Skinny came into the Drop Out that night I bought him one pint. He had no news. I said, 'Finish that and I want you to go to the Riverview Bar. D'you know where it is?'

'I do but I was never in it.'

'Walter Nix drinks there. He plays in some solo school. I don't think he goes in there until late. You be in before him.'

'What do I do?'

126

'Just keep your eyes open. Here's twenty. You can have a few pints on top of your tenner.'

I had ordered Skinny to stay away from Toots Books in case a visit would coincide with Droney being on the turf. Next morning I didn't get to the coffee table. As sometimes happened I had a woman in who couldn't make up her mind. She had two Maeve Binchys. 'I know I've read one of these but I can't remember which one.' I offered to make an unbusinesslike sacrifice. Maeve Binchy fetched a good price. 'This week I have a special deal. Two for the price of one.' The woman quickly made up her mind which Maeve Binchy she hadn't read. Then took half an hour to find a Catherine Cookson to go with it.

That was the afternoon I had to go out for fags and got soaked. Droney was waiting outside the shop when I came back.

'Jasusbastarinfuckingrain, where would I get a peak cap?'

'Go into any church and try the confession boxes.'

'I should have known better than to ask you.'

Inside the shop Droney said, 'I must remember to get it transcribed on my arse later because it's the last thing I look at in the morning. SCB. Scout confession boxes.'

He hadn't been in the shop as much as usual since he met Madeleine Brown. I had an excuse now to follow his cue.

'When do ye do it? When the poor husband is up on a ladder cleaning windows?'

'We're only singing.'

'Your honour, we were only singing. Case dismissed. Where do ye do it? Her house? Out the back here?'

'Toots, join us. Sing.'

'It's that kinky already? Ye want a threesome?'

'No. You know what I mean. Shake it off. Break free. Sing.'

'Get out of my shop.'

'I'll have a peak cap for you in the morning.'

'Out.'

I decided Walter must be off his game. Droney was as normal as Droney could ever be. I was relieved. Almost – what was that word again – happy?

Skinny had nothing to report that I might not have anticipated before the crazy letter arrived. The game of solo was played in dead silence except for an acrimonious post mortem after every hand. 'I was in the pub ten minutes before Walter came in. For the next hour and a half he drank three slow pints while I had six on top of the one I had while I was waiting for him to come in. All the other customers were pensioners. I stuck out a mile. No telly. As cover I had to keep looking at my watch and check with the old lady behind the counter that her clock was right. That I was supposed to meet a bloke. And then have to go through a gang of lies when she asked me who would that be, invent a name, ask her this is the Riverview Bar, I'm in the right place, there isn't another one around here with a name like that, so that I was dripping sweat with guilt and lashing back the porter and all the time thinking, come back euthanasia, all is forgiven. At closing time your man left with one of the card players. I followed them around the corner. I heard them say goodnight. They were living next door to each other. So I tore all the way back and up the town to the night club for three more pints.'

'You had seven pints in the Riverview? That means I owe you for two. The night club comes out of your own pocket.'

Peak cap day. I wore it to the coffee table. I wore it at the coffee table. I poked the peak up with my finger.

'Guess how much?'

'Let me see it,' Valelly demanded. He dropped the cap as fast as he picked it up, flicking infection from his fingers. 'That cap wasn't born yesterday. That thing is maggoty. The Oxfam shop. Although I thought those places were supposed to wash the stuff before they sell it.'

'Not Oxfam.'

'The market. A pound.'

'Not the market. It came from a confession box. Free. Courtesy of Mr Droney.'

'I have to tell the truth, Toots. I told you a white lie.'

So we got the saga of the church on its knees, no altar boys, winos in the porch and the old man who couldn't go into the Augustinians without having his cap robbed. They lapped it up. Even Walter. I said, 'Tell them where you went then.'

Droney held up his griddle cake. 'Mother Kelly's Doorstep.'

'Before that. After you threw the cap into the shop.'

'Oh. You mean, up to the labour exchange to sing "One Cornetto"?'

It wasn't my form to show an interest in Droney's idiot romanticisms. But I did it to show Walter that Droney was still himself. Peak caps and cornettos. The coffee table had a ball.

Then Skinny came in that night to the Drop Out and the fun was truly over.

THE ABYSS

'Your man, Droney, the mad guy. Is he . . . is he a friend of yours?'

'Why?'

Skinny was in the Drop Out before me. I don't know if Sherlock Holmes himself would have been as much on the ball as I was. Skinny's glass was a quarter full. Only a skim of a head fought for expression on the surface. I'd often thought that Skinny was a better advertisement for the product than Mr Johnson. You could count Skinny's gulps and his pace by the frothy rings on the glass. But now the glass was clear. I put it down to him having had to nurse the pint, that he was skint. But I wasn't a second in the door when he called two and put the money on the counter. Then I looked at him and saw the apprehension. He had been distracted from his pint.

'Go on. What have you to tell me?'

'Fuckit. You know my mate that drives the cab? I was on my way home and I met him as he was knocking off. He said, hop in, I've something to tell you. He doesn't know anything about what I'm at. The day we followed Droney to Clarina Woods, he thought that was just all for a laugh. Anyway, the first thing is, my mate was stopped earlier around quarter past two at the traffic lights near the Augustinians? He saw Droney in the porch with this wino that's always thrown on the ground with a bottle of cider. Have you seen this guy?'

'I think I know who you mean.'

'Well. From what my mate could see, Droney took off his

jacket, it seemed a terrific leather jacket to my mate, and then Droney helped the wino to stand up and the wino takes off this manky raincoat. And they swap. That was all right but the next thing my mate got a run about ten to three out to Blackthorn Heights and on his way back in who does he see but Droney wearing the wino's coat coming away from St Gabriel's holding this kid by the hand. My mate doesn't know why but something made him stop the car. He was thinking like he hadn't placed Droney as a married guy, you know, with the . . .' Skinny made a vague gesture towards his own face. 'The kid was so young he'd have to be a grandson anyway, or then my mate thought Droney might be helping out some neighbour. But next thing that he sees really makes him sit up. You know when you come from St Gabriel's there's that burnt-out building used to be Costelloe's cabinet factory? Droney turns in there with the kid . . .'

I was sick.

'. . . it's just a waste kind of a yard at the back of the factory. So my mate nips out after them. Next thing my mate sees the young fella having to reach up to put his hand in the pocket of the old raincoat and he thinks he sees, he can't swear to it, but he thinks he sees Droney fiddling with his own fly. Just at that minute Droney looks around and spots my mate and Droney quickly pulls a sweet out of his pocket and my mate hears him say, run along home now like a good boy. And Droney vamooses himself. My mate goes to the kid and asks him where he lives, which turns out to be only around the block. My mate gave the kid a lecture. Not to talk to strangers ever again and all that. My mate thought about going to the guards but then he started thinking about Droney and his face and that business out in Clarina Woods and he just couldn't bring himself to do it.'

I thought of Walter. Could he possibly have known about this as far back as when he sent the letter and only brought me into it the day of Mad Martin's funeral? Skinny was quiet, letting me think. He wasn't the iconoclastic Skinny anymore. He was now an all-bets-are-off-they-should-be-castrated recidivist. I said, 'Do you feel the same as your mate, about not going to the guards?'

'I don't know what way to feel. Is this what you were expecting? Is this why you had me follow him?'

'No. I didn't know what to expect. But it could be the answer. You could be out of a job.'

'All good things come to an end. Hello, canal. Although, I have to be honest with you, if it is this whatever it is, if it's the type of thing that . . . I wouldn't want to be involved, even from a distance, no matter what kind of a misfortune the guy is, you know . . .'

'OK. Look, thank you for everything you did. I appreciate it. The one thing I can tell you is this. Nothing is going to happen. I'm going to sort it out. I can promise you that. The other thing is. Your co-op business, the government pays for that, is that right?'

'Of course.'

I was afraid I'd be turned down. It was like applying for a job myself. 'If it would work for you, clean the bike, mind the shop, whatever you like, if you don't go for the canal . . .'

I drove on: 'But I could only think about that after I sort this business out. You understand that?'

'Of course.' Relieved.

When Skinny left I rang Walter in the Riverview Bar. I asked him to call into the bookshop at half-nine next morning.

I let Walter in and closed the door again, didn't pull the blinds. I invented a nameless friend who knew I was a friend of Droney and who had seen what Skinny's mate saw and who told me out of concern for Droney, the misfortune.

'Did you know about this all along, Walter, and send the letter?'

'Of course I didn't. What do you take me for? The question is, what are we going to do?'

'I'm not going to the coffee table this morning. What I want you to do if Droney is there, and it might be just our fucking luck that he wouldn't be there, is tell him I'm caught up and I saw you passing or something or you were in here anyway and that I asked you to ask Droney would he call in and see me. Right?'

'What are you going to do?'

'I don't know. I'm going to put it to him some way.'

He came in at twelve o'clock. 'God bless all here.' I had three customers but I put the 'Back in five minutes' sign up and closed the door. Droney gave me an eyebrow. Two men and a woman. I remember what they bought. The woman was the first to show with *The Heart is a Lonely Hunter*.

'Good stuff,' Droney said to the lady from his usual commentary position near my table. She gave him a polite smile. The first man bought two by Dick Francis. I let both of them out and locked the door again. The second man said, 'Sorry, am I keeping you?'

'No, no. Carry on.'

But the second man rushed himself anyway. He bought *The Henry Root Letters*. Everybody buys *The Henry Root Letters* when the pressure is on. Or *The Diary of Adrian Mole*.

'You sent for me, Sire?'

'What are you at?'

'At?'

'What were you doing with the child at St Gabriel's school?'

'I beg your pardon, Toots?'

'Three days in a row you were with two girls outside the Model, giving them sweets.'

'Are you following me?'

'No. But whether I am or not is irrelevant. What are you up to?'

'A man can't sing anymore now. A man can't give a sweet to a child . . .'

'Jack, tell me. What is it? What's the problem here? I'm your friend, right? Let me help you. If I can help you.'

He walked away from me and looked towards the window. With the blinds down he had nothing to look out on. He went to the corner made by the street wall and the first shelf of books. He crumpled onto the floor and sat with his knees up and his elbows on his knees. He drove his face into his hands.

'Toots.'

'What?'

'Help me.'

'Did you send the letter?'

'Yes. Yes yes yes yes yes yes yes. Oh, for fuck sake, Toots, help me.'

'What is it? Help you how? What's wrong?'

'I don't know what's wrong. Or I'm what's wrong. Or I'm fucking mad or the world won't sing. I'm telling you, I'm tortured . . .'

His two fists grabbed the sides of his long grey hair. 'Am I somebody who would harm a child? Am I, Toots?'

'No.'

He crossed his thumbs and put them under his chin. 'After I met her – Madeleine – I was home having my boiled egg and griddle cake. I started to think about how I had everything now. I have loads of money. I own property. I'm happy as Larry going around the town a free man, not afraid to sing. And on top of it all I get a woman. That was never one of my hopes. Unless I met a bird of a feather from a circus. And I get one of the most beautiful women in the city and we have a ball. We fuck and she writes on my arse. You'd say I had it made, wouldn't you, Toots?'

'You have. So what's wrong? You should be singing like you're saying everyone else should be.'

'I hadn't eaten half the boiled egg and I got this flash of my father. Sitting outside the door. Yackie. And my mother. The day I came home from school and she's sitting there crying, after Father Cletus had been there. All I had to say to her was, Mam, I never wanted to be a fucking priest. But I kept my mouth shut. Poor Mr Hassett, who gave me everything, I let that man suffer. Even Mr Spencer. He was a good man. A bit of a bollix but a good man. I let them all carry the heaviness while I'm a sneaky little fucker, taking advantage of this, this thing on my face. I acted the victim when I'd be coming towards Mr Hassett, I'd let the head fall and the shoulders stoop. Why didn't I say to them, everybody be happy, I'm grand, it didn't bother me, I could light candles for Father Cletus. It was an awful wrong I did, Toots, I mocked God . . .'

'Stop it. Jack, you were only a young fella. It was natural, anyone else would have done the same . . .'

'. . . I started thinking then, just not wanting to be a priest, that wasn't so much insulting God, but going on as though I

134

was some sort of chosen person, that me and God together were thwarted, that was a wrong thing to do . . .'

'It wasn't your fault. You were only a kid.'

'I wasn't a kid when I ducked away from him. My father, I don't know what was in him that he didn't even want to know I existed for so long. He was a rough man. He wasn't a great thinking man. It was something he probably wasn't able to handle. But then, when he was woken up, after Father Cletus, for three and a half years he couldn't have been better. He was a great father. And I couldn't look at him when he was crippled and I was nearly a man then. I let the smell get at me and the "Yackie". I ran away from it. A fucking coward. I let him die without me. I let my mother die in a bingo hall in the middle of strangers. I'm damned I'm damned I'm damned . . .'

'Horseshit. Come on, Jack. Shake yourself out of it. Look, God gave you something very few people have got. He gave it to you at birth. Was that fair to you? But you did great. You did your best. Why would anyone want anymore from you? The maddest God wouldn't ask for any more than you had to carry . . .'

I couldn't be sure that he was listening to me. He heard me but was he listening?

'It was like, is this it, all over again. Except what was being said inside in my head was – was crazy. What punishment should you have. That's what was being said inside in my head. You thought you'd get away with it but you have to be punished. And it was to fit. Mr Hassett, a lovely man, gave sweets to children but nobody can do that anymore. Because the world is all – bad now. But you have to give sweets to children because you owe it to Mr Hassett. That's what was going on inside my fucking head. And I was agreeing with it. I was saying, why shouldn't I give sweets to children? I can do it with my face. I can't turn away from Mr Hassett and everything he stood for, like I turned away letting on I might have wanted to be a priest. I thought my head was telling me that that was going to be my punishment. That I'd give sweets to children and maybe have people laughing at me or telling me, get away out of that, you dirty old man. And I thought I could take this, give sweets to children and be pure and it would be singing and the world could mind its own dirty business. And then, whatever was inside in my head, I thought first it was laughing at me, that was my first feeling, but it was stern, it was a patriarchal thing, it was like, this is for your own good, it has to happen, you have to pay. You'll be like the people who give sweets now to children but you won't know what's happening to you because mad people are the last to know they're mad. I said that at the coffee table after Mad Martin. I was already half-mad but I didn't know it. Up outside the Model there were people around near the bus stop and I knew that giving the sweets to those girls was leading me on and I said nothing will happen to me. And then I said, fuck 'em, why can't I do it in an out-of-the-way place? Why should I need minders when I'm giving sweets to children? Why should I have to be chaperoned? Toots Toots Toots, if you knew what I nearly did. That young kid from St Gabriel's, were you following me? Was it the fellow who saw me, told you? It doesn't matter. I got a dirty raincoat off that wino I told you about, that hangs around the porch of the Augustinians. I knew it was all wrong, that it was going too far, but I couldn't stop. I didn't even have to make the hole in the pocket of the raincoat, it was holes already and I got this kid, Toots, I was only so much away from it, I was just about to finger out my mickey so the kid's hand would go into the pocket and grab . . . Toots, I need help. Help me, for God's sake, Toots . . . help me . . .'

I went over to him and put my hand on his shoulder. 'Stand up, Jack. Come over and sit at the table.' I got the climbing stool and sat opposite him. I said, 'Look, there's no harm been done, right? We just have to talk through it. We have to make sure it can't happen again.'

'I'm frightened. I was expecting to be hauled in all day. The fellow who saw me . . .'

'Don't worry about that. You don't need to know him but he's a friend of mine. It's from here on in we have to think about. All that stuff going on in your head is shit, d'you hear me? It could be like you said, you're having such a good time, with Madeleine thrown in. You often hear of people who worry because everything is going too well. You don't have to give out sweets for a start. That belonged to a time when a sweet was

136

a big deal for a child. Go into the supermarkets. Look what the women load up into their trolleys on the way out. Scoops of kingsize chocolates, crisps, sweets, magnums of orange. The world doesn't need you for that anymore.'

'That's where you're wrong, Toots. Supposing *I* need it. Supposing I want to give out sweets. Or I want to pat a child on the head. Why should I be persecuted? Some things are beautiful. Or they were. They should still be allowed to be. The world should sing. It did once. I know it did. If I didn't have to sing alone. I know it's madness but I thought, I had some idea I'd have converts. But all I get is more and more people thinking I'm screwy. If there was only some bit of hope. If there was only one person could see it. I wouldn't be like this. I know I wouldn't. Everyone needs a bit of a clap now and then. I'm the same. I bury it but it's there.'

'Look, I know what you mean. I mightn't even let on but for what it's worth I agree with you. A man should be allowed to give sweets to children. Right? That's what you're saying. But he's not. Are you listening to me here now? He's not allowed to do that anymore. He's not allowed to smoke in government buildings, hmm? I smoke. But I don't smoke where I see the fucking signs. Some cunt will nab me, I'll be brought to court and fined and if I don't pay the fine I'll be fucked into prison. These are facts. I don't like it but I can't do anything about it. Now, society doesn't want you giving sweets to children for a start. There's mothers out there. They'd tear you apart. And you say that you're afraid, that even if it was like years ago and Mr Hassett, you're afraid, this voice is telling you that you must give sweets but your punishment will be you'll go mad and do something terrible? OK. It's a load of bollix imagination but even if it was true, even if there was a voice inside in your head, you just told me about it rationally. All you have to do is do whatever you want to do, but no sweets, no children. Well, no strange children, right? Just cut that out of your life. You have plenty of other ways of singing. Fuck off out to Clarina Woods and give sermons.'

'You saw me?'

'By a fluke I happened to be passing there, giving the Mini a run. I saw you getting out of a taxi. But fuck that. You have a repertoire, you don't need this children fucking sweets lark. Cut it out.'

I thought I made sense. I thought he took in that I was making sense. But he looked at me like someone I'd whipped. He stood up and walked past me towards the door. I didn't want to let him out yet. Was it safe? But he stopped with his back to me.

'Cut it out. And then what? What's next? You let them get away with that and will there be signs in the labour exchange saying "This is a 'Sing One Cornetto' Free Zone"? And what after that? You mean well, Toots. But even you, you can't see it. You won't sing. You're a decent man. You're a good man. How can I expect,' Droney waved his hand at the street, 'how can I expect the mob who know no better, how could I expect them to sing when decent men, good men, people with a soul and a conscience, who still believe there's such a thing as beauty, when even they lie down . . .'

I got angry. I couldn't take this. 'Jack, let me out of it. I have fuck-all to sing about. D'you understand? Crying. I have a lot to cry about. I have a lot to rage about. Mad. Who is more entitled to go fucking mad, with my wife mad locked up, my son dead? Sing my arse. Come on now. Snap out of it . . .'

He shook his head. 'No. I'm sorry for you more than anybody. But no, Toots. If it never happened. If you were at home with your wife and son, a happy family the way you should have been, you still wouldn't sing, Toots. Would you? Be honest? Would you even sing if it was allowed? If it was encouraged? If I asked you, like the Lord, would you sing one hour with me, would you do it? Even if I swore to you that I'd . . . try and be normal, if it could be proven that you'd be saving me, would you sing then?'

'"One Cornetto" in the labour exchange? No. I wouldn't.'

'Would you sing on the stage? It's still allowed there, on the stage.'

'The stage is for people like John McCormack. Right? OK? I'm Jimmy Imbusch, remember. Not McCormack. Imbusch.'

He turned towards me. 'Not right. Not OK. You don't have to be McCormack. There's little villages out there, putting on amateur drama plays. Do they have names like Olivier? They don't. But they do their own business. They sing. Take our fucking coffee table. If we put on a show, hey kids, let's put on a show, there's none of them McCormack, nothing to frighten you, and you were asked to help out, would you do it? No. You'd rationalise your way out of it. I'm talking to you and I'm asking you for help. All I'm saying to you is, don't let me alone. Don't let me be the only one. Do something, do anything. Hold my coat. Don't send me out of here the way I came in. Don't let the thing come back into my head.'

'Well, what the fuck can I do?'

'You could *sing*, Toots. Will you sing?'

'It depends. Don't get any ideas into your head. I'm talking about a once-off. But not "One Cornetto". You get one outing from me and no more sweets. That's the deal. So make up your mind.'

Droney put his hand on his poll. Drew the hand down to his neck. 'I think I have it. It'll make it easy on you. The coffee table. So you'll be legit. We will put on a show. We'll put on a concert and you can be part of it, yeah? I can't make it easier than that, can I? But it will have to come from you.'

'How do you mean?'

'You must suggest it.'

'Why?'

'To give it . . . to give it, to give it, to give it . . . legitim-acy.'

'A concert.'

'Yes.'

'They'd laugh at me.'

'There you are. We're not even up and running and you're afraid you'll be laughed at. Who? Who'll laugh at you? Not me. I'll back you up. And if I do, Madeleine will go along. That lady is singing, thanks to me. I don't know about Walter . . .'

I did. I said, 'There's something you should know about Walter.'

'What's that?'

'He knows about you. It was Walter saw you up at the Model. He came to me. I had to tell him about St Gabriel's. He knows

139

why I asked him to ask you to call in. I'm going to have to be above board with Walter.'

'I suppose I have to accept that. But that means he'll go along, Toots. He can't say no in the circumstances. You only have Valelly to worry about. Right?'

I walked past him and opened the door. I said, 'Let me think about it. Is that fair? But no more of the . . . you know what I mean?'

THE COFFEE TABLE PLAYERS

Skinny Mitchell came into the Drop Out later than usual, edgy, looking at his watch a second inside the door. 'I have just time for a quick one, have to meet a mate up the road, so how is everything?'

'I investigated that.'

'Yes?'

'I have good news. It won't happen again. The whole thing was an experiment.'

'An experiment?' Another glance at the watch. Experiments. We were just experimenting, your Honour.

'You know Droney, the way he goes around. He has this philosophy that the world has lost its way. That things were better before. We shouldn't be worried about what other people think of us. We should sing when we feel like it. We should shout out loud if it takes our fancy. Salute strangers. Be ourselves. Whatever we are. Be loose, he calls it. Not uptight . . .'

'He's dead fucking right there. Tell us, Mr Mitchell, why you'd like to join us. I always wanted to become a Manufacturing Team Member since as far back as I can remember. And I was reading up on the company where it's well established as progressive and there's room for self-advancement and I need the fucking money to get pissed, you stupid prick. Sorry, you were saying our friend is experimenting?'

'He believes men should be allowed to give sweets to children, like in the old days. Without people assuming he's a pervert.'

'A fair point. A fair point.'

'So he thought he'd get that dirty raincoat. Find a child. Take him some place out of the way like the old cabinet factory. Have the sweets in his pocket and let the child put his hand in and then pat the child on the head and send him home. And he would have been able to prove to himself that it should be allowed. But your friend came along and Droney panicked. That's it. But the main thing is, I got through to him and showed him that he can't do it again. I pretended that he was spotted by, that your mate was actually a friend of mine who knew I knew Droney and that I persuaded him not to go to the guards. I told Droney it had to stop. I made him see sense!'

Did he believe me? I couldn't figure. He took a slug of the pint that brought him one third of the way down. I didn't know whether he was tasting the drink or my story.

'The oul fella was on to the bollix he knows in the Civic Trust. I think I have to take it. Oxfam here I come. Have you thick woolly socks, please, for use on the canal? But that's good. I'm glad you're happy with your friend. All the lads love him. I better catch up with my mate. See you again.' One more swallow and the glass could have been entered for a competition.

I got a cab to the Riverview Bar. I ordered a pint and had it served before Walter looked up from the game and noticed me. He hurried over. He said, 'Well?'

'Can we talk?'

I had Walter in the bookshop at half-nine that morning. Droney came in at twelve. There was Skinny in the Drop Out earlier. And now Walter again. With Walter and Droney my story was that a nameless friend spotted Droney and the kid from St Gabriel's. Reporting to Skinny I had diluted Droney's obsession and insisted the danger was past when I was sure of no such happy news. And now with Walter I had to deliver the truth, shorn of Droney's relationship with Madeleine Brown because Walter respected her. Any more and I would end up telling myself lies. But I managed to bring Walter along as far as:

'A concert? I don't understand a concert. All he wants you to do is one mad thing and he's happy.'

'I have no intention of doing any mad thing, Walter. We have to help him. I've thought about it all afternoon. We have to do something but I can tell you Toots Books is not going to be the martyr on his own. I'm going to do my bit but I'm going to do it hiding inside that coffee table. If there's a gang of us making apes of ourselves I won't stick out. And remember, he knows you know. I told him I'd be telling you. He said himself that you'd have to go along.'

'A concert. What kind of a concert?'

'What kind of a concert is there? We'll bring it up tomorrow and see what the reaction is. Droney says Madeleine will be game. He's saved her life or something the way he has her on the dry and seeing the bright side. It only leaves Valelly.'

'But what reason can we give Ignatius for putting on a concert? Apart from the fact, what can I do? What will you do? Can you juggle for instance?'

'That's where I have a sleepless night tonight, Walter.'

But seven pints a night seven nights a week men don't have sleepless nights. All I had ready in the morning was a half plan to suggest: I have an idea. And think on my feet from there. What I did not have in the morning was the drink-induced confidence of the night before. Even with Droney, Walter and Madeleine carrying the train of my robe, I was nervous approaching Valelly's throne. I got my coffee and sat down and while I was reaching for the sugar took off: 'I have an idea. It just came to me.'

I spoke while Valelly was dismantling his Zippo. 'I bet it's the flint. I knew it. It couldn't be the fluid. Look at that. You'd have to put that under a microscope to see it. But I always carry a spare. Now. Let's see. I was right. One flick. Perfect. There's no lighter will light as fast as that . . .'

'I have an idea . . .'

Since the idea, whatever it might be, wasn't an idea that Valelly had, he kept flicking his fucking Zippo. Walter tried to help me. 'What idea have you, Toots?'

'I think we should put on a concert.'

Madeleine put her hand on Valelly's Zippo-flicking wrist: 'Toots wants to put on a concert.'

'What's that, my love?'

'Toots says he wants to put on a concert.'

At last Valelly looked at me. 'A concert for what?'

143

'I didn't say I. I said we should put on a concert.'

'Why?'

'Why not? There were concerts when you were a buttons, remember?'

'They were in aid of the foreign missions.' Vallely spoke out of his infinite patience.

'So. We put on a concert in aid of the foreign missions.'

'Do you go to Mass? They've stopped the Sunday night Mass in the Franciscans. They did away with the quarter past twelve in the Augustinians. Because they do not have enough priests. There probably aren't any foreign missions. We haven't enough for ourselves here.'

Droney came in: 'You could be wrong there, Ignatius . . .'

'Wrong? How could I be wrong?'

'. . . I saw a poster in the Augustinians. It's called after a priest who used to be there years ago, when I was on the altar myself. Father Cletus. He was in Nigeria for years. He died out there. It's the Father Cletus Bursary where they raise funds to sometimes send a black priest over here for experience and that helps with the shortage problem here as well.'

'You can't call that foreign missions. You'd have to call that home missions.'

I had my imprimatur. 'Right. We put on a concert in aid of the home missions.'

Valelly was annoyed. 'Have you thought of how much it would cost us? Do you know about putting on concerts? The work that goes into it? You might find one big name and get him free, like we did, say, with John McCormack, but everyone else has to be paid. We'd be better off putting our money into the box for this Father Cletus. There's no point in raising money if you spend as much as you're raising.'

'You don't understand . . .'

'Don't understand? Ignatius Valelly doesn't understand? Doesn't understand *concerts*? I've heard it all now.'

'I meant, we'd put on the concert. There's no need for big names. We'd be the big names. Remember we were the "wide circle of friends"? It won't cost any money. Everything will be a profit.'

'And have you thought of how you'll get people to pay their money if you haven't big names? Let me tell you that show business is a hard business. I was there. I know.'

'I only said I had an idea. I didn't say I knew everything. As a matter of fact I was hoping . . . I thought maybe you'd run it.'

I had him.

'If a concert had to be put on, I could do it better than anybody. I could put on a great concert. I could put on the best concert. There isn't anything I don't know about concerts. But you're not telling us why. Why do you want to put on a concert?'

'It was just an idea. Look, we'll forget about it. I was never on a stage in my life and I got this idea that it's something I missed out on. Even though I can't do anything. And now that we know it might help to bring a black man over here we'd be doing good. But you're right. We probably wouldn't be able to bring it off.'

'Who says we couldn't? That isn't the point. There would be no need to worry about that part of it. I could organise like a general. You want us, all of us here at the coffee table, to *be* the concert? Walter, have you a specialty . . .'

'My specialty is, I'm going home now before this crazy . . .'

'No no no no. Sit down. Sit down there now, Walter. We'll have a vote. Those for the concert raise your hands. Madeleine, lift up your hand. Good man there, Jackie Droney yourself. And myself and Toots. Walter, you're outvoted.'

Valelly turned towards the bar. 'Andrew, something to write on, please.'

Walter searched his pockets and offered a failed lottery card.

'Something proper to write on, I meant, Walter. Andrew, give me that notebook you take stock on. Things must be done properly, Walter. And this, thank you, Andrew, this is just to make headings until I buy a diary on the way home to plan a meticulous campaign. First, tomorrow, you all have the day to think about it. I want to know what you feel you can offer by way of performance. Everything must be timed. Everything must be on schedule so that it will go like clockwork!'

Valelly wrote a heading, flicked the page, wrote another. He was lost talking to himself. 'Hall. Programmes. Advertising. Posters . . .'

Droney called in that afternoon. 'Brilliant, Toots. Masterful. You

145

should have heard him after you left. I'm surprised he doesn't want to put it on tonight. Ignatius believes in action not talk, he says. I thanked Walter by the way. I told him I'm cured already. I am too. Just think, you're going to be on the stage, Toots.'

'Unfortunately I can think of nothing else. And it's frightening the shit out of me.'

'What will you do? What's your act, Toots?'

'I haven't the faintest idea. I don't have a trunkful of turns like you have. Now get out and be good.'

Part Three

Part Three

AND MANY, MANY MORE

Skinny Mitchell didn't turn up in the Drop Out that night. I thought about my own performance. I exhumed an old talent and with it another resurrection – my last hope of Nellie. She'd *have* to come out of the convent to see me on the stage.

The bookshop was empty at coffee time next morning but I made sure to be half an hour late going into the Market Bar. I wanted to hear what everyone else was going to perform before I was stupid enough to open my big mouth.

Valelly looked at his watch. 'We can start now at last,' he rebuked me on the way to get my cup of coffee. 'This is my diary.' A yearly planner job. 'That's our first expense. I'll write that down. Twenty-nine ninety. I started yesterday. I saw a Father Gerard in the Augustinians to clear that the concert will be under their auspices. Let this be a lesson on how to handle people. I didn't go in there like a fool. I knew what to expect. Priests aren't like nuns. Nuns will take money from drug dealers. They don't philosophise. They survive. I explained our concert in aid of the Father Cletus Bursary the way I would to a child. Father Gerard tried to look the gift horse in the mouth. What type of concert? he wanted to know. Did I bite his head off and say, do you think I have a concert all wrapped up here in parchment with an elastic band around it looking for a home? No. I indulged him. I said it's an old-fashioned concert with clean acts and no smut to re-establish the old Christian values and auditions were already taking place. He wanted to know who was putting it on. I told him the Coffee Table Players. I stared into his face. He was afraid to let on that he didn't know the famous Coffee Table Players. It all took half an hour where another man would get bogged down. Then I secured the Gaelic League Hall as the venue. Is that to everybody's satisfaction, the Gaelic League Hall?'

It most certainly was to mine. I was saved from the theatre where Valelly had worked as a buttons because it was now an Omniplex. The bingo hall next door to the Drop Out had once been a theatre too. From the minute I thought of having to make a fool of myself in public, I saw the disaster taking place in the Arts Centre, the establishment venue, where they had Patrons and Friends of the Art Centre who would go to watch anything. Now I could hide inside the coffee table and the coffee table would be hidden within the Gaelic League Hall.

'Now it would take another man two weeks or even three weeks to get the Gaelic League Hall. Because that's the way they operate. I got it in an hour. Because, you see, I knew what to expect. The man in charge is Padraigh O Maolcathaigh. He's a retired clerk and runs the hall in an honorary capacity. A decent man but the Gaelic League isn't the popular cause it used to be. Now the first thing, when you approach such people, you don't tell them you want the hall for a meeting of the British Legion. Or to show French films with subtitles. I introduce myself as the Chairman and Founder of the Coffee Table Players and say we're looking for a venue to put on a concert in aid of the Father Cletus Bursary for the propagation of the faith. But that our problem is we can only pay three hundred pounds for the use of the hall for one night. Any fool would get it off them for fifty if he waited a month while they had committee meetings. But I knew my man. Tell me more about the concert, he wants to know. He doesn't say a word about the three hundred pounds because he has it already spent on behalf of the Gaelic League. I shovel it on. Concert reflecting traditional Irish values. I tell him we'll have the Bob Nesbitt School of Irish Dancing. Which, of course, we will have even if it's Bob Nesbitt, the grandson. We'll have people singing "Shall My Soul Pass Through Old Ireland" and so on. I take out my cheque book while I have him. I say, Padraigh O Maolcathaigh is synonymous with the Gaelic League, you don't have to have meetings with people under you or anything like that. So we're

150

there. Of course we'll have to get the three hundred back through sponsorship.'

Madeleine Brown congratulated him. 'Well done, Ignatius.' Walter, the debater, said, 'Hear hear.' I was sucked in. I offered, 'I might be able to help with the sponsorship.'

'Yes?'

'I used to be sponsorship manager with E. M. Hamilton.'

'Were you? Good man, Toots. I'll appoint you my second in command.' Praise.

'We have the venue. The Augustinians are squared. I'll get Bob Nesbitt. His dancers can appear twice, once in each half. When we know what we're doing ourselves and add it to Bob Nesbitt, we'll see what we need to fill out the time. With an interval to sell raffle tickets.'

I blundered in, flushed with the praise, power-mad as second-in-command. 'We could fill the bill with public house singers.'

'And have them steal the show? No, thanks. Think of why we need Bob Nesbitt. When I was captain of Trojans, I only played with them for two years. We won everything, the Lawson Cup, the League, the Saxone Cup, we swept the board. But what I always did when picking the team, I put our weakest player up outside left. Now, in the theatre the same principle applies. Our weakest act will go on straight after the Bob Nesbitt Irish dancers because the audience will always be glad of anything after the Irish dancing. That's strategy. That's why we won't be having any public house singers that no one could follow without being a let-down. Let's try and calculate what we have. Toots. Toots Books, now that's a grand theatrical name. What will you do, Toots?'

'Do I have to go first?'

'Of course not. We'll put you on anytime. You can go on after Bob Nesbitt if you like.'

'I meant, do I have to go first saying what I'll do?'

'What's the difference?'

Just saying what I would do, giving it birth, I was expecting to be laughed at by my own Coffee Table Players.

'I was thinking of singing "I'm Falling In Love With Some-one".'

'Excellent. Excellent, Toots. And?'

'What you mean "and". That's it.'

'Anybody who has one song has two. We'll all have to do two turns.'

'I wasn't expecting an encore.'

'One in each half, I'm talking about. But if you do want an encore you'll get an encore. I'm the emcee.'

'"The Magic of Your Love".'

'No wonder you wanted to put on a concert. Toots Books, Ireland's own Nelson Eddy. Two songs, with me introducing you and waiting for the applause to stop. Six, maybe eight minutes. Taking that as an average. Five of us at eight minutes is forty. Throw in fifteen to twenty minutes of an interval. Bob Nesbitt twice will take at least half an hour, although it will seem like a month. We have the raffle. And the full company sketch. Madeleine, what will you do for us, my love?'

'"Shall My Soul Pass Through Old Ireland".'

'Can you? Terrific. And'?

'"The Old Refrain".'

'You must be our star. I might give you joint billing with me. Mr Droney.'

'I can't sing.'

'What do you mean you can't sing? My sister can't play the piano but she does. Didn't you sing "Just One Cornetto" up at the labour exchange?'

'I only do things like that because they're the first thing that comes into my head.'

'So do the first thing that comes into your head. We'll build the concert around you. The Great Droney. The Great Droney will play the Great Kusacki in the full company sketch. Madeleine, you'll be the wench. I'll play OUR HERO. Walter, what have you for us?'

'A monologue.'

'Our Bartley Michaels. Dan McGrew? Sam McGee?'

'"The Blacksmith of Limerick". "The Burial of Sir John Moore at Corunna".'

'And I'll do a couple of easy listenin' songs as well as emcee and starring as OUR HERO in the full company sketch. Toots, you have your concert. I'll arrange the printing today. I'll go to Corrs. An ad in the paper for the weekend. We're on next Wednesday. Ignatius Valelly, actor manager.'

Eddie Hamilton was now a tea and coffee broker with a small office in a business centre. He had a staff of one receptionist. I could see Nellie sitting in the front row. That's how I had the balls to present the concert to the sane scrutiny of a sound man like Eddie Hamilton. The last time I saw him he had seen me first and he let himself be sucked into a department store. He couldn't handle a Toots Books who had once been Jimmy Imbusch. But there is a way of humouring people. Eddie had it.

I got a big welcome.

'Jimmy. Come inside. Angela, tea or coffee, Jimmy?'

'Whatever's handy.'

How was I and all the rest of it. Nellie? Still in the convent? So sorry about that.

'Eddie, can you do me a turn?'

'Shoot. If I can you know I will.'

'I'm involved with a group putting on a concert.'

'Are you? Good man. What kind of a concert?'

'Old-fashioned. I got involved for something to do.'

'Of course.'

'It's going on at the Gaelic League Hall.'

'Is that place still there?'

'Just about. The concert's in aid of charity. The missions. But the hall is going to cost us three hundred quid and we're trying to get it sponsored. I don't know how you're doing here . . .'

'Done. You want me to sponsor the hall? Done. Is that it?'

'Yes.'

'Do it now. Just a tick. Angela, the company chequebook.'

'You'll be credited in the publicity.'

'Don't, Jimmy. Not concerned with the public anymore. It would only lead to a queue outside the door. Good to see you in action. Who do I make it payable to?'

'The Coffee Table Players.'

'I'm out of touch. Don't seem to have heard of them. You're their fundraiser?'

'Just for the hall. It's a once-off.'

Eddie wrote the cheque. He wouldn't hurry me off the premises. Out of politeness he asked about the concert. Who had we lined up? When were the Coffee Table Players founded that he hadn't heard of them?

'You're appearing yourself? Really? I didn't know you had it in you. Put me down for two tickets. Not complimentary.'

The humouring had begun. I'd picked it up from Droney, could see myself the way Eddie must see me. Jimmy Imbusch? As sound as anyone I ever knew. But after the tragedy. If I could only have kept the firm going. Toots Books. And now this.

But I could see Nellie in the front row.

I had to sit on myself to frustrate a premature visit to the convent. Skinny Mitchell was next.

'. . . my oul fella knows the head bollix for the canal but that guy doesn't do the interviewing. I had to go through the motions with this other guy. You dropped out of Business Studies I see. Cocks an eyebrow at me. The cunt. I got this opportunity to go to Amsterdam, I tell him. A colleague of mine had an apartment there. A fucking *colleague*. The language they make you use. A wonderful opportunity to establish a base from which to see Europe before I was too old. The cunt in his fifties, seconded from the corporation with his shiny suit. I wanted to travel. To broaden my mind. He sees. Your last position before you returned to university was a Manufacturing Team Member. What exactly were your duties? Scratching my arse and watching the clock. But I tell him Assembly and Wrapping. He sees. And now you intend to teach? More eyebrow. Like I was a rich man's son flirting with vocations. Which is true only I'm a poor man's son. But fuck him. How are things with yourself?'

Skinny listened. 'You're kidding?'

'No.'

'A concert?'

'A concert.'

'That you're all putting on yourselves?'

'Yes.'

154

'Why not. Droney, he'll be in it? What will he do?'

'The first thing that comes into his head.'

'The whole town is getting that off him already for free. And you're in it yourself. What are you doing?'

'Singing Nelson Eddy.'

'I think I heard my father mention him. Sounds great gas. Why are ye doing it?'

'In aid of the missions.'

'But why are ye doing it, no matter what it's in aid of?'

'We just got the idea.'

'Of course. Of course.'

'Why aren't you falling off the stool laughing?'

'Can I bring my friends? You want to hear laughing? Bunch of cynics. How much to get in?'

'That hasn't been discussed yet.'

'Don't forget the unwaged.'

When Skinny left I sat on my stool looking at Nellie in the front row. I went to sleep singing to her.

Valelly was telling them when I came in: 'Have to find a pianist . . . ah, Toots.' I gave him the cheque. 'Toots, you're a wizard. I was always good at delegating. Corrs the printers. Another grandson. Admission a fiver. Raffle. Cloakroom tickets will do. Ad in the paper. It's only a matter of countdown.'

I went to the convent. It was all a hoax, I told them, the heinous crime letter. It was Droney. We should have guessed. And for no reason, the same as the way he puts dogs' deaths in the paper. But we have a new development. Sister Mary Monica picked up. The soap was back on the road.

I give Droney the credit. Droney wants us to put on a concert. Nellie hugs the Harlequins jersey. She is delighted. Jimmy is active. Now Jimmy is smug: 'You should have seen Valelly. He jumped at the idea. It was all he could do not to put it on that night. He must have been waiting all his life for another chance to show what he could do.'

I can't wait for Sister Mary Monica or Nellie to ask: what will you all do? I tell them. Valelly. Madeleine. Walter. The Great Droney. The Bob Nesbitt School of Irish Dancing. And I wait. Nellie just smiles and is patient. Sister Mary Monica obliges. 'What are you going to do yourself?' I give my answer to Nellie.

'One song I'm going to sing is "I'm Falling In Love With Someone". The one I used to sing when Tom would get me going? You used to love it, Nellie?'

She saw what was coming. I could see it behind her eyes. For just a second I saw it and then she pulled the curtains.

'Jimmy, that's *wonderful*.'

I ploughed on. 'And for the second half, your old favourite, "The Magic of Your Love".'

I was trying to hold myself back. Don't say it in a brutal fashion. Slide it in. But then a miracle from Sister Mary Monica that will make it all oh so easy. 'Will you have an orchestra?'

'I doubt it. Valelly was talking about he has to find a pianist.'

'If I wasn't so rusty.'

'You play the piano?'

'It's been so many years.'

'You're hired. I insist. I'll tell Valelly call off the dogs.' She has to come out now, if not for me, I can pretend, for Sister Mary Monica. 'You'll do it? Nellie, tell Sister Mary Monica she has to oblige.'

Nellie says to Sister Mary Monica, 'You will.'

'If you can't get anybody else . . .'

'We don't want anybody else.'

'I'm so out of practice.'

'Nonsense.' Time to nail it down and get out of there while I'm winning. Don't risk being alone with Nellie.

'Nellie, you're going to love it. Accompanied by Sister Mary Monica . . .'

Sister Mary Monica answered, 'Jimmy, no publicity. Not for me.'

I was looking at Nellie. She was trying to fight. This was an attack she could never have anticipated. I let it go. 'I must find Valelly and tell him we have our Franz Liszt.'

I kissed Nellie on the cheek. She gave me her sweetest smile

156

when I said, 'Roll on Wednesday.' At the front door I told Sister
Mary Monica my own agenda. 'I'm counting on you. It's your job
to get her there. Promise?'

'Jimmy, everything in my power.'

Skinny called into the Drop Out. 'Start on Monday. Feckin' off
for the weekend. The condemned man's last meal. How are the
Coffee Table Players? Is it really true? It's not a ballhop.'

'Read it in the paper tomorrow night.'

'I told my mates. They're all on. Except they don't believe me.
They'll have to believe me when they see it on the paper.'

He didn't stay long, just the one pint. The usual got-to-meet-a-
bloke type of escape. He wasn't the same Skinny since his mate
spotted Droney with the child from St Gabriel's.

On Friday morning, Valelly congratulated himself by praising me.
'A nun? Marvellous. Well done, Toots. Can I pick a team or
can I pick a team? Corrs will do the printing for nothing. The
McCormack programme is in their glass case. I'm a legend in the
Corr family. Bob Nesbitt is delighted to appear. A pity the Quay
Lane Male Voice Choir is no more. Broke up after Dan Fitton took
to drink in his fifties. Mr Kleiser will provide the piano. He used to
help old Ned Toomey in St Munchin's Boys Club. He remembers
me driving Mr Toomey. It's easy when everyone knows you. We'll
be in the paper tonight. Mr Kleiser asked me how rehearsals were
going. I told him we don't believe in rehearsals. Rob a show of
spontaneity. This nun, though, can I ring her, she might want to
test the piano?'

I got back to the bookshop at twelve. Instead of going to the
Drop Out for soup I bought a sandwich and stayed in Toots Books
with the door shut and the blinds down. I rehearsed. I went into
the back and sang. Five nights to go. How would the time pass?
Not even Skinny for company in the Drop Out. I got the idea
to feck off myself. In the Drop Out that night I rang Droney in
O'Brien's to get him to do Saturday.

Nobody in the Drop Out ever spoke to me except the odd

157

goodnight from a bingo refugee. Tonight I got a few looks. The barman hovered. 'I see a concert advertised in the paper with a Toots Books appearing. Would that be yourself by any chance?'

Out of the tens of thousands of Toots Books. The barman didn't pursue it. Guy sits by himself and never watches the games. Odd, some people.

I ate the thigh and superchip sitting at the kitchen table with the paper in front of me:

GRAND VARIETY CONCERT
In Aid of THE FATHER CLETUS BURSARY
Presented by THE COFFEE TABLE PLAYERS
Featuring IGNATIUS VALELLY
Also appearing
MADELEINE BROWN
WALTER NIX
TOOTS BOOKS
THE GREAT DRONEY
THE BOB NESBITT SCHOOL OF IRISH DANCING
Master of Ceremonies IGNATIUS VALELLY
Produced by IGNATIUS VALELLY
At the GAELIC LEAGUE HALL
WEDNESDAY at 8pm SHARP
ADMISSION £5.

I drove to Galway and mooched around the bookshops. I went on out to Spiddal and paddled in the sea, not asking, but thanking: Jesus, thank you for doing it this way.

I stayed in Salthill. I scoured the pubs. They were all packed, but it's easy for a man. The pint and the fags and an old mirror to stare at. Inside in one of those mirrors I saw a woman looking into her mirror at my reflection. In her forties with two other women of the same cut. I was sorry for her. She had no point hoping. Wasting her time. Nellie was there in the front row.

I was back on the road after breakfast. The leisure centre was on my way home. I did my eight hundred metres, had lunch, read the papers and thought about the concert. I felt sorry for poor Valelly. He was demented, rushing out a fiasco of a concert, trying to recapture his glory as a buttons. I went to Mass and gave thanks and settled into the Drop Out. Skinny didn't come in, must have been late getting back from his weekend. But Maurice did.

I was cocooned by the coffee table and my dreams of Nellie. And the world of the Great Droney. A concert? Of course. Why not. But there were people out there running as normal. I'd had a taste of it when I went to Eddie Hamilton for the sponsorship. People to whom a concert might sound like bringing back TB. I should have anticipated that Maurice would saddle his horse.

He only had a half-pint. The draconian drinking and driving laws. Here we go: 'That is you on the paper, I suppose?'

'The ad for the concert?'

'What's going on?'

'Mostly singing. Monologues. A bit of Irish dancing.'

'That's not what I meant. How did you get involved? Did you join a drama group? I never heard of the Coffee Table Players.'

'That's just a title we gave ourselves. *Ad hoc.*'

'Who's we? This Great Droney, is that that nutcase landlord of yours?'

'The very same.'

'Is that why you're involved? Has he a hold over you?'

'Of course not.'

'People who know you're my brother have been asking me. Why didn't you tell me about this? Not have it come out of nowhere on the paper, making me feel a fool. You're always doing things without telling me. I don't know what to say to people. What part have you in this concert?'

'I'm Nelson Eddy.'

'What?'

'Well, Ireland's own Nelson Eddy. I'm singing a couple of songs and taking part in a bit of a sketch.'

'Since when could you sing? I didn't know you sang.'

'Maurice, you often heard me singing. I'm not a crow.'

'That was at home or in a pub. You can't just walk up and do that on a stage.'

'Why can't I?'

'Because . . . for Christ sake. What's got into you? You're going to make a fool of yourself in public. I'll have people coming up to me. You have to get a grip on yourself. I know you've had your troubles but there's no need for . . . and this friend of yours, he's the laughing stock of the whole town. Who are these other people? I've never heard of any of them except Bob Nesbitt.'

'They're friends of mine. We meet for coffee in the Market Bar. That's where we got the name. Ignatius Valelly used to be a buttons years ago when McCormack sang here. Jack Doyle and Movita, Vic Loving, Tauber, he knew them all . . .'

'I never heard of him.'

'You wouldn't. He's way older. He's not a star. This is just an amateur thing for a good cause. Walter Nix is an ex-taxi driver, he's doing monologues. Madeleine Brown, her husband is Bobby Brown the insurance . . .'

'Brown that fiddled all that money? That Brown?'

'He's OK now. He's a window cleaner. They seem happy.'

'*They* seem happy? No wonder they would. What about all the people they took the money off of? Look, how did you get involved with a crowd like that? Do you realise what you're doing with your life, do you? Just because Nellie is . . . how did you get roped in? Who's idea was this?'

'Mine.'

'Christ. I don't know what to say to you. Why? Why did you get such a mad idea?'

'Something to do.'

'There's a million things for a person to do. Everyone doesn't have to go jumping up on stages putting on concerts . . .'

Maurice was always the older brother, circumscribed by having to be the rock. But now I saw him through the Droney conjunctivitis, his rectitude begged to take the mickey.

'It's only for one night, Maurice. I'm not going to throw up Toots Books to become a strolling player.'

He heard the threat of finality. But he had to try once more. He couldn't go home and have his wife say: but didn't you point out to him. He had to be able to say to his wife and himself: I tried everything.

'Do you read the appointments section? I see jobs you could do all the time. I know technology's gone mad but lots of places look for people who can run things. Where you'd be more occupied, have more responsibility. Where you are you have too much time to be thinking, that's not healthy.'

'I'm happy in the bookshop, Maurice. I don't want to change.'

'I don't know. I don't know what to say to you. If only . . .'

'Say you'll come to the concert.'

'Think about what I said. Ring me if you want to talk. You don't need this, you know. If you think about it, maybe in the morning, give it some thought, ask yourself, do I need this. Ring me in the morning. You might find it good to talk to someone. I have to go now.'

I was early on Monday morning but they were all there before me. Valelly had the posters and the programmes. The poster was a blow-up of the newspaper ad. The programme was a meagre folded sheet.

In order of appearance
IGNATIUS VALELLY, Tenor,
Easy Listenin'

THE GREAT DRONEY

WALTER NIX,
Monologuist

THE GREAT DRONEY

MADELEINE BROWN, Soprano,
The Golden Vale Queen of Song

THE GREAT DRONEY

THE BOB NESBITT SCHOOL OF IRISH DANCING

THE GREAT DRONEY

TOOTS BOOKS, Baritone,
Ireland's Own Nelson Eddy

INTERVAL

IGNATIUS VALELLY, Tenor,

Easy Listenin'

THE GREAT DRONEY

WALTER NIX,
Monologuist

THE GREAT DRONEY

MADELEINE BROWN, Soprano,
The Golden Vale Queen of Song

THE GREAT DRONEY

THE BOB NESBITT SCHOOL OF IRISH DANCING

TOOTS BOOKS, Baritone,
Ireland's Own Nelson Eddy.

RAFFLE

FULL COMPANY SKETCH

Man Drinking Bottle of Guinness.................... The Great Droney
Wench... Madeleine Brown
Mine Host.. Toots Books
Ensemble.......... Walter Nix and Members of the Bob Nesbitt
School of Irish Dancing
Our Hero.. Ignatius Valelly

The programme was as fittingly miserable as the concert surely
would be. Ignatius Valelly had long lost his touch. 'Costumes,'
Valelly said, 'Toots and Walter dress suit. Go to Todds and ask
for Gerard Lewis. He handles all my clothes. I spoke to Bob
Nesbitt. He'll accommodate Madeleine the Irish Colleen, has all
the gear there. Toots and Walter will sell the programme in their
dress suits. A nice touch. Madeleine says her husband will do
box office. I was on to your friend Sister Mary Monica. She's
coming in this afternoon. Kleiser's men are delivering the piano.
Padraigh O Maolcathaigh will be there to see what else we need.
Anything else? Can anyone think of anything else? Have I left
out anything?'

I was curious. 'What will Droney wear?'

'The first thing that comes into his head.'

Of course.

So Sister Mary Monica would be in the Gaelic League Hall in the afternoon. I was afraid to go and see Nellie on my own in case she'd trap me. Jimmy. Please, Jimmy. I didn't want any more of that. It was never-take-no-for-an-answer time. But I thought of Nellie all afternoon. I saw mountain streams. We were on river banks. Picnics. Blue skies. Hampers. We ran hand in hand through tall grass. We sat with our backs to a haystack. We hired bikes. We never used to do things like that but they were the images. It didn't matter a damn that they'd come from cigarette ads.

I brought the programme with me to the Drop Out to show Skinny. '. . . can't wait to bring my CV up to date. I see in your last position, Mr Mitchell, you were a grim reaper? There's this foreman, he does the canal and a lot of other places that the Civic Trust are fucking around with, a most considerate chap. He gives me this yoke on a pole to slash the reeds, a dangerous bastard of a thing altogether. The foreman tells me, whatever you do be careful, don't cut your foot off. There's five of us all issued with wellies and this thing with the slash hook at the end of it. No one wants to use it because the foreman was deadly serious. The other blokes just wade in, pulling bikes and prams out. Romantic . . .'

Skinny studied the programme. 'Very nice. Your friend Droney must be a talented man. Man Drinking Bottle of Guinness. I could play that part.'

It could have been Skinny's frayed soul from tooling about on the canal. The old spark wasn't there. There was no fuck-me-pink reaction to Walter the Monologuist or Valelly as OUR HERO. The real Skinny would have laughed in the face of Ireland's Own Nelson Eddy. He was still afraid of us. Or me in particular. I had to accept that a bag of sweets and a dirty raincoat cast a long shadow.

Walter and I were sent to Todds by Valelly. Tuesday morning is a quiet time in the drapery trade. Gerard Lewis abandoned trying to affect realism in his adjustment of the suit racks when he saw us. He came towards us, rubbing his hands. 'Nice morning gentlemen.'

Walter explained: 'Ignatius Valelly asked us to call . . .'

'Ignatius?'

The dress suits were new. 'Ignatius insisted,' Gerard Lewis explained. Suits, dicky-bows, shirts, socks, shoes. All new. First time out. No one had worn them before us. Sponsored by Todds. Return at our leisure.

I went back to the shop to leave the suit and stuff and there I got a better idea. Bring the gear with me.

I hadn't been to the convent before at what I thought of as coffee time. Nellie was in the laundry. Sister Mary Monica had to send for her. She came into the parlour, taking off her apron and rolling down her sleeves. 'Jimmy. How *are* you?'

God, if I let her beat me now I'm finished. I won't get this chance again. 'Look Nellie, this is how Ireland's Own Nelson Eddy will be accoutred. How do you think I'll look?'

'Jimmy, you'll be dashing.'

'I bet you can't wait to see me.'

I got no answer. Nellie had tried to fold her arms when she sat down. That didn't agree with her. She changed to gripping the sides of the armchair. She'd come straight from the laundry and didn't have the Harlequins jersey. I said to Sister Mary Monica, 'What about transport? Will I collect you?'

'Ignatius is sending a taxi. He's a lovely man.'

'So will you go with Sister Mary Monica, Nellie, or what, or will you come with me?'

'You'll be busy, Jimmy. I'll go in the taxi.'

Get out fast. 'See you both on the night.' I gave Nellie the kiss and let her hand take its time slipping out of mine.

Maurice rang. 'I'm ringing you all morning. You were to ring me. Where were you?'

'I had to collect a dress suit and then I was at the convent.'

'Dress suit? What's on?'

'The concert.'

'Did you think about what I said? Were you listening to me at all?'

'I did listen to you, Maurice.'

'Well? You're not insisting on going ahead with this?'

'Maurice, it's just a concert. What the hell is the matter with you? For Christ sake, what harm is there in a concert?'

'Don't get snappy with me. Look, I'm just trying to save you from yourself. A concert is a public thing. It's not *like* singing in a public house half-pissed. A stage is for people who are meant to be on stage . . .'

I cut him off.

One of my customers had mentioned the ad on Monday afternoon.

'Is that yourself?'

'Yes.'

And the look that said: how could he be on the stage? Don't I know him from going into his bookshop.

Skinny came into the Drop Out on Tuesday night but didn't have a drink. 'Just passing on the way to meet a mate. I said I'd check to see everything OK with your concert. It's going ahead?'

It went ahead.

THE CONCERT

I arrived at the Gaelic League Hall at twenty past seven. The main street entrance leads directly to the back of the stage. Even though I'm short-sighted the hall was so intimate that I could see the biscuit tin holding Bobby Brown's float on the table just inside the door of the emergency exit where the audience would gain admission from a lane at the back. The setting for the concert was arseways from the start.

Ignatius Valelly was directing Padraigh O Maolcathaigh and a handyman to position the full company sketch props. He greeted me: 'What do you think of my hat? And my stool?'

It was a trendy theatrical trilby to go with Valelly's fawn suit. The stool was a bar stool. Walter and I came in our formal dress. Droney was togged out in the old overcoat with the belt of twine and the jeans and the wellingtons and the cravat and the long grey hair and the port wine stain. Madeleine Brown was in the changing room with the Irish dancers. I said to Valelly, 'It suits you.'

'Of course it does. Toots, Bob Nesbitt. Bob, Ireland's Own Nelson Eddy.'

I shook hands with Bob Nesbitt. He'd been around. I took his face to read: where's this guy been hiding? Padraigh O Maolcathaigh and his handyman carried tables and chairs onto the side of the stage for the full company sketch. The makeshift counter was one of those screens behind which you might expect a whore with a heart of gold to undress in a cowboy picture except that in place of the titillating silk stockings the Market Bar sign was hung.

166

On the floor, hidden from the audience by the screen, lay the bottle of Guinness and a crate with glasses and cans of orange. The piano was centre-stage beside an optional microphone. Anyone with half a voice wouldn't need it. A performer could almost reach out and shake hands with the front row. I counted a possible capacity of about one hundred and fifty.

'Well, Toots. All set?' said the Great Droney.

'Tomorrow don't come into my shop. Stay away from my door. You madman getting me into this.'

Walter said, 'We have an audience.' Bobby Brown sold his first ticket to an elderly lady. I looked at my watch. Twenty-five past seven. I thought they'd be here by now. Sister Mary Monica getting the feel of the piano. The handyman closed the curtains. Valelly finished with his props. 'Toots, Walter. Programmes.'

Walter made the first sale to the lady. Seven or eight dribbled in during the next five minutes. One of them Maurice. He sat in the back row. When he saw me approach in my dress suit with the programmes I think he had a last hope that this was my intended capacity all along, that I'd been having him on. But after he looked at the programme, I said, 'Small company. We have to double up.' He'd come alone. Without his wife. Without a nephew or niece to see Uncle Jimmy. Uncle Toots.

Just gone half-seven. Gerard Lewis and his wife came in. I offered them complimentary programmes. Gerard Lewis shovelled the money at me. 'Do you want Ignatius to kill me?'

Almost twenty-five to eight. I went backstage. Valelly was experimenting with casual perches on the bar stool and adjusting his hat. 'Is it better at this angle?' he asked the Great Droney, Padraigh O Maolcathaigh and the handyman. I cut in: 'The taxi. What time was it to collect Sister Mary Monica?'

'He was to be at the convent at quarter past seven. Don't worry. I handpicked him myself. She'll be here.'

Walter and I served an aisle each. The way the punters trickled in didn't presage a full house. Eddie Hamilton and his wife arrived. Walter dealt with them. They waved at me. I sold a few more programmes, one to a priest, another to a customer of the shop, one to a woman who introduced herself as Walter's wife. I couldn't be brusque. She'd heard so much about us chat.

She didn't seem worried that her husband had suddenly taken to the stage. The crowd began to back up at Bobby Brown's table. A minute after quarter to eight. I rushed backstage. Madeleine was out of the dressing room, wearing an Irish dancing costume and a scarf decorated with horses' heads. 'They're not here,' I said to Valelly. I shoved the programmes at Droney. 'I'm going out front to look.'

I ran from the main street entrance around the block to the lane where the queue included Skinny and his mates. I ran back and looked from the stage. Droney was out there now, flogging the programmes. I was sweating, didn't dwell on the incongruity of Walter in his dress suit and Droney in the duds. Ten to eight. I ran out to the lane again. Then back to the main street entrance. Fuck Valelly and his handpicked driver. I stayed at the main street entrance and ate a cigarette.

The taxi came at five to eight. Sister Mary Monica was alone. Valelly came out from backstage as I went to open the taxi door. I said to the driver, 'Hang on there one second.' And to Sister Mary Monica, 'Where is she?'

'Jimmy, she says she'll follow on.'

'Follow on? What does that mean? Why isn't she with you? You were supposed to bring her.'

'Jimmy, do you think I haven't been trying for the past half an hour? She says Johnny is with her.'

'What? What are you saying?'

'Jimmy, believe me. I tried my best. She's the way – the way she often is. She said she couldn't leave him but she promised she'd come in time for you. She knows where you are in the programme. I'm to send back the car . . .'

I didn't care that Valelly had heard. I sat in the car. Valelly's head was at the window on my side before I could turn to the driver. 'Look after my friend,' said Valelly.

The driver spoke about knowing Walter and Walter being in the concert but once I'd told him to get me to the convent as fast as he could I stopped listening. All I could hear was my head throbbing and feel the sweat. We were there at seven minutes past eight.

The nun who answered recognised me. 'I have to see my wife

immediately. Tell her I'm in the parlour. Tell her if she can't come down I'll go straight up. Hurry.'

I sucked a cigarette and looked at nine, ten minutes past eight. The lucky people would have already got Easy Listenin' from Valelly. They might have had a taste of the Great Droney. Eleven minutes past. She came in with her arms around the Harlequins jersey. 'Jimmy.'

'Hi. I said I'd come back up with the taxi to kill the nerves.'

'Jimmy, I can't leave him yet.'

'Nellie, please. Just come in the car. Everything will be all right. Do this for me, Nellie.'

'I can't, I can't. I can't leave him. I can't leave him yet. Please Jimmy, please understand. Don't make me.'

I couldn't look at her and I couldn't hold in the rage. I shook my fists at the ceiling. 'Jesus . . .' I gave up. Sat down in the armchair. This time Nellie knelt down beside me.

'Don't cry, Jimmy. Please don't cry. I'm going to come. I'm not ready yet but the minute he's all right I'm coming. I told Sister Mary Monica. I promise.'

'If we went now we'd be lucky to be there on time. It's too late . . .'

'No. You sing near the end of the second half. I'll be there then at least. I know I will. I promise, Jimmy. You go and send the taxi back for me. It's the best way. I'll be ready then. You must go, you can't let them down.'

'How do you know you'll be able to come? How do you know you'll be able to leave him?'

'Because I know. Jimmy, I'm promising you. Send the taxi back for me. I'll be there.'

'Nellie, I'm begging you. Promise me. Swear to me that you'll come.'

'Jimmy, hurry. I promise you I'm coming. Hurry and send the taxi back. I'll go upstairs now but I'll be there. I promise. Now hurry . . .'

It was just after half-past eight when I reached backstage. Madeleine was singing, 'Shall I see the little chapel, where I pledged my heart and hand'. Valelly and Bob Nesbitt and the Irish dancers were over in the far wing. I stood beside Walter and Droney. I got the ratings later from Skinny. The handyman threw the house light switches. Padraigh O Maolcathaigh and Bob Nesbitt ran the curtains open to reveal Valelly sitting on his stool. He let the audience savour his perch. Then he took off the hat and fiddled with it as he approached the edge of the stage. Sister Mary Monica gave him the flourish of a few bars of an intro.

'Good evening, ladies and gentlemen, and welcome to tonight's feast of entertainment gathered here at no expense. Chuckles. Sit back and enjoy yourselves. Take it easy. It's easy listenin'. Look, I'll show you.'

Valelly sat on the bar stool and put on his hat.

Well, I woke up Sunday mornin' with no way to hold my head that didn't hurt . . .

He sang with such confidence or else it was the honeymoon tolerance towards a first act, or he bowed so many times when he finished, Skinny wasn't sure, but the audience gave him a decent hand. Out of a hundred and fifty, eighty-three seats were occupied.

Leaving out Maurice in his capacity as a helpless bystander there were Walter's wife, one daughter of Valelly's and her husband, a couple of neighbours of mine and a few customers from the bookshop, Eddie Hamilton and his wife, Gerard Lewis and his wife, who were blackmailed into attending by Valelly's account in Todds, and Skinny and his game-for-a-laugh mates.

The rest of the audience were people of a certain age. Withered. They were representative of all those who had withdrawn into hibernation from about the mid-1960s and the emergence of here's-me-tits tabloid entertainment in all branches of the industry. They would have retreated further back into the cave as even the newspapers began to print the word 'fuck' and interviewed old pop stars of thirty-five who reminisced on those who gave good head.

This audience would have known the gramophone circle. Soap operas about families who shout at each other all the time couldn't fill that vacuum. Most of the small audience would have seen the ad in the paper as the long-awaited sound of the 'all clear'. They came to the Gaelic League Hall expecting the same satisfaction due to a street of urchins from liberating American soldiers bearing candy bars. Their long dark night was over. They brought goodwill.

Valelly introduced the Great Droney. The audience would have seen from the programme that the Great Droney was due to appear seven times. A reasonable interpretation would have deduced that the Great Droney was a snappy performer. Valelly danced to his stage-right exit. The crowd waited. So did Droney in the wings. He waited until the sound of polite coughing suggested he had waited long enough. Keep them guessing.

Then, to Sister Mary Monica's accompaniment, the Great Droney sang 'Just One Cornetto'. This was instant meat and drink to Skinny's gang. Also, they recognised when he had finished. They clapped and whistled and stamped the floor and got shush looks. On with the Great Droney.

How do you write to a fish?

In his introduction, Valelly had admitted: 'For your delectation, the Great Droney, to perform the first thing that comes into his head.'

It's easy. Simply drop him a line.

This was a wow with Skinny and his cynics but generally Droney left the stage to a restless silence. The concert was now well on its way. Downhill.

Walter was a disaster. He began: 'Ladies and gentlemen, "The Blacksmith of Limerick".' The selection itself was popular. The crowd knew the piece from their schooldays. But Walter was a debater not a declaimer. Stuff like

The first that gained the rampart he was a captain brave
A captain of the grenadiers with blood-stained dirk and glaive.
He pointed and he parried but it was all in vain
For right through skull and helmet the hammer found his brain

needed a show-off. Walter wasn't Bartley Michaels. He couldn't carry it – coughs punctuated the thirteen verses. The applause was in thanksgiving that he had finished.

The Great Droney came on again as was threatened in the programme. Valelly did not introduce him a second time. The Great Droney wandering onto the stage the way he roamed around town, that was the form. He spoke to Sister Mary Monica. They performed an instrumental duet of 'Colonel Bogie'. The Great Droney played the comb wrapped in silver paper. Skinny and his crew had tanked up at the happy hour. They laughed their heads off but they were on their own clapping.

This was the fiasco so far when I arrived during Madeleine's 'Shall My Soul Pass Through Old Ireland'. She was terrific. A sweet voice. I joined in the applause myself. The house shouted 'Encore', and good as Madeleine had been there was an element in the shouts of encore of the next item on the programme being the Great Droney again. The Great Droney did go on stage but the crowd tried to shout him off with 'Encore, encore'.

Valelly went on to appease them. He gave them his promise that of course they would hear the Golden Vale Queen of Song again. But for the smooth running of the programme, that was designed to go like clockwork, for their further pleasure now, the Great Droney.

Some of the audience persisted with 'Encore, encore'. And some, not so well versed in euphemism, shouted 'Boo'. That was what inspired Droney's next turn.

I'd told the taxi driver to rush back up to the convent. Was there a chance she'd make my first number?

> '. . . and says, bless me father, for I have sinned. It's a month since my last confession. I made love to a woman . . .'

It wasn't at all in his canon. Droney didn't tell jokes. He was witty but not a joke-teller. Not a dirty-joke slob.

> '. . . the woman is your wife? That is not considered a sin, my son . . .'

The hall was quiet. Censure or anticipation, either would do to compose a silence.

'. . . it's the way I do it, father . . .'
'. . . and what way is that . . .'
'I like to do it from behind . . .'

The only sound was that of faces going red.

'. . . I see. Again, that is not necessarily a sin. You are referring to coitus, I trust?'

Droney watched them squirm. Fuck them booing me.

'Yes, father. But you see, I like to surprise her. I like to come at her when she has her back turned. When she's not expecting it. Especially when she's bending over the freezer. That's my favourite. To surprise her from behind when she's bending over the freezer . . .'
'. . . again, it is not another woman. She is your own wife. It may be unorthodox. You may have your reasons. Does your wife object to be so taken by surprise?'
'No, father. She enjoys it . . .'
'Then, again I say to you, there is nothing wrong my son.'
'. . . are you sure, father . . .'
'. . . yes, my son. I'm sure. Now for your penance . . .'
'But why am I barred from Tesco?'

The elderly lady who had come in first was now first to leave, after standing to shout, 'Disgusting!' She was heard above the adulation from Skinny's people who had now become a claque for the Great Droney. The priest and three more followed the elderly lady. Eddie Hamilton and Gerard Lewis clapped but their wives were quiet. Maurice was a stone. He looked twice over at Bobby Brown, as though it must be somebody's job to throw Droney out.

Valelly trotted on. 'And now, ladies and gentlemen . . .'

He gave them the number of Munster Belts and All Ireland

Titles and World Championships won by the Bob Nesbitt School of Irish Dancing. Valelly succeeded in taming the audience. Irish dancing. What could go wrong? There were six dancers, three boys and three girls. They opened with jigs and reels in soft shoe and nipped to the sides of the stage to slip into buckles for the hornpipes. They danced all six together. They danced in pairs and in threes. One pair danced and the other four stayed stiff and still. Each had a turn on his or her own. I thought of what I'd learned of permutations and combinations at school. In how many ways can two people be chosen from a group of six? In how many ways can one boy and one girl be chosen from three boys and three girls? Two boys? Two girls? Any one of six? I calculated thirty-six ways. They must have rationed themselves to half a minute because throw in the whole gang dancing together and the Bob Nesbitt show lasted twenty-one minutes.

There was still a chance Nellie might make it for my first song.

Bob Nesbitt himself was surprised by the cries of 'Encore'. I had only the Great Droney between me and me. I was glad to have Droney going on again otherwise I might have been the first act in history to dread having to follow a school of Irish dancing. Valelly had to go out and promise more of Bob Nesbitt in the second half.

It was the first time the port wine stain failed Droney as a prop. Those who knew him from around town were anaesthetised. The rest, taking the affliction in conjunction with his old overcoat and rags, might have thought he painted the thing on. His long grey hair might have been a wig *à la* Great Kusacki. He went on again to silence and spoke to Sister Mary Monica. Then he faced the audience and made a great show of searching his pockets. Then he mimed 'found it'. A skipping rope. Sister Mary Monica led him. He sang 'Singin' in the Rain'. He skipped in his wellingtons while he sang, tripped a few times, got up, and sang on skipping. I thought of the nun who wasn't allowed out to our wedding who now accompanied a man skipping in wellingtons. And I thought of how, if it hadn't accommodated my own plan in relation to Nellie, I'd been such a dumb prick to have landed myself in it. Just being an accessory to Droney's act I had paid my dues towards his no longer having an excuse to pester children with sweets.

Droney's audience was now down to Skinny and his pals. Two

other couples left before the Great Droney finished singing in the rain. Theirs was a quiet exit, as though blaming themselves for not knowing better. The acclamation from the Skinny seats couldn't hide it. This concert was a joke too far.

The Great Droney pulled at his face and looked around the stage. Inspired, he dashed to the wings and returned with a brush that he hoisted on his shoulder rifle-fashion. He marched across and back the stage. 'Oh, let me like a soldier fall upon some open plain . . .'

She would hardly make it now to hear me in the first half and yet I had no fear of going on after Droney. I was ready. But Droney hadn't finished yet. He stared brazenly out at the hall as only he could, a man who didn't give a fuck who thought what of him. Then:

'. . . man goes in and says, bless me father for I have sinned . . .'

Five people immediately stood up and left. Two couples and one gentleman on his own, who shouted back at Droney, 'You should be ashamed of yourself.'

'. . . the priest listens and says . . .'

What if everybody leaves? As long as Nellie came why should I worry.

'. . . very good, my son. Now for your penance say three Hail Marys and the Angelus. You do know the Angelus, my son?'
'. . . does it go Gong Gong Gong . . .'

Valelly introduced me. To bring us up to the interval, during which we would have the raffle, the one and only Toots Books, Ireland's Own Nelson Eddy.

I was Ireland's Own Nelson Eddy but I was no Nelson Eddy. Yet to the vintage in the hall – excepting Skinny's sceptics – Afghanistan's Own would have been welcome singing 'I'm Falling In Love With Someone'. Sister Mary Monica asked me, 'Did you see her?'

'She's coming. She promised she'd be here before the end.'

'What key?'

'What?'

'For your song.'

'I don't know. I'm going to be talking most of it.'

'E flat.'

Her intro charmed the house. We were winning before I started. I had a lot going for me. I wasn't the Great Droney. I wasn't Walter.

I've a very strange feeling I ne'er felt before,
It's a kind of a grind of depression.

I sang at the emergency exit, hoping Nellie might come in. I sang well, even when I was drawn to see Maurice with his head bent, looking at his knees. If he couldn't see me, maybe I wasn't there.

... believe me I'm telling you truly;
I'm gay without pause and sad without cause,
My spirits are truly unruly.

It was the stuff to give the troops. I had order. I'd be even better later, singing to Nellie. I finished:

I'm sure I could love someone madly
If someone could only love me.

Then I got the kick in the arse. The applause was for the song not the singer. The only cries of 'Encore' came from Skinny and Eddie Hamilton.

Padraigh O Maolcathaigh and the handyman closed the curtains.

I told Sister Mary Monica, 'I'm going to ring the convent. If she comes, hold onto her.' I ignored Valelly, calling after me, 'Toots, the raffle tickets.'

I went to a pub two blocks away where I wouldn't meet any of the audience. I ordered a pint and rang while the pint was settling. I got the engaged tone. There was a switchboard in the convent to connect callers to the secondary school, the offices and the residence but the switchboard clocked out at half-five. The number I rang was the one I used when Nellie first stayed away from home. I checked the directory. It was the same number. At night that number was answered by whoever heard it ringing. The phone was on a table in the hall between two chairs. I had some of the pint and tried again. It was still engaged.

I had the Mini. I could drive up there. But suppose Nellie came down while I was going up. Nobody would know her outside of Sister Mary Monica and Nellie wouldn't know anybody unless she spotted Maurice. If Sister Mary Monica had to take a leak or was back on stage Nellie might run. I tried again. It was no longer engaged. But it rang out. They went to bed at all sorts of early hours up there. But when I rang again it was engaged.

Ten minutes gone. I ordered a second pint. I'd left the house with the intention of not having a drop. I saw us getting into the car and going home. With every minute lost I was less inclined to drive to the convent in case I'd miss her. Then, of course, she was already in the Gaelic League Hall, talking to Sister Mary Monica and waiting for Jimmy. That was it. Or was it? I rang again. Engaged. Ringing out. Engaged. Some mad nun ringing relatives at the cheap rate now that the nuns were emancipated and Sister Mary Monica was out. After twenty minutes I knew that Nellie was in the Gaelic League Hall, waiting for me. I ran back.

She wasn't there. Neither were twenty-eight of the audience last seen listening to Ireland's Own Nelson Eddy. Valelly was on stage helping the survivors to make it through the night. 'Yesterday is Dead and Gone'. She said she's coming. She's coming. You saw her face. You heard her. She was sincere. She meant it. She's coming. Or was it that you try and try and try and give it your best and suddenly you have nothing left anymore and that's why I'm not running out of the hall now to go and collect her? No. Relax. You have three more Great Droneys going on as well as Madeleine, Walter and the Bob Nesbitt School of Irish Dancing.

Valelly was well received again. He had a daughter out there with her husband. Gerard Lewis and his wife cheered Valelly's account with Todds. Skinny and his gang would clap anything.

I looked out at Maurice. He didn't applaud. Valelly said, 'Wasn't that lovely, ladies and gentlemen?' From the edge of the stage he dominated the audience with his self-belief. 'Was I good?' Yes, Skinny's crowd shouted. 'Will I come on again later? Everybody now.' YES! Valelly gave them his last bow.

The Great Droney went on and recited

> *Tom and Joe are twins and so*
> *We find it very hard to know*
> *Which is Tom*
> *And which is Joe.*

The Great Droney bowed. The Great Droney stared at the audience who stared back at him. It was too much even for Skinny's people. Too pathetic. Skinny clapped but couldn't bring anyone with him. The Great Droney persisted:

> *Up the airy mountain*
> *Down the rushy glen*
> *We daren't go a hunting*
> *For fear of little men.*

Another staring match.

This time I went to the nearest pub. I recognised some of the audience. They looked at me and looked away. Whispering to each other: that's one of them. I rang. Ringing. Ringing out. Engaged. Back to the hall.

Walter was on. He'd reached:

> *No useless coffin enclosed his breast*
> *Not in sheet nor in shroud we wound him.*
> *But he lay like a warrior taking his rest*
> *With his martial cloak around him.*

Five more seats were empty since I'd left.

> *Slowly and sadly we laid him down*
> *From the field of his fame fresh and gory;*

We carved not a line, and we raised not a stone –
But we left him alone with his glory.

Walter did well, much better than he had done with 'The Black-smith'. But the 'Burial of Sir John Moore' didn't need an actor. Walter got a great hand. Even a call for an encore. Again, though, the Great Droney was due on next. The Great Droney caught my arm: 'What will I do? I can't think of a thing.'

'What did you do after "The Fairies"?'

'"Old MacDonald Had a Farm".'

'How did that go?'

'They ignored me. They just sat there except for one guy who's cheering me all night. Quick. What will I do?'

'How do I know? Tell them if they don't like you to sing themselves. I have to make a phone call . . .'

'Brilliant . . .'

Engaged. Drive up, batter down the door, drag her out. I wouldn't make it on time. Drag her out wouldn't work. Pray. Rush back. She might be there.

The Great Droney had threatened them. He had three more good ones about the man who went to confession. Or would they join him in community singing. They were at 'The Northern Lights of Old Aberdeen' when I got back. The concert graph had climbed off the floor with Walter. The Great Droney in his capacity as the audience himself kept it on a plateau. They had to clap themselves.

Madeleine sang 'The Old Refrain' and the graph soared while I was again across the road ringing. Ringing out. Engaged.

The audience roared for Madeleine to sing again but Valelly was out reminding them of the smooth running of the show.

'Quick,' Droney said.

'What?'

'What will I do now?'

'Show them your filofax. Hold on, I'm joking, I need an audience.'

I needed my wife. After Droney now there would only be Bob Nesbitt. Then Ireland's Own Nelson Eddy . . . and no Nellie. And have to hang around for the fucking raffle and the fucking full company sketch as a bartender, with Valelly acting as OUR HERO.

'Think of something. Quick . . .'

I did think of something. I ran around the back of the stage to Valelly's wing. He was taming the crowd with the promise that Madeleine would sing again after the full company sketch. He saw me waving at him to come off.

'. . . but first once more the Great Droney . . .'

Boos.

'What's wrong, Toots?'

'The sketch. OUR HERO.'

'I'll be fine. Don't worry about Ignatius.'

'Swap. Let me be OUR HERO. You be the barman. Sing something after Bob Nesbitt instead of me. Let me be OUR HERO.'

'Of course, Toots. If you want to be OUR HERO be OUR HERO. I can be a terrific barman.'

'. . . I know. We'll have a quiz . . .'

I'd bought time. I ran out of the hall and up a block to the Mini. I put the key in the ignition. The full company sketch with Toots Books as OUR HERO singing 'The Magic of Your Love'. Show Maurice. The younger brother could pull off the big one. I had the time. I could taste it. I was already punching the air. Yes!

Nellie took her seat in the front row. She'd brought the Harlequins jersey. She looked up at Ireland's Own Nelson Eddy in his dress suit. I walked across the stage to Sister Mary Monica, rubbing my hands with the confidence of OUR HERO. I let the audience think I was instructing her E flat. Sister Mary Monica led me as I went to the front of the stage. I didn't look at Nellie yet.

> *Until I met you*
> *I never knew*
> *What life could hold for me . . .*
>
> *Until I met you*
> *I never dreamed*

180

> *How sweet a song could be . . .*
>
> *I drifted along*
> *My lonely way*
> *With never a song or a smile*
>
> *Until I met you*
> *And then I knew*
> *That love made the waiting worthwhile . . .*

Already the hall was expectant. There was a hush out there now. I saw Maurice lean forward and rest his arms on the empty seat in front of him.

I went on:

> *The music, the moonlight, the starlit sky*
> *Have woven their spell round my heart*
> *The nightwind is saying that you and I*

At last I looked at her –

> *Should never be far apart.*

Bobby Brown stood up from his table and biscuit tin. He walked halfway down the aisle towards the stage. Droney, Walter and Madeleine stepped out onto the stage from one wing, Valelly and Bob Nesbitt from the other. Padraigh O Maolcathaigh and the handyman went down the steps to stand by the edge of the front row of seats. The six Irish dancers edged on to stand behind Valelly and Bob Nesbitt.

> *The music, the moonlight, the starlit sky*
> *Have all been around us before*
> *But we walked so blindly we passed them by*
> *'Til now we have found something more.*

I put out my hand. Nellie left her seat and walked over to the steps leading to the stage. I went to meet her. I took the Harlequins jersey and put it on my shoulder. I held Nellie's hands and led her centre-stage. The audience stood up. Those near the side aisles moved down to gather in front of the stage. I sang into Nellie's eyes.

> *In the magic of your love*
> *I have found a world so new*
> *In the shelter of your arms*
> *Every golden dream comes true.*

The rest of the audience abandoned their seats to collect in front of the stage. Maurice was on his feet at the back of the hall. Nellie and I became a duet.

> *Tho' this lovely night will end*
> *And the stars no longer shine*
> *All my life I shall know*
> *There was one perfect moment*
> *When you were mine.*

Valelly moved forward and stretched his palms and drew them towards himself, calling on the audience to join in the refrain:

> *Tho this lovely night will end*
> *And the stars no longer shine*

Everybody sang. Maurice had his head thrown back.

> *All my life I shall know*
> *There was one perfect moment*
> *When you were mine.*

The stage was rushed. We were hugged and kissed and slapped on the back. I led Nellie out of the hall with my arm around her. We were cheered all the way.

There was something wrong with my fingers and thumb. They wouldn't turn the key in the ignition. She was over there now.

I missed Droney's quiz and Bob Nesbitt's Irish dancers and only caught the finish of Valelly's 'Solitaire'. Droney had divided the hall into two teams, front rows and back rows. He gave them five questions each. The winning side was granted the honour of nominating one of their own to draw the raffle ticket.

'. . . what is the name of Hopalong Cassidy's horse?'

Valelly dragged his stool off stage and threw his hat into the wings. He bounced back out with the cloakroom tickets in a plastic bag. 'Now ladies and gentlemen, before our full company sketch, may we have a nominee from the victorious quiz team to come up and draw the winning ticket in our raffle for . . .'

I was standing beside Droney, Walter and Madeleine. Valelly rushed over to us. 'I forgot a prize for the raffle. Someone run across the road and get a bottle of whiskey.'

'I'll go.' I was thinking: one last call.

I ignored the deserters from the concert and bought the whiskey. The payphone was through the lounge in the passage leading to the toilets. I put the whiskey on the ground and tapped the number. But I put down the receiver before the phone could ring. If she were there she wouldn't be here. I sat down on the ground beside the whiskey and lit a cigarette. A man passed me on his way to the gents and back out again. He didn't enquire. Chap in a dress suit sitting on a dirty floor, holding a bottle of whiskey and a fag. Assume the remains of a hunt ball or otherwise have to ask, are you all right? I had to lift myself up and dust myself down. One last confident prayer: she's over in the hall now.

'. . . worn once, ladies and gentlemen. Once and once only at his last public appearance . . .'

Valelly was raffling what he told the audience was Frank Sinatra's hat.

The full company sketch was revealed to the audience. Valelly was the barman. The Great Droney ordered: 'A bottle of Guinness please,' so that everybody would know he was the Man Drinking Bottle of Guinness. The Irish dancers and Bob Nesbitt and Walter asked for orange. I did not go on stage until this farrago was accomplished. The Great Droney drank. Madeleine, the wench, beseeched him: 'Droney, I love you Droney.'

Enter OUR HERO to whom the wench does not give a second look.

I stretched my hand out towards the wench and sang 'Until I met you I never knew what life could hold for me' before I engaged the audience. I knew, when I turned to face them, I would see Nellie running past Bobby Brown down the aisle to her seat in the front row. I knew it because it was the only thing left that life could hold for me. That is how I sang so confidently with my hand stretched out towards the wench.

I turned to the audience.

Maurice brought me home. He wouldn't let me drive the Mini. Sister Mary Monica came with us. Maurice put me in the back seat. He has an up-to-date car. The driver has sole charge of all controls. I could hear the click of the back doors being locked. He might have been afraid that I would throw myself out of the speeding car.

I was looking for an accident. I looked out all the way, hoping to see the taxi hit broadsides at a junction, with the guards taking measurements and Nellie and the Harlequins jersey shocked but safe, standing on the footpath. But the taxi was parked outside the main door of the convent. Maurice told the driver he could go. I went in with Sister Mary Monica. Nellie might have tripped on the stairs and sprained her ankle.

She was sitting on one of the chairs in the hall beside the telephone. She said, 'Jimmy.' She had let the phone ring out and taken the receiver off the hook to give me the variety of the engaged tone. She knew what she was doing. Sister Mary Monica was the worst ally I could have had all along. Believing in prayer, Sister Mary Monica could see miracles and hope where anyone else would have seen, as I saw now, that my wife was insane.

I thanked Maurice. There was no need for him to come in to the house. I'd be all right. He said, 'I tried to stop you. Look, I'll call into you. We'll go for coffee and talk it all out. You need someone to talk to you. You mightn't think it but you do.'

I had loads of cigarettes because I had seen us sitting up late into the night. I undid the dicky-bow and put it on the table beside the ashtray while I drank coffee and smoked and accepted the last few lashes of not being able to forget the humiliation.

I turned to the audience and I croaked 'Until I met you I never dreamed'. And then I died. I pitied the audience now. Having to vacate their seats as quietly as possible and tip-toe out of the hall to spare the man crying up on the stage. When they saw Sister Mary Monica leave the piano to put her arms around me and Maurice run down the aisle and up the steps of the stage the audience understood what to do even if Valelly was never miming to them that they should leave.

FULL COMPANY SKETCH

I woke in the ash-spattered dress suit, puzzled that I had slept after only two pints. It could only be that I was worn out after the latest suck-in. I was whipped and weary with no hope left. Still sticky with shame, I had to drag myself upstairs to the bathroom. I'd learned to pee with my eyes closed so as not to notice the fetid toilet bowl. The ceiling was black with condensation and there were streaks left behind from the cobwebs I'd swiped with the sweeping brush. Gunge was superimposed on the grout between the tiles. More than the house was manky. I'd accumulated my own grime. From Advertising & Sponsorship Manager with E. M. Hamilton to Toots Books of the naked bulb and the stone floor to coffee-table junkie my palimpsest read: self-disgust.

Without hope my last bolt-hole was that of the zombie. Put one foot in front of the other. I looked down at my hands hanging out of the dress suit. Change clothes. Yet even in a catatonic state I was given a function: I remembered the Mini. Some vulture of a traffic warden was probably getting ready to lick his pencil. I changed, cycled to the shop and rescued the car.

I bought the paper and read the horses. I didn't want to face Maurice today. He'd come in. It might be worse than coffee. Lunch. I wanted to hide. But already I'd been hiding in the coffee table, the leisure centre, the Drop Out, at Mass, behind the Sunday supplements after the once-a-week hot dinner. I'd been hiding in the snack box.

Take out the packet. Light up. Breathe. Watch the clock crawl towards coffee time. Don't go to coffee. Stay in the shop. Take the money and put the book in the bag that says Marks & Spencer. Wait. About now. Droney came in.

'You all right?'

'I'm fine.'

'When we didn't see you at coffee . . .'

'Coffee isn't roll call.'

'Can I do anything? Do you want to go off some place, I'll mind the shop.'

'What you can do for me is tell me, did I meet your requirements. Are *you* going to be all right?'

'That's finished, Toots. Any voices come into my head again, I'm going to tell them, fuck off.'

'How can you be sure you'll be able to do that?'

'I'm so sure, Toots. Look, you ever see or hear of me giving a sweet to a child I want you to contact the guards. I just know that's over. I can't ask for more than that concert. Toots, that concert was *singing*.'

'Sure? You have loads of money. You have property. You're a free man about town. You can *sing*. You have a beautiful woman. And now that you've had your concert . . . what I'm telling you is Ireland's Own Nelson Eddy is retired. If there is a next time or anything like a next time you can be damn sure I'll go to the guards.'

'I have a confession to make.'

'What?'

'The bit about Madeleine Brown. It's not true. I made that up. She's happy with Bobby. I wouldn't do that anyway, interfere in a marriage.'

'But you showed me your arse. Here in the shop. The *Si* and the *ng*.'

'That was someone else.'

'Who?'

'A woman in Dublin.'

'What woman in Dublin?'

'You don't know her. Toots, ladies' choice at dances wasn't on for me. I don't know my way around Dublin like I used to in London. I got the address from a guy who sells papers outside the GPO. He was the fourth guy I tried. The first three told me to fuck off.'

'What did you do, say to him where would I get a woman?'

'Yeah.'

'So why did you tell me it was Madeleine Brown?'

'Wishful thinking.'

'What's this Dublin woman like?'

'She wouldn't be top of the range.'

'What does that mean?'

'She's not battered or anything. About our own age.'

'What does she look like if she's our own age?'

'She's well preserved.'

'That sounds like a euphemism for something. Drop the other shoe, tell me all about it.'

'I had to give your man twenty. She was forty and an extra tenner for the writing. But she can't allow any shouting.'

'What shouting?'

'When making love. The way it should be. What with the neighbours.'

'Were you with her more than once?'

'Just when wanting it becomes too much. Maybe four or five times a year.'

Back in my E. M. Hamilton days and even in Regional Development I knew colleagues who had split up and went into what they called second relationships. They weren't afraid of what they'd been brought up on. I thought of their coitus being interrupted by cheering crowds, reminding them that they should go naked hand in hand to the window to wave at the Popemobile. When wanting it becomes too much . . .

'Is she still in business?'

'She was a couple of weeks ago. Why?'

'I was thinking of going to Dublin. Take the Curragh races in on my way back tomorrow. I need a break.'

'Do you mean . . .'

'Yes.'

'You want me to arrange it?'

'Yes.'

'She's within walking distance of the GPO but you should take a taxi to be on the safe side. You could drive the Mini but it wouldn't be outside the door when you came out. Are you talking a full night or what?'

'I don't know. Can I play it by ear?'

'I can find out. If you're sure it's what you want to do I can ring.'

'Ring.'

I stopped in Kildare for a pub-grub dinner. After shepherd's pie I ordered coffee to go with the fags. A woman of our own age. Well preserved. Not battered or anything. Not top of the range. And I couldn't shout. There were nine butts in the ashtray when I asked myself: why am I not on my way? So I woke up and drove home.

I was back in town at ten to seven. I'd make the leisure centre at the usual time. My routine would not be affected. The comfortable old coat.

Odd. Skinny Mitchell was looking in the window of the bookshop. Did he think I worked late? What could he want? I was almost past the shop when I realised he was knocking on the window. As I parked, the door of the shop opened and Skinny went in. I crossed the road and put my own key in the door.

Droney was arsed up against the bar of my bicycle. Books were moved out of the way so that Valelly and Walter could sit on a table. On the floor, with his elbows on his knees, sat Bobby Brown. Madeleine had the stool. Sister Mary Monica presided from my own chair. Skinny had reached the middle of the floor when I slipped in behind him. I didn't go any further than stand with my back to the door.

I watched their shock. They looked at me and from me to Droney. Droney said 'Toots' but Madeleine Brown cut him off. She said, 'Let me tell him.'

To reconstruct:

While I was in London, picking my winning doubles and trebles, Madeleine Brown fell in the door of the Market Bar. She was confused from the booze, didn't know what side of the road she had, the way tourists are lost when they come out of a shop in Oxford Street. Droney knew her from O'Brien's. He brought her across the road and fed her coffee and tomato juice. She was down, burying it all in the drink. Droney tried to help her.

Droney knew, like everyone else, that Bobby Brown had been a financial consultant. He showed Madeleine that Bobby Brown cleaning windows was *singing*. Bobby Brown hadn't been knocked out of the ring. What was a few misappropriated shillings. Madeleine and Bobby were lucky to have escaped the life they only thought they missed. They were free now. Droney dispelled the fug of low pubs and Madeleine's acting the slattern to show her that she, too, was *singing*, standing by her man. He gave her the guff for nearly two hours.

It was Madeleine's first gee-up since Bobby was caught. Sober, she had walked the streets with her head down. Sobering up now after the coffee and tomato juice she wanted to believe in Droney. She said. 'You don't see what happened to us as a tragedy?'

'A tragedy?' Droney was indignant. 'Do you know what real tragedy is? There's a friend of mine . . .'

When Droney went to O'Brien's that night, Madeleine and Bobby were there waiting for him. Madeleine was already on spring water. She asked Droney to explain to Bobby how both of them were singing. Then she said, 'I've been thinking all day about your friend . . .'

Next morning Madeleine entered the coffee table. She made Droney tell Walter and Valelly about Toots Books. Walter spoke for himself and Valelly: 'We didn't know.' He continued – speaking for himself – 'it doesn't sound to me like there's anything we can do.'

Valelly took over. When Valelly captained Trojans he was also their penalty-taker. He never missed. Before he started his run he saw the ball in the left corner of the net while the goalkeeper had dived to the right. Valelly worked backwards from the premise that he had already scored. Now he saw Nellie out of the convent to see her husband getting his honorary doctorate or having the mayoral chain placed around his neck. But Valelly could not walk backwards to the penalty spot. He was handicapped by not knowing every blade of grass on the pitch. To wit, he didn't know Toots Books. Droney was Toots's best friend, was that right? Droney said, near enough.

Then, Valelly commanded, tell the coffee table all about yourself and Toots.

Droney told them his own story and as much of mine as he knew. Valelly put it to Droney: you shout after him in the street, Toots, *sing*. Can he sing?

Droney explained *sing*.

Valelly told them: I'll have the answer in the morning.

Something out of the ordinary was called for, Valelly laid it out for them next day. He had stayed up for hours thinking. He saw the ball in the back of the net in the shape of Toots on stage and his wife in the audience. But they were already well served by Droney *singing* at the command of voices in his head, first heard while sitting on the landing in the house of Deutsch. With that sort of outlandishness accepted by Toots as a norm where Droney was concerned it should be possible to nurse Toots towards the notion that the voices might turn malevolent and lead Droney into trouble. Assassins derived their authority from voices in their heads. Why not Droney?

So, the ball was in the back of the net. But where to begin? Walter pointed to the penalty spot. He took an envelope from his pocket and, drawing on a lifetime's experience of detectives, fictional and factual, he wrote the message: ONE OF YOU IS ABOUT TO COMMIT A HEINOUS CRIME.

The battle plan was laid out. Enter Skinny.

Droney's lifetime experience of seeing himself through the eyes of others sussed Skinny after Skinny's first ten minutes in O'Brien's. Nowhere, not in any part of Droney's wanderings about town, never in any of his jobs in London, not even as a child, had he ever come across anyone who wasn't drawn to Droney's face. Skinny's exaggerated nonchalance in not once looking at Droney in O'Brien's was discordant. Droney figured: that fella who isn't watching me is watching me. Why?

Seeing Skinny in the Crow's Nest again affecting a rigid lack of interest when Skinny hadn't been to the Crow's Nest before and had only recently begun to come into O'Brien's convinced Droney that Skinny was acting the spy for what reason Droney could not grasp. Droney's usual route from the Crow's Nest to O'Brien's was through the sheltered community and the park.

191

He was open to the idea that Skinny might actually follow him. Droney stopped behind the third corner in the sheltered community. He heard Skinny coming. When Skinny put only a tentative head around the corner Droney grabbed him by the throat. Why was Skinny following him? Skinny croaked that he wasn't. Droney threatened Skinny by pointing towards his own face. He told Skinny that the handicapped were compensated at birth. In Droney's case his two hands had the strength of ten men's. He'd choke Skinny. Why was Skinny following him?

Skinny sang.

Droney loosened his grip and apologised for manhandling Skinny. He invited Skinny to O'Brien's where he sat him down with Madeleine and Bobby and then Droney rang Valelly at home and Walter in the Riverview Bar. They came in.

Skinny was turned.

They showed Skinny how Skinny would be helping me. They made him aware of the cause. Skinny didn't have to get up off his arse in O'Brien's. Droney wrote the script for him. The award of the silver paper cup to the worst garden was one of Droney's lunacies that I'd heard of before from Droney himself so I was hooked when Skinny claimed to have seen Droney at it again. The business of Droney preaching the sermon to the cows was fiction. And Skinny didn't have any mate working as a taxi driver.

While I was still in London, Valelly, Walter, Droney and Madeleine called Sister Mary Monica to get her imprimatur. Sister Mary Monica agreed to act as a mole to give the plan a push.

I saw the *dramatis personae* as they used to appear in the credits at the end of the old movies in cameo shots of the parts they had played. 'Oh wonderful,' Sister Mary Monica clapped her hands after I told her we had a lady now at the coffee table. She already knew and was ahead of me all the way in my soap opera from then on. 'No watermark,' Walter said, holding the paper up to the light. 'The usual shite,' Skinny reporting on the Crow's Nest decor. Skinny and his non-existent mate of a taxi driver following Droney to Clarina Woods to hear the sermon to the cows. And the hackney mate having to tell his base the destination which meant that Skinny had to pay him. Verisimilitude again. After Mad Martin's funeral, Walter telling me how he saw Droney giving sweets to girls outside the Model School three days in a row. And Skinny: 'Your man, Droney, the mad guy. Is he . . . is he a friend of yours?' Skinny's mate seeing Droney swap the good leather jacket for the wino's dirty raincoat and catching Droney about to molest the child from St Gabriel's. And more Skinny: '. . . if it is whatever it is, if it's the type of thing that, I wouldn't want to be involved even from a distance, no matter what kind of a misfortune the guy is, you know . . .'

Walter: 'The question is what are we going to do?'

Droney: '. . . I'm talking to you and I'm asking you for help. All I'm saying to you is don't let me alone. Don't let me be the only one. Do something, do anything. Hold my coat. Don't send me out of here the way I came in. Don't let the thing come back into my head . . .'

If a concert had to be put on I could do it better than anybody. I could put on a great concert. I could put on the best concert. There isn't anything I don't know about concerts . . .

Valelly sacrificed his own reputation to put on a fiasco of a concert for my sake. Offstage, the Coffee Table Players brought the house down. For my sake, they made a total ape out of me.

They waited now for my reaction.

'What are you all doing here now?'

They were shifty about what they were all doing here now. This time they didn't look at Droney. They let Valelly have the floor.

'We were planning our next move.'

I searched for the grace to thank them. The coffee table was an open door ready to be pushed in the name of any lunacy. And yet they were all I had. They were only trying to help. But they hadn't seen Nellie sitting by the phone in the convent hall. They didn't know there wasn't a next move. I put my finger under the door latch. 'You meant well and I thank you. But there isn't going to be a next move. Your next move is go home.'

I held the door open. I would keep my eyes on the floor while they filed out and save us all embarrassment.

'Did you go to see the Pope?'

I looked up to see Valelly on his feet. I pointed to myself. 'Me?'

'Yes. Did you go to see the Pope?'

'No. I was in New York when he was here.'

'Did you go to see him in Rome, I meant.'

'No. I was never in Rome.'

'Are you sure? Didn't you go and they wouldn't let you in and you knocked two Swiss Guards down and burst into his private chapel?'

I began to shake my head, indulging the insane. But Valelly flew on: 'How did he disguise himself? When you brought him back with you and smuggled him into the convent to talk to your wife.'

I was with him now. 'Look, I tried everything. Sister Mary Monica will tell you . . .'

'Who held the sheet?'

'What?'

'Was it yourself and Droney and your brother Maurice held the sheet the time you burned down the convent. Sister Mary Monica had got all the pupils and the nuns out first and your wife jumped out into the sheet.'

I snapped at him. 'All right. All right. You're saying I haven't tried. So tell me your next move. You think I want to give up?'

I let the door close behind me and backed up to the table where Valelly had been sitting beside Walter. Valelly stood where he could see us all and none of us would be deprived by having to look at his back. He began, 'Ignatius Valelly never came up with the wrong answer in his life!' I set myself to be ten times more of a devil's advocate than Maurice ever could have been. Valelly went on, 'I got one hundred per cent in maths in my Inter cert. When Ignatius Valelly's answer was different it meant the answer in the back of the book was wrong. Or the teacher wrote the sum wrong on the blackboard. The concert should have worked. Why didn't it?'

Valelly let the question dangle, even though he wasn't looking for an answer. Satisfied that we were tantalised he said, 'I stayed up all hours until I figured it out. You would be wasting your time getting the Pope. Burning down the convent won't work either. Even though you should have considered getting the Pope and burning down the convent. But you see, the wrong sum was written on the blackboard. We shouldn't have tried to bring your wife out to the concert. We should have brought the concert to the convent!'

I was glacial in my detachment. Valelly was getting on to becoming an old man now. Probably long before he chanced on our coffee table he must have recognised that he had wasted his life. But couldn't accept it. True, he had saved the dignity of John McCormack and had the memorabilia to prove it. But what had he done after? He didn't let his children leave school at fifteen and a half. They were graduates. He'd tooled around the buildings, the pubs, the garages in London and New York. He'd only landed on his feet in the end by sitting on his arse, driving the decent Ned Toomey for twenty years. Without that piece of luck he'd be on a state pension and going to Eddie Benson's for a haircut instead of Figaro's.

When Madeleine made Droney tell him and Walter about my problem, Valelly saw a last chance to shine. There was an integrity to his effort in putting on the concert. I would grant him that. It was in harmony with all he knew. And I had to admit I had let the concert give me hope. But it hadn't worked. When I went to the convent after the concert I saw that Nellie was too far gone. Now, the Mohammed and the mountain scenario that Valelly was plucking from his sleeve was another manifestation that he could not face being washed up. Maurice could not have seen that any clearer than I did now. In a way, my mind was off my misery. I pitied Valelly. I took the rest of them in. Walter was just a lost soul who found a haven in the coffee table. He would abide by the rules of the sect just for the company. And poor Madeleine and Bobby had found port in Droney's conferring on them the aura of *singing*. Even Sister Mary Monica, an educated, charitable and good lady, was seduced by having been cloistered for so long. She felt guilty for missing out on the world. Here was a chance for her to play a part in affairs. Here, I did not belong. It was true for Maurice. I'd let myself slip. Wasn't that the way to look at it, I was thinking, thinking like Maurice.

Then, '. . . because what we have to consider is: what if she is right in not wanting to come out?' Valelly aimed the question at me but he quickly pointed to Droney. 'That man there. He told us himself. He asked himself the question: *is this it?* And he said "no". I'm not having it. And he *sang*.' Valelly turned back to me. 'Supposing your wife did that?'

I began to nibble.

'Supposing your wife isn't the question at all? Supposing *you* are the wrong answer in the back of the book? Supposing your wife said: *is this it?* My son is gone? Pardon my French, Sister Mary Monica, but supposing your wife said: *is this it*, it is in my arse. Fuck this. Why should I cope? You take my son, you can shove the rest of it as well. I'm taking back my comics. Your wife could be like that man there. She could be *singing*. You wanted her to bear up. It's what everybody expected of her. But you were wrong. Everybody was wrong. But she was right. That's why my concert didn't work.'

My wife isn't deranged? My wife is sound? My wife is *singing*?

Maurice was waiting outside the bookshop next morning when I landed the Raleigh. He was bouncy. And that was not his form. He was looking at his watch. 'I must say, some people have a great life. Open any time. Close any time.' I was to be humoured. But like Valelly I too had stayed up all hours. I knew what I was doing.

I put the bike in and hung up the sign. We went to the Drop Out for coffee. Maurice was in a hurry to begin. 'I called a few times yesterday. Anytime I looked in the window your friend was sitting at the table.' 'Your friend' meant Maurice had taken a deep breath to approach the patient gingerly. 'Where were you?'

'I was in Kildare.'

'Kildare? What brought you to Kildare?'

'I was on my way to Dublin. Droney knows this woman in Dublin who's obliging, for around forty quid. It's been so long for me, I thought why not. But I stopped in Kildare for a bite and got cold feet.'

Maurice was embarrassed and elided into, 'Look, I'm glad you mentioned him. I said to you before the concert. There's something you don't see here. Think of it in terms of your position in society, and I'm not talking about snobbery or anything. That Droney was never in your league. He can do what he likes.

Good luck to him as far as I'm concerned. But you can't let yourself down mixing with these people. You could justify him by accepting he's mad. But you take Brown's wife. Brown is a criminal. You're seduced by a spurious glamour here. You don't need people like that. There are other people who care for you. I'm your brother. Talk to me. Eddie Hamilton. I saw him at the concert. I blame myself. Years ago, I should have tried harder to get you to see sense. We talked it over last night at home. I know, I know. I know what you're going to say about what Nellie said. But you have to admit now – it's not Nellie's fault – you have to admit that we can't just go on what Nellie wants when it's not doing any good. It's not doing any good for her and it's not doing any good for you.'

'Maurice?'

'Yes, Jimmy.'

'Will you help me?'

'That's what I'm here for this minute.'

'Will you hold a sheet?'

'Pardon?'

'I got an idea. I was thinking of burning the convent down. I could get Sister Mary Monica to have all the students and nuns out safely and then I could spread petrol all over the place and we could stand under Nellie's window, you, me and Droney, say, holding a sheet that she could jump out into.'

'Why are you talking like this? Are you trying to be funny? I came here to help you and you start raving.'

'Maurice, it might get her out.'

'Now stop that. Stop that stupid talk. You don't mean it, so what are you saying it for?'

'It's only a building. Put against a life. Lots of places get burned down and they get built up again.'

'Sane people don't burn them down. Jesus, Jimmy, I can't blame you because you're not thinking straight. I know you're disappointed that the concert didn't work. Look, all I'm asking you is to put it in my hands for a change. You tried hard in your own way but it didn't work. It's just, let it be tried a different way, people who know about these things . . .'

'Maurice, there might be another way.'

197

'What?'

'I don't watch the goggle box or read the papers much. How is the Pope?'

'What in the name of God has the Pope got to do with anything?'

'I thought I might go and see him. Ask him to come over and see Nellie. On the quiet. Sort of smuggle him into the convent in disguise . . .'

'Why are you talking like this? You can't mean one single word you're saying. It's this rotting away in that bookshop. And it's these people, isn't it? They have a hold over you. Talking like that about the Pope. That's not you. You were never like that. That Droney guy is mad. You stop anybody in the street and ask them. They'll tell you straight to your face that Droney is mad. And that woman married to Brown, she can't be right in the head either. As for the older guy, do you realise he raffled a hat that he said was Frank Sinatra's? Does he think we're all supposed to be eejits? A piano accompanying Irish dancing. A bloody piano on its own . . .'

'Actually it was Ignatius Valelly suggested the Pope might be the answer.'

'See? See what I mean? All of them mad. If only you could see them the way an ordinary person . . .'

'It was Ignatius also said I should burn down the convent and get you and me and Droney to hold the sheet.'

'Sweet God. Answer me. Answer me one question. Agree with me. Is this Valelly, is he or is he not mad?'

'No.'

'What do you mean, no? Just to descend to that madman's wavelength for a second. If you burned down the convent and Nellie did jump out, don't you understand that you'd be in jail? That if you were found insane you'd still be locked up. Does that lunatic Valelly not understand that? I can tell you, I'll have him locked up before I'm finished. I'll have them all put away . . .'

'Maurice, I'm not going to burn down any convent. I'm not going to see the Pope.'

'Thank you for that. So why did you say it in the first place? Do you think I have nothing to do getting off work to listen to wild talk? And how do I know now that you're not just starting to be clever with me? Tell me you're not in their clutches. Tell me the truth. Have they a hold over you? You might think they have. Tell me, and I'll show you that that can't be. Whatever fix you might think you're in, I'll show you the way out. Look Jimmy, you have me, you have the likes of Eddie Hamilton, you have some of our old neighbours. You want shoulders to lean on, all I'm saying is look in the right direction . . .'

'Maurice, I want to get my wife back.'

'Of course you do. Now you're talking. That's why I'm sitting here.'

'I'm going to get her back in my own way.'

'How?'

'I can't tell you yet.'

'Listen. Jimmy, please listen. There's been enough of you going off doing things without telling people. You tried your way. It didn't work. You turned to madmen for help. Let me tell you why I came here this morning. Here's my proposition. I want you to sit down with me and Dr Chrichton. Not do anything. Just the three of us sit down and have a chat. You can bring Sister Mary Monica along if you like. I'm not asking you to do anything. Just listen to what he has to say.'

'Fuck Dr Chrichton.'

'Just like that. Professional expertise simply dismissed. After you taking advice from mad people and criminals. You won't listen to your own brother. Have I done something to you that I don't know about? Have I ever done you any harm?'

'I'm going to get my wife back.'

'How? Two minutes ago you wanted to bring in the Pope. You talked of burning down the convent.'

'There's a better way.'

'What way?'

'I can't tell you. It's a way that wouldn't be there if I told you.'

'What does that mean? I'd go to the police and try and stop you? Is that it?'

'I don't think so.'

'Think? Don't think so? You mean you're not sure? You're not

199

sure whether I'd go to the police or not? Christ. Jimmy, listen. Let me help you. Tell me. How can I help you?'

'You can't help me, Maurice. Nobody can. That's what I've learned at last.'

SING!

On the train back from Dublin I considered the psychotherapist's verdict. Even after five years he knew me when I telephoned. He must have had the odd update from my own doctor. He said over the phone, 'Of course, if you think I might be any use. By all means.' He may have anticipated a madman. After listening to me this morning I was afraid that he might think his prescience to have been on the ball.

I brought the psychotherapist to my meeting Droney again and the establishment of the coffee table. I gave him the potted biographies of Droney, Valelly, Walter and Madeleine. I introduced Skinny. I described the concert and how I had been set up. I threw in Maurice.

Droney goes to the Model School or St Gabriel's every other day at half-three. He waits until the last child has been collected or gone home on the bus. Then he holds out the bag of sweets to the lollipop man. Passers-by give a benign nod to his philanthropy. On pension day Droney stands outside the general post office and when it's not raining he tours the seats in the park. Just like Mr Hassett used to do, Droney says, guess which hand to the old boys. And think of a number between one and ten. Far from hunting Droney the fifty-seven-year-old park ranger wants to join in but Droney told him to go way and come back in twenty years.

Between the main street and the market there is a pedestrianised shopping centre. Toots Books marks the spot where six arteries converge. This is my pitch. Under the canopies of the

201

department stores on the main street there are people selling stolen cigarettes: buskers with coats thrown on the ground; long-haired beardies with suitcase stands of jewellery; pavement artists; merchants selling pop-star posters; periwinkle pedlars. I could have blended there, huddling under the canopies with my back to the wall. But I knew what I was doing. You can't half *sing*.

Out of the concert proceeds Valelly withheld the price of the dress suit to give to Todds so that I am fittingly accoutred when I throw back my head: 'When the melancholy shadows fall. My heart is melancholy too. Then I hear the balalaika's call. And life is gay and bright and new.'

I began by singing to Droney. The first morning he stood outside the door of Heirlooms, having advised me not to take my eyes off his port wine stain so that I wouldn't be intimidated by the people looking at me as though I was some sort of oddball. Now I don't need him. I can look at the people now as though they are some sort of oddballs.

I have my admirers but they got me into trouble the first day by lobbing money at my feet. A guard said, move along now please. I got a placard. 'PLEASE DO NOT GIVE MONEY TO THE SINGER'. Then Droney came up with the embellishment of a smaller sign to put on the ground next to the tin of sweets. 'PLEASE TAKE ONE – NOTE: ONLY ONE BULLSEYE PER PERSON'.

I gave up the thigh and superchips. Now it is a cup of coffee and a fag while I listen to the tapes. The repertoire is entirely Nelson Eddy. I get up early and have a boiled egg and a few slices of griddle cake. I shower. I shave. I leave for work at a quarter past eight so that I can salute the neighbours again. Lovely day, thank God. I'm back dealing at the corner shop. Everybody was happy to see me out and about. But now they're not so sure, since the talk was brought up about what goes on downtown.

I cleaned the grout off one tile in the bathroom and stood back to admire my industry. A little every day. I repapered our room.

Maurice didn't catch up with me for a week. The health board offices are further up the town. He was almost on top of me on his way to the market on Saturday and didn't recognise me in the dress suit, he being naturally inclined to skirt all can-rattlers as a matter of ideology. Although he had in fact been looking for me.

When he did see me Maurice let his wife continue onto the market while he stood occupied by the window of Heirlooms. I did not need Droney as a prop there anymore but I did have Valelly, Walter, Madeleine and even Skinny, who mixed with the crowd and showed the way by clapping when I finished a song. Three-card-trick men do it. Also that first week, I let my glasses rest on my chest so that the audience would constitute a blur if I strayed from Droney's port wine stain, so today I was not put off by being able to see Maurice forcing his grim mouth shut. Maurice waited until I finished. 'At the Balalaika'. He called me from a safe distance by using his hand. I gathered my placards and tin of sweets. When I was a couple of yards from him he spat, 'Follow me.' He walked off in front, keeping the yards between us.

Maurice passed café after café and pub after pub until he slipped into the snug of what he would have called a dive had I been the host. In there with me he wouldn't be seen in there with me. He ordered two coffees through the hatch. I placed my placards and tin of sweets on the seat between us.

'Put that rubbish on the ground.'

When he paid for the coffees and could close the hatch, when he'd sugared and stirred and had a swallow, he said, with an effort at trying to stay calm, 'What do you think you're up to?'

'In what way?'

'Don't patronise me. Don't try to be so smart. I went out for a late drink last night. John Collins, the chemist from the regional, came in. I was sitting at the counter with two of my neighbours. John Collins said, is that actually your brother that does the singing? I thought he meant the concert. And that would have been bad enough. I was about to give him some story, that you obliged someone in aid of charity as a once-off, when he went on: in the shopping centre. I had to listen to him with the shame creeping all over me. So what the fuck do you think you're doing?'

'*Singing.*'

'I said, don't get smart with me. I saw you, I heard you. I know you were singing. Why? And what's that ridiculous dress suit in aid of?'

'That's my outfit for the shop now as well. They're not necessarily my *singing* clothes.'

'Singing clothes? What's that supposed to mean? And you're not answering my question. What do you think you're up to singing in the streets?'

'What's wrong with the streets?'

'You're a prick, do you know that? Do I deserve this for being your brother? You know what's wrong with singing in the streets. Don't insult me by making me spell it out. Of course I know the score but you won't admit it. It's those people. That Droney headcase. You're different since you met him. Have you any consideration for other people anymore? Did my wife do anything to you that she has to suffer this? What about my children? When people will say to them, isn't that your uncle? And what is this business of those sweets and the signs?'

'The first day, people started giving me money. They misunderstood. That's why I have the placard. The sweets are just to drive the point home that I don't want anything.'

'They misunderstood. Jesus. They're not the only one. Can I ask you one question? One simple question? Think of mam and dad. The family we were lucky to come from. Would you see anything wrong in what you're doing if mam and dad were alive? Hmm?'

'I'm not doing anything wrong.'

'You won't listen to me. That's actually what you're saying, isn't it? That no matter what you say I'm hopping my head off a stone wall.'

'Maurice, I have to get back to the shop.'

'The shop. That was the start of it. A man of your background – listen to me. The problem here is that you no longer have proper judgement. It's not your fault. I shouldn't lose my temper. I have to catch up with my wife. You still didn't tell me why. Why you're acting like a lunatic? Do me a favour. Think of mam and dad over the weekend. Think how they'd feel if they were alive. I'll call in on Monday and we'll talk it over. I have to help you to see sense.'

'Maurice, can you make it at a quarter to four on Monday?'

'Quarter to four? Why that time especially?'

The convent was at its busiest at four o'clock with the girls clocking out. Maurice saw me in action on my sixth performance there. On my first Monday the school handyman tried to shush me out of the grounds. When I ignored him he gave me a go-on-now fist in the shoulder. Sister Mary Monica had to come down and establish my bona fides.

Maurice stopped ten yards inside the gate when he saw Valelly, Walter, Droney and Madeleine sitting on the railings around the statue of Our Lady. I went on and stood under the window where Nellie sat holding the Harlequins jersey. It was Sister Mary Monica's job to have her there. Many of the girls were already waiting. Some of them sat on their books. Today I got two requests before I started. 'Sir, sing "The Balalaika". Mister, do the one about "Rose Marie".'

The first day I sang to Nellie she gave me her 'Jimmy, how *are* you' smile. I wasn't put off. I'd been expecting the filibuster. I told Sister Mary Monica: I don't want to know her reaction. Nellie was a match for me on Monday, Tuesday, Wednesday and Thursday. But on Friday her smile thinned. I began to think I had a chance. I didn't risk Saturday or Sunday without the back-up of the coffee table and the girls. Today, with Maurice inside the gate and the breadman with his arms full slowly closing the back door with his knee, and the girls and the coffee table and the school handyman pretending to be poking about the flower beds, Nellie couldn't keep the smile going while this aching heart of mine was singing. The smile thinned again and during 'Softly as a Morning Sunrise' I saw the terror in her eyes. Just as I launched 'I'll See You Again', she fled from the window. Maurice had fled before her.

The girls know by now. More and more of them stay behind after school. A junior cert. Student asks all the time for 'Smilin' Through'. Somebody not yet sixteen asking to hear a Nelson Eddy song. I said it to Maurice. I said: if only

205

for that alone. But he didn't listen. He stayed away for two weeks. Then he came in to ask me, in the name of God stop. That half the town must know about it now. People in the job suddenly cut the conversation when he walked into an office.

But he's right about half the town. The city is full of churches yet a cadre of old ladies suddenly discovered no better place to say a few afternoon prayers than the convent reparation chapel from where they emerge every day at four. Add the pensioners who just happen to walk their dogs down a cul de sac that leads nowhere *but* a convent.

I admitted to the psychotherapist that there were some days when Nellie did not appear at the window at all even though I saw the curtains move. I sang anyway and the crowd was patient. I told him that when she did appear she couldn't even begin to manage her 'Jimmy, how *are* you' pose. And neither did her terror last. All I can see there now is 'Jimmy, please don't make me'. But I don't think she means it anymore. She must know now that she no longer has to *sing* alone.

It's been five weeks and today is the day, I explained to the psychotherapist. Could it work, that's what I wanted him to tell me. Or am I rushing it. I'm getting the midday train back so that I'll be on time. I've been giving 'The Magic of Your Love' a rub of the cuff and I believe I'm ready and Nellie is ready.

> The nightwind is saying that you and I
> Should never be far apart.
> The music, the moonlight, the starlit sky
> Have all been around us before
> But we walked so blindly we passed them by
> 'Til now we have found something more.

That's when I'll start walking towards the convent door. I hope to meet her halfway on the stairs.

Could it work?

He gave me his professional opinion and also his opinion as a layman because in this case they were the same. He was delighted to be able to say to me: I don't know.

ALSO BY MICHAEL CURTIN

Michael Curtin

The Cove Shivering Club

'Brilliantly and warmly done . . . a major discovery.'
Kaleidoscope, BBC Radio 4

'Michael Curtin is one of Ireland's national treasures; a superb comic novelist who deserves to be far better known . . . Curtin's hilarity is shot through with impeccably judged moments of poignancy, even tragedy.'　　　　*Sunday Express*

'Sparkling and hilarious, full of characters and lines that lovers of Michael Curtin expect . . . very funny and very, very human.'
Roddy Doyle

'Real comic writing, with not a dull moment.'
Times Educational Supplement

'Witty gem.'　　　　　　　　　　　　　*Scotland on Sunday*

'Brilliant comic novel.'　　　　　　　　　*Belfast Telegraph*

It all began on Good Friday, 1955, when, aged ten, Junior Nash and Dunstan Tucker swam each way across the bay defying the freshness of the Atlantic in spring and thereby became full members of The Cove Shivering Club. The rules were simple: you don't piss in the water and you don't bring a woman. Years later the club members reconvene to decide how to deal with a rule-breaking woman, and indeed with modernity in general.

With its maze of comic twists and turns, *The Cove Shivering Club* brilliantly demonstrates Michael Curtin's wicked sense of the humorous absurd and his deeply affectionate understanding of the most human of moral frailties.

4th

Michael Curtin

The League Against Christmas

'Curtin is one of Ireland's best writers'   Roddy Doyle

A glorious nostalgic farce set in the unforgiving 1980s. The
League Against Christmas are five solo whist players who meet
every Wednesday night in a dowdy pub – The King's Head – in
Shepherd's Bush: Percy Bateman, a drifting Irish social misfit who
once spectacularly failed on the rugby pitch; Kenneth Foster, an
accountant who harbours desires to cross-dress; Arthur Ellis, a
former area manager of NatWest finance who want to convert the
world to using lino (not a popular flooring in the chrome-plated
1980s) and carries a piece with him at all times for the purpose;
Ernie Gosling, the King's Head potman; and Diana Hayhurst,
shoulder-padded editor of *Unipolitan* magazine for the modern
woman.

   Each hates Christmas and the league decide to pursue an
alternative: a diddly club robbery in Ireland, carried out under
the hangdog eyes of a couple of the Metropolitan Police's finest,
who have mistaken the league for an IRA cell. This is Curtin at
his irreverent, loveable best with a delightful cast of characters in
a plot of pure devilry.

'Michael Curtin is one of Ireland's national treasures – a superb
comic novelist.'   *Sunday Express*

4th

Michael Curtin

The Plastic Tomato Cutter

'Curtin's books are marvellous achievements, very funny and very, very human. He has also created some of the best barmen in modern literature.'
Roddy Doyle

Mr Yendall, one of life's great antiques even as a young man – deputy-manager of Montague's outfitters and the habitual occupant of the corner table at the Draper's Club – charts the downward progress of society as a wave of Beatlemania and unisex boutiques sweeps through the sixties. Of another age, Tim Harding, snooker champion and member of the society of bellringers – despite him being a 'black Protestant' ex-Trinity College man of doubtful parentage – is so besotted by the local beauty, Celia Sloane, that he can hardly see straight. She insists that they pursue a perfectly romantic courtship, traditional almost. Well, almost . . . This a rare love story, that is about chalk and cigarettes, waistcoats and tradition, plastic, religion and the taking of glorious long shots.

'Good on modern dialogue, clever with ticklish set pieces and screamingly funny about male eccentricities.'
Daily Mail

'The effect at first of tuning one's radio into the middle of a garrulous Irish soap opera . . . Curtin's is a wit that touches the heart.'
Daily Telegraph

4th

All Fourth Estate books are available from
you local bookshop.

For a monthly update on Fourth Estate's
latest releases, with interviews, extracts,
competitions and special offers visit
www.4thestate.com

Or visit
www.4thestate.com/readingroom
for the very latest reading guides on our
bestselling authors, including Michael Chabon,
Annie Proulx, Lorna Sage, Carol Shields.

London • New York